"A compelling, exciting story! The author has a way of combining spiritual concepts, intrigue, and a love story, which takes place on two continents. The writer's familiarity with Africa and its culture makes for fascinating and spellbinding reading. The book should appeal to most any reader."

Arliss Bottom
Bedford, Texas

"The reader quickly becomes aware that the author intimately knows the subject he is writing about: medicine, Africa, and the Christian life. Interwoven in these subjects is a story of war and terrorism, but also of friendship, love, and what happens to lives given over to God. The book is a 'must read' to the surprising conclusion."

A.M. Regier
Madrid, Nebraska

"From the emergency room of a U.S. hospital to the heart of Africa, this novel takes us on a journey through the dawn of love but also through acts of war and terrorism taking place on the Dark Continent. The narrative carries the reader through conflicts of unrestrained evil with Christians lives. The battle between good and evil finally terminates in a shocking ending. It is an exciting and fulfilling read."

C. McLaughlin
Grant, Nebraska

FOREST OF **FEARS** *a novel*

FOREST OF FEARS *a novel*

paul fay

Tate Publishing & *Enterprises*

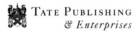

TATE PUBLISHING
& Enterprises

Published in the United States of America

ISBN: 1–5988674–7–4
06.12.08

To my wife, Kathy, who worked, agonized, and sacrificed at my side through years of medical practice in the U.S.A. and the demands of life in Congo, Africa. Without her love and support, this novel could not have been written.

FOREWORD

I believe the chief gift from Africa is the continent itself, its presence which for some people is like an old fever, latent always in their blood; or like an old wound throbbing in the bones as the air changes. This is not a place to visit unless one chooses to be an exile forever afterwards from an inexplicable majestic silence lying just over the border of memory and thought. Africa gives you the knowledge that man is a small creature, among other creatures, in a large landscape.

Doris Lessing
African Stories

So do not fear, for I am with you;
do not be dismayed, for I am your God.
I will strengthen you and help you;
I will uphold you with my righteous right hand.
All who rage against you
will surely be ashamed and disgraced;
those who oppose you
will be as nothing and perish.
Though you search for your enemies,
you will not find them.
Those who wage war against you
will be as nothing at all.
For I am the LORD, your God,
who takes hold of your right hand
and says to you, Do not fear;
I will help you.

Isaiah 41:10–14

Dr. Zachary Wylie–Surgical resident at large Midwest teaching hospital

Susan–Zach's wife

Desiree–Zack and Susan's three-year-old daughter

Dr. Ben Wells–Missionary surgeon with years of experience in the Congo, West Africa

Dr. Pascal Mutamaya–African surgeon and emergency room specialist. Trained at a Protestant mission in the Belgium Congo, Switzerland and the USA

Colonel Ching–Congolese; trained in Catholic primary and secondary schools in the Belgium Congo; greatly influenced by the politics of Lenin; trained in China, returned with strong Communist teachings; colonel in Simba army

Joel Lusombo–Nurse, protégé of Ben Wells and his adopted spiritual son

Angela Lowell–American nurse, born in the Central African Republic to missionary parents

CHAPTER 1

An uncanny sound drifted in on the stale, stifling air that moved up from the antiquated courtyard below. The smell of stale bricks, sewage pipes, and hospital exhaust created a sinister concoction, to be inhaled against one's will. Two and one-half years into the surgical residency and the mournful sound of the ambulance still caused forlorn feelings and a deplorable apprehension. Zach's stomach began to churn, as it always did, waiting for his phone to ring. Staring at the ceiling, he began to sweat despite a cool breeze that had suddenly swept into the small cubicle-like room used by the on-call surgeons. The area consisted of a cot, a bed stand with phone, a lamp, and sink. You could wash your hands, but other necessary functions required a trip down the hall.

In that indistinct zone between sleep and wakefulness, the history of ancient medical facilities flashed through his mind. In seconds, a reshuffling of time took place, and he was thinking of what he had learned in college about the origins of hospitals. Professor Raynard, in his eccentric manner, had spoken of the great temples of the ancient gods, some 4000 BC, that had been used for the treatment of the sick and were the training schools for doctors. Some years later, the great temple of Asclepius was built to the Greek god of medicine and had become the great center of medical learning. *But they didn't have wailing ambulances and the torture of telephones*, Zach almost spoke aloud. The cooler air still carried the stench from the darkness below, gagging his gloom into further wakefulness. The phone shattered the silence, startling him despite his anticipation.

"Hit the deck running, Doc, you got two gun shot wounds bleeding their way into the ER!"

"Darn him, why is he always so cheerful!" Zach slammed the phone down, cursing the always-jocular night operator. He felt angry at everything, but hateful at nothing. The clock next showed 2:10 a.m. He had laid down thirty minutes ago, the first rest since the shift had started at six o'clock the morning before. A vague shadow moved across the wall, shaking him further awake and causing a strange, cold fear in him. Something was there, a presence—an existence—that he could feel, but not see. Zack felt far more frightened than the situation deserved. Good grief! He was not irrational or superstitious! The phone rang again.

"Yeah, I'm coming!"

"Sorry, Doc, don't want you fallin' back to sleep on me." From his lonely telephone operator's center, Rod knew these men and women and respected the incredible physical and mental stress they were under. He allowed a great deal of range for their moods and their raging outbursts of expletives. They weren't striking at him, but only at the frustrations, fatigue, and demands they experienced minute to minute.

Shaking off the cold fear he felt in his spine, Zach did "hit the floor running," down two flights of bent, wooden stairs, each creaking to its own tune. He found himself taking two and three at a time. He was running full speed when passing Rod's small workstation, yelling out as he passed, "You've got sadism down to a fine art!" Zach grabbed the door jam, stopping his passing abruptly, and peered in for a split second. Rod was leaning back, his huge frame engulfing the chair. He wore his usual laconic smile. It was quiet on the switchboard this time of night, and Rod had freedom while plugging in the ancient telephone system with mechanical movements. He knew Zach well enough to sense when he was serious. He had actually followed his career back to his college days when he was an All-American football player for UCLA. How and why he had gotten all the way to this mid-western charity hospital was a mystery to him. He also knew that the hospital underground gossip system had it on *good* authority that he was recently separated from his wife. Some *observers* had it that it was an ugly situation. But he liked Zach and knew him to be one of the most respected of all the current surgical residents. The clandestine word in the coffee shop was that he would be the chief resident next year, that is, if Dr. Tharp were still head of Surgery. But everyone knew that Dr. Tharp's position as the Chief of Surgery, in the hierarchy and politics of a large teaching hospital, was in a more precarious position than a bull rider's bones.

The quietness of the hall changed to the sights, sounds, and stench of organized chaos as Zach swung open the large doors and entered the domain of the emergency room. Shifting around a police officer guarding at the bedside of a young bearded man with bloody bandages around his head, Zach rushed toward the activity near the minor surgery room. He passed a gurney where nurses were transferring a man to a bed. He had a gaping hole in his leg with bone protruding through the skin, and a string of profanities spilling from his mouth—he was probably stable for the moment.

"We have a nasty one here, Zach!" Seeing Dr. Mutamaya's presence in the emergency room always had a reviving effect on him, but he never quite understood why.

Three nurses, Pascal Mutamaya—the Chief trauma surgeon—and an intern Zach had seen but didn't know, were working frantically, taking blood pressures, drawing blood, attaching electrodes, and pushing intravenous fluids. Someone had already intubated one patient and the respirator was moving his chest rhythmically.

"Get X-ray in here! We need a chest, stat." Dr. Mutamaya never yelled or cursed, as many did, but when he spoke, his dignified voice had an almost mystical effect on the staff.

"And get a chest tube tray in here!" The nurses responded immediately and he looked up at Zach. "This man has taken two shots in the chest! We cannot get a blood pressure and he is not breathing."

"How about the others?"

"He has taken one in the leg," his head motioning to the gurney. "That woman over there has at least one bullet in the abdomen."

"And she's a hundred percent dead in the lower extremities," someone else said, "but her vital signs are stable." A few feet away, someone was screaming with high-pitched, hideous shrieks.

Someone on amphetamines or PCP, Zach thought.

Cracked and strident noises escaped around the tracheal tube as he turned all his attention back to the patients. For the next few hours, time did not exist for any of the team as they strived to stabilize blood pressures, support breathing, control bleeding, and make some sort of restoration out of the horribly tangled mess of humanity—chaos caused by hate, drugs, rage, and ugliness, with which they dealt daily.

Man's inhumanity to man. What a dumb statement, thought Zach, *it is his barbarity and savageness because man is inhuman.* He shook off these thoughts. *I must be more exhausted than I realize when I start this tacky philosophizing.*

He and Pascal had gotten the chest tube in, still using old suction bottles and negative pressure created by gravity. They had also stabilized his pressure by pumping in two units of blood and a couple liters of Ringer's lactate. His airway was secure, and they had managed to get an arterial clamp around the large severed axillary artery before they shipped him off to the operating room and the team of surgeons waiting for him. No neurological procedure could be done for the pretty young woman with the abdominal wound. A bullet had entered her abdomen just below the umbilicus, leaving a small, insignificant entry wound. But as it exited her back, above the bony crest of the pelvis, it created a gaping hole surrounded by torn flesh and blood. It had obviously had missed the aorta. If it had hit that large artery, she would have bled to death before hitting the ER. But the projectile, flattening as it hit tissues, had unmistakably severed her spinal cord. She was stabilized to be sent to the operating room to have her abdominal cavity explored. All emergency room physicians knew that a stab or gunshot wound in the abdomen almost always meant perforated loops of bowel. The ragged holes spilled contamination into the abdominal cavity leading to peritonitis, sepsis, and death. *They will probably be able to save her,* Zach thought angrily, *to be just half a body!*

Dawn was breaking over the city when their efforts finally culminated in total weariness and mental exhaustion. He and Pascal had not spoken except in curt, essential medical terms. Yet, once again, Zach felt the inexplicable strength and self-control of the man. Above and beyond his surgical skills, he knew little about him personally except that the other surgeons often referred to him as the "Bible Doc." But none ever seemed to say this in a demeaning way. He was probably in his forties, Zach had guessed, based more on the fact that his dark black hair was slightly gray at the temples and deep crow's feet formed quotation marks on each side of his brown eyes. From his movements, physical strength, and intensity, one could easily believe him to be many years younger. His accent was alien to Zach, but he had never asked where he come from. Good grief, he had enough problems without delving into the life story of another staff man! But Zach had heard that he had come from the Eastern University Surgical Department in Boston to become the Associate Professor of Surgery and head of the Trauma Center here at County Hospital.

With an enormous effort, Zach straightened himself, stretching the spasms from his back. As he did so, his eyes met those of Dr. Mutamaya. For a second, he was startled. What was in those eyes he found so absorbing, and why was the aura around this man so fascinating?

Dr. Mutamaya spoke with the same low, reverberating voice with which they had worked during the past four hours, "Thanks, Zach, you work with great competence. I'm truly impressed!"

Whether it was from the experience of the accolades thrown his way during his football years or the experiences of a disastrously immature relationship in his marriage, Zach had developed a cynical attitude toward compliments. *Most compliments were hypocritical and manipulative*, he often thought. But from this man, this dedicated surgeon—whom he hardly knew—he felt sincerely complimented by his words. Yet, all he could mutter was a weak, "Thanks."

Pascal smiled. He looked relaxed and vigorous despite the hours in this battleground of horror. With the night almost gone, the moans of pain, the screams of patients reacting to illicit drugs, and the cranky respirators were silenced. The auto accidents and multiple injuries had stopped coming, so the X-rays and laboratory tests were temporarily halted. The battered women and their intoxicated, foul-mouthed abusers were now less defiant and sullen. The floor was covered with soiled masks, dirty linen, and empty intravenous containers. Scattered papers and bloody gauze lay where they had been hastily discarded in the frantic attempt to save lives. One nurse was slumped in a chair, another lay face down on a gurney, while another leaned against a scrub sink; all in various states of physical exhaustion and mental delirium.

Zach found it mildly disturbing that he could look at this slaughterhouse of human tragedy and feel almost nothing. He turned away, dull with fatigue, and started the walk back to his call room, to silence and sleep.

CHAPTER *two* 2

The air hung heavy and moist. The light from the kerosene lamp formed an unmoving triangle of light, making his writing easier. Ben wished for a slight flow of air to relieve the oppressive heat. The silence of the African night he found to be both comforting and harsh. Only the sounds of insects and the occasional echo of voices drifting in from a long distance disturbed the stillness of the night. There was little to block the sounds. Solitude and loneliness were having their schizophrenic effect on him as he bent closer to see the paper on which he was writing. In this isolation, one can experience an extraordinary awareness of the universe and its Creator, and simultaneously be consumed by the magnitude of its greatness and infinite mystery. Yet, one could also be easily reduced to having an almost infantile need for security. Dr. Ben Wells looked up from his desk, rubbing his eyes to clear the fatigue. *One of these days I'm going to have to get those glasses*, he thought, staring into the dark night. His thoughts allowed a brief repose from the research paper on which he had been working. *There are people out there in the silence*, he pondered, *trying to sleep on the bamboo mats protected by grass roofs. Most were friendly, usually gracious and displayed a propensity to generosity. Yet, language and culture continued to separate. These were barriers irrevocably present that a lifetime could only chip at, but never completely subdue. Their speech, culture, and thought patterns, all so unfamiliar, formed a vast channel in which one could swim but could never completely traverse.*

During his twenty years in Central Africa, Ben had learned to both love and hate the country. The people and the vast beauty of the land became inexplicable and veracious ingredients that penetrated one's soul. But the poverty, superstition, corruption, and suffering were things that one had to handle with countless defenses. Ben had traveled through many; the most destructive was the formation of an emotional barricade to keep out the anguish and pain surrounding him. However, such an apathetic defense might be protective, but left a barrier around an empty shell, devoid of human response. Ben had learned, through hardship and time, to deal with the endless progression of disease, deformities, and death by treating them with all the skill he possessed and then let God carry them both.

Ben leaned back and closed his eyes for a few moments, reflecting on how often he had been asked the questions, "Why are you doing this?" "How were you called to give your life to this dark country?" "Why do you want to waste your good years like this?" These were profound questions, many without ultimate answer. Human beings lived and believed on such diverse perception in life. From the recess of his memory, he recalled the words of the great Prophet of God, Isaiah. When confronted by God, Isaiah wrote:

"I heard the voice of God saying, whom shall I send?" And Isaiah was so sensitive to God that he could reply in no other way but to pour out his heart. "Here am I, send me!"

Ben reached into his desk drawer and retrieved his daily journal. A few weeks ago, he had wrestled with some of these same thoughts. He found and read aloud the words he had written:

"Christians speak of the call of God, as others speak of the call of the wild or the call of the sea. The calls are undeniable and sincere, heard by a few because they are strongly attuned to the very nature of God. But these 'calls' do not reveal the person's nature, but that of a mighty God. The 'call of the sea' or the 'call of God' has to come from the very nature of God. The prophet Isaiah was so overwhelmed by the presence of God and so attuned to His presence that he announced from his amazed soul, 'Here am I, send me!' This amazing declaration had to have come from God's nature, not from Isaiah's."

There were some further words Ben had written, and then he completed the journaling for that day with the following assertion:

"Why am I here, why am I working and living here in this African country? Why was I called? I hope and I pray that it is because my 'call' is an expression of God's nature and my attempt to serve is because I am so attuned to God's will that I am truthfully saying, as Isaiah did centuries ago, 'Here am I, send me.'"

Suddenly, Ben heard a different sound; strange and unearthly. It seemed to be shriek, like the high-pitched sound air makes as it rushes from the lungs of a wounded animal. He recognized the sound from a deep alcove of past experience. He knew the noise! He had heard it before! It was a human scream altered by air being forced out through swollen lips and a throat filled with blood. The soldiers had come! He had experienced it before; the vicious kick of heavy boots; the stocks of rifles slamming against flesh and bone; the screams of women being attacked as clothes were being torn from their trembling bodies! Girls thrown with brutal force to the ground, their bodies viciously penetrated in senseless acts of animalistic lust!

For the past three nights, there had been Short Wave radio reports of soldiers coming, leaving their military base at Kahila, and moving westward toward their mission station. The communication earlier tonight had been filled with static and hard to hear, but the voices of the Catholic missionaries at the neighboring station of Masula had not seemed to carry any particular alarm. Sister Bernadette had joked at the end of their communication about seeing some of the soldiers using their automatic rifles as walking sticks, the barrels firmly held in the palms of their hands. To the north, the Baptist mission station had reported an uneventful day.

Hideous screams again penetrated the darkness. Ben shivered despite the heat and his spirit of resolve. Abruptly, he felt a presence in the room. It was frightening, and despite himself, he turned quickly to the direction of the force. Nothing was there but the shadows thrown from the kerosene lantern. He knew very well what could happen if the soldiers came into their Station. Three years before, he had experienced the ugliness and anguish that had occurred during the last uprising. The chaos, the hate, and wrath that had been held in check for so long had spilled over into looting, stealing, burning, and devastation. Many had died! The sense of the presence in the room remained. The screams had stopped and total silence rushed through the open window, almost more frightening than the tortured shrieks. Why was he not more panicked? He should be! He had seen the alcohol and drug induced fierceness in the eyes of soldiers before. And he had tasted blood from his own smashed lips and broken teeth and had felt the imminence of death. Why the relative sense of peace? The presence seemed stronger, holding the room in its grip.

"Turn and read!" It wasn't a voice and yet so undeniable that it could have been. Was it real or from the recess of an unsettled mind? He sighed deeply. He would never really know, but he turned and picked up his worn Bible. With no forethought, he opened to Psalm 124. This ancient document expressed the thoughts of a man experiencing similar circumstances nearly three thousand years ago. He read aloud, comforted by his own voice and deeply moved by the words:

> If the Lord had not been on our side when men attacked us, when their anger flared against us, they would have swallowed us alive; the flood would have swept over us, the raging waters would have swept us away. But praise be to the Lord who would not let us be torn by their teeth. We have escaped like a bird out of the fowler's snare; the snare has been broken, and we have escaped. Our help is in the name of the Lord, the Maker of heaven and earth.

Ben closed his frayed Bible, thanking God for these words. He had long ago forsaken any attempt to explain why he could be drawn to open his Bible to such crucial passages. He laid the Book back on his desk, listening again for the sounds from the darkness. A gunshot collapsed the stillness, bursting in his ears, and at the same time shattering the door. The latch and wooden splinters were thrown across the room, striking the chair in which he had been sitting. The door was kicked open and a breeze swept across the room, extinguishing his lamp. There in the doorway, silhouetted in the moonlight, stood a specter, a man in combat clothes. He held a heavy automatic weapon in his hands. His African face was partially hidden in the darkness, but his eyes were white and flaming. Ben instantly had the feeling he was looking into the very fires of hell.

CHAPTER 3

The early afternoon sun drifted above the old bricks of County Hospital, casting its rays through the west window, jostling Zach awake from his exhausted slumber. In the stage between wakefulness and sleep, he was again encountering the aura he had felt earlier. But now it was less frightening; more amicable and sympathetic. Shaking himself awake, he became aware of his perspiration saturating the pillow and the gritty sensation in his eyes as he blinked. Sitting up on the edge of the cot, he shivered, as if to rid himself of this unusual feeling. Old habits drifted back and made him wonder how long it had been since he had awaken and immediately driven himself to do vigorous exercise. It had been a long time. He dropped to the floor, forcing himself to start push-ups. After several minutes, he noted moisture on his face. *Sweat*, he thought at first, but it was not sweat at all but salty tears flowing down his face. He stood, shaking himself to break the mood. He gathered his towel, comb, and shaving kit and entered the hall that took him toward the communal shower. He heard raspy snores coming from behind a closed door. *Probably some other poor slob; a piece of meat exhausted beyond restoration*, he thought.

When he returned, he found the door to his room ajar. In his lethargy, he must have failed to close it. It didn't matter; he had nothing one would want to steal. Entering his small call room, thoughts of the coming day were totally occupying his mind. He was startled to see Dr. Pascal Mutamaya sitting on the edge of his cluttered bed.

His visitor arose quickly with effortless movement and extended his hand.

"Please forgive me for entering your room like this. Your door was open."

His voice was low and resonant, causing Zach to strain to hear his words. But his handshake was bold and there was kindness radiating from the Cimmerian eyes that were set in a strikingly handsome face. Only the broad nose, ample lips, and ebony skin displayed his African heritage.

"It's okay, please sit down." Zach self-consciously grabbed the hard wooden chair from the desk and sat facing him.

"What can I do for you, Dr. Mutamaya?" Zach felt miserable and knew that his Chief must sense it.

"Please, call me Pascal." He was obviously trying to make Zach feel at ease. "I know that you have some time off today, and I do not want you to waste it talking with me. I just came by for a few moments."

"So what brings you here, Doctor Mutamaya?" Zach spoke with unnecessary sharpness and immediately wished he could draw the words back.

Dr. Mutamaya smiled, displaying a perfect row of white teeth. Deep furrows appeared on each side of his eyes as he smiled. He arose effortlessly. "We will speak another time. I would like to know you a little better."

"No, no, please sit back down. I don't mean to be so ill-mannered." For the first time in weeks, Zach smiled. Again he pondered what there was about this man's presence that made him feel so exposed.

"I will take only a few moments of your time, please." His quiet voice and reserved manner seemed to contrast completely with the incredible surgical skills and firm decisiveness of the surgeon he knew from the ER. His torso was lean and his stature lithe, revealing a fluidity of movement. Sitting here in this small room, Zach realized that he was not a large man at all, only seemingly so by the dominance of his personality and abilities.

To break the uncomfortable silence, Zach spoke, "Doctor, may I ask you where you are from? You are African, are you not?"

"That is correct. My village is in the southwestern part of my country of the Belgium Congo." As he spoke, the soft, melodic accent seemed more pronounced. "But one day, I will tell you more about my land. Now, I will not take your precious time to speak of myself. Later, perhaps. But now I came only to greet you and to encourage you. I enjoy working with you on emergencies. I believe you to be one of the most capable residents with whom I have worked since I came here three years ago." He seemed to want to say more, but then checked himself.

"Thank you, sir!" Zach replied with deep feeling, "Those words mean a great deal, especially from one such as yourself." Zach stared at the floor thinking how this man's words had swept away much of his fatigue, indecision, and growing desperation.

"I must let you go now." Dr. Mutamaya extended his hand. His grip was firm and dry. At the doorway, he turned back. There was softness in his dark face. "I see in your eyes something that should not be there. There is too much anguish for one so young and talented. I sense in you something very disturbing. The door to my office will always be open."

With those words, he was gone. Even the old wooden floor did not creak under his step. Zach sat on the edge of the cot with chin cupped in trembling hands. Compulsively, he again wondered why this man disturbed him so much. He sat there a long time staring at the floor, and then, without warning, tears again began to well-up and flow down his cheeks. He no longer knew what he was going to do that day.

Zach sat for a long period of time, the separation and sense of failure so deep it was a physical pain. Where had it all gone wrong?

"I'm a good doctor!" He spoke only to the four infertile walls. But knowing this fact did not help him. Medicine had been the most important thing in his life for so many years. But now, it oddly no longer seemed to be the central force driving him. Its meaning and purpose were being torn asunder by the ugliness in his marriage, the hate-love he felt for Susan, and the overwhelming love he had for their flaxen-haired infant daughter. Desiree's face was there before him, through the tears. Her presence seemed so real. Zach had never anticipated feeling such incredible love for a helpless baby. So many hours cramming in Anatomy, Physiology, Biochemistry. Then came the Clinic years, continually involved in supervised patient care under demanding and scrupulous professors. There were the months writing two or three page Histories and Physicals, quoting excerpts from Cecil and Loeb's textbook of Internal Medicine, as if from the sacred Torah. Then there were the extensive hours spent examining and researching far into the early morning hours in order to skillfully and efficiently present a differential diagnosis on the surgical patients scheduled for that morning. Added to this were the constant attacks from the Chief Resident and Staff Surgeons and from surly nurses who took pleasure in tormenting young residents. In addition to all this, there was the constant swallowing of pride and battling numbing physical and emotional exhaustion. He knew some of his classmates took Dexedrine to cope with the long hours, but he had always resisted their use. None of the physical or emotional stresses had ever impeded him. In fact, he had welcomed the demands, thrived on pressure, and grew more resourceful as the stress increased. Zach had never required much sleep to perform well and couldn't remember the last time he had slept four or five hours in sequence.

But the circumstances with Susan were different than anything he had ever encountered. It wasn't difficult for him to remember a time when they had been passionately in love. However, during these past several months, Zach had often conjectured that it might have been more passion than love. Did he really know what *love* was? Their passion had been real, healthy, and Herculean. They had made love for hours, often rejecting family and friends. Theirs was a passionate and fiery island, in and for themselves. It was more than a year before the island began to crumble. Then, it was quickly and violently taken apart. The end began with small tremors, followed by more and more furious eruptions that shook their relationship. They had been married in a small church service, her mother and his brother had been there with the appropriate tears and slaps on the back. Having just finished his Internship, he had no money for a honeymoon—not on the salary of two hundred dollars a month. But by cashing a five thousand dollar US Savings Bond that had been a high school graduation gift, they spent five exciting days together traveling from the west coast through the desert of California, arriving in Las Vegas about midnight. Their motel was not the most elegant in the spacious city, but to them it was revered as a bit of paradise. Susan had known very little luxury in her life. Her father had drunk and abused her and her family until the day he died, his flesh turned yellow and abdomen swollen tight with fluid. At the end, he hemorrhaged from the huge veins in his esophagus. His alcoholism and cirrhosis was a deadly disease. Her mother had raised the three children on the income from teaching in a primary school and added to the earnings by cleaning houses on weekends.

From Las Vegas, their next three days passed quickly while hiking hand in hand on the rim of the Grand Canyon and making love on a hastily thrown blanket in the Rocky Mountain National Park. Arriving at the County Hospital was like stepping from the confines of heaven into the quagmire of a stagnant swamp. Not until she found work could they afford a decent apartment. His salary as a first year surgical resident was totally laughable. But it didn't seem to matter. Being together was all they needed, until the birth of their daughter merged with the harsh demands of his surgical program. It was then that Susan's moods began to change. Suddenly, she was becoming angry for reasons he couldn't fathom. She progressively became more jealous, accusing him of staying at the hospital to have affairs with the nurses. Sometimes he would leave early in the morning with Susan loving and attentive, only to arrive home after thirty-six hours on duty to find the apartment's dead bolt latched and his knocking met by a venting of profanity and irrational accusations. More and more often, he had to sleep in the Resident's call room and make various excuses to his fellow residents. Yet, through this time, there were moments of calm and happiness. Zach began feeling as if he were walking a tight rope. There was a constant dread gripping him with an imperceptible icy hand.

◇◇◇◇◇◇◇◇◇

Zach was shattered suddenly from his deep solicitude by the telephone. He cursed loudly and then was attacked by guilt for the use of stupid profanity. But he struck back at his own irrational thoughts, "Forget all that religious rubbish. I long ago got rid of that nonsense."

The phone rang again. His sense of duty struggled sadistically with his desire for freedom. But his call to medicine won and he picked up the ringing instrument, warning signs going off in his head.

"Sorry to bother you, Doc. I know that you're not on call, but the Chief asked me to contact you." Gertie's voice from the hospital switchboard seemed more odious than ever. Zach must have waited longer than he had realized because her Midwestern accent again gushed from the phone, "Hey, Doc, you there?"

"Right, Gertie, I'm here, but not for long 'cause I'm out of here. I haven't had four hours off in a row for . . . I don't know when!"

"Yeah, I know how you feel!" She didn't. She had never worked more that an eight-hour shift in her life. "But we've got a big one. A plane crashed at International. They're taking some to St. Luke's and some to Mercy and some are arriving here already." The emergency crews knew that County was the closest. He slammed the phone down without replying and quickly grasped his white coat and started for the door. Suddenly, he stopped, as if held by an invisible hand. Once more, he sensed something there, not really a presence, but more a force. Real or imagined, Zach suddenly felt calmer inside than he had for weeks; weariness drained from him. Unexplainably, his mind was clearer and he felt physically revived. Once again, Zach just waved off this strange sense of a *presence* as being due to lack of sleep.

Sunday afternoons in the ER were normally a time of relative repose. Until now, this day had its normal run of lacerations, accidental poisonings, sore throats, and fevers. But when Zach entered the long ER room, the dozen beds lining the wall were filled with patients in varied states of injury. The two minor surgery suites were connected to one another by a thin wall and were enclosed with glass on three sides. Each was filled with patients and teams of doctors, nurses, and paramedics. There was an explosion of cries, orders being barked, and staff darting from place to place in what might seem to the untrained eye to be total chaos. However, to Zach, all the turmoil was purposeful and efficient. He found himself unconsciously seeking out Dr. Mutamaya, knowing that his attendance would be a stabilizing force. He did not see him and had no time to search because a young nurse was shaking his arm.

"Dr. Wylie, Dr. Mutamaya wants you in OR two, stat!" As quickly as she had appeared, she was gone.

Glancing through the glass window, Zach saw Dr. Mutamaya in the process of intubating a patient. He looked up briefly as Zack entered the OR and then finished advancing the endotube down the patient's trachea and attaching the respirator.

"Zach, they need me upstairs—an internal bleed. The peritoneal taps were positive. The patient is still in shock after three units of blood. Probably a spleen or lacerated liver. This woman here has a flail chest and a pneumothorax. She needs traction on the sternum and a chest tube, stat."

Zach's mind kicked in quickly. "Vitals, please!" Turning to the nurse and realizing that it was the same pretty face that had told him that he was needed here.

"Blood pressure 60/30, pulse 150. Her respirations are too erratic to count."

The patient obviously had multiple rib fractures and her boney thorax was unstable so that when she breathed in to expand her lungs, the negative pressure caused her chest to collapse instead of expanding to draw air into the lungs. This *flail chest* with its paradoxical breathing would be rapidly fatal. Also, the collapsed lung, caused by the penetrating edge of a broken rib, was viciously robbing her body of oxygen. This, they all knew, allowed the pressure from the expanded lung to push the heart and large vessels to the opposite side. The result of these two conditions was swiftly making death inevitable.

Zach saw that the chest tube tray was opened and the patient's chest had been prepped with an antiseptic. "Get me a couple of large towel clips, some rope, and small pulleys and weights. You can get them out of the orthopedic supplies. Stat!" His command was somewhat louder than he meant it to be. He turned to say something to Dr. Mutamaya, but he was gone.

Within minutes, Zach had a tube between her fourth and fifth ribs in the lateral chest wall, no anesthesia being necessary; the patient was too far in shock to need it. The nurse quickly attached this tube to the drainage bottles on the floor, creating a negative pressure and allowing the lung to expand. While the nurse was arranging the bottles, Zach collected the sharp-pointed towel clips that were made to hold surgical drapes around the wound. He quickly clamped them to the mid portion of the fifth ribs on each side of the breastbone. He then tied a thin nylon robe to their handles, and, using IV stands, he attached pulleys and small weights. This effectively pulled the dying women's chest out, allowing her to reverse the paradoxical breathing. Her chest, diaphragms, and lungs were again functioning as the billows they were meant to be.

"BP 110/62, pulse down to 100, and respirations not so labored. Her color is a lot better. Do you want arterial blood gases again, Doctor?"

The nurse's voice was professional and efficient, but Zach thought he sensed something else. Was it admiration for his work? He wanted to think so, but it was more likely relief he was hearing in her voice. A few minutes ago, this young patient was near death. Now she was stabilized and had a chance to live. The entire setup was crude, but effective. It would keep her alive until she could get to the Intensive Care Unit and the more sophisticated technology.

"Can we transfer her now, Doctor?" He noticed for the first time just how pretty this very skilled nurse was. Her short cropped, almost boyish haircut seemed to accentuate her natural beauty. It perfectly framed her large brown eyes. She squeezed his arm ever so briefly.

"Yes, take her way. And order the blood gases." Zack replied, somewhat self-consciously.

"I will, and . . . uh, good job, doctor."

He was right, there was admiration in her eyes, and he suddenly felt less exhausted. But from either fatigue or a distorted ego, he once again couldn't accept a compliment for a job well done—so he expressed nothing. He turned away from her and started toward the next disaster area. But he could feel her eyes on his back and so he turned back to her and mumbled weakly, "Thanks."

CHAPTER 4

An aide with a kerosene lantern moved up next to the man at the doorway and the flickering light cast shadows on this horrible mirage before him. Ben stared back at the fiery eyes and knew instinctively who this man must be. Although he had never met him, the vicious face, military bearing, and the ugly scar along the left side of his face had all been described to him. Ben now saw for himself that scar which started near the eye and meandered over his cheek to find the corner of his mouth. The hideous wound retracted his upper lip into a perpetual sneer that was made even more ghastly by the flickering light. This grim apparition had to be Colonel Ching.

The odor of alcohol struck Ben, even from the distance between them. The man stepped in and closed the door. Now there was darkness again and the Colonel was visible only by the moonlight from the window. Ben heard Ching's heavy booted steps coming toward him and then stop. Only a silhouette was facing him. Suddenly, there was an enormous pain across the left side of his head and a kaleidoscope of colors flashed before his eyes. He felt a severe burning sensation over his face—then there was nothing.

◇◇◇◇◇◇◇◇◇

Colonel Ching Mugaba had been born Antonio Ansaka in the small, rural village of Mukaka, near the trade city of Bindu in the West-Central part of the Belgium Congo. His father had been a very famous Ngangu Ankisi, who the white men termed a *witch doctor*. Power and cautious esteem were awarded to Antonio's father because he knew the secrets of the dead and the living. The night Antonio was born was a story that was repeated many times around the night fires. The winds and rains that night had come with a force which had frightened even those familiar with tropical storms. Mutando, the brother of his mother and the third wife of his father, had related this birth story to Antonio many times.

It had been the middle of the night when his first cry was heard from the hut of Bangogo, the village midwife. Many nights, as Antonio grew to manhood, his Uncle had retold the story of how the men in a nearby hut, talking and celebrating with palm wine, had heard the cry of a newborn carried upon the wind. With that first cry, the rains abruptly stopped and a cold, lurking silence descended. Antonio's father had never spoken of that night, nor did the boy ever dare ask him. But the other men had told him that when they had exited their place of waiting, they saw in the parting clouds and moonlight a creature of short stature. There was dense hair on its face and body and it had a red mouth with large protruding teeth. The feet were like those of an animal, only backwards. The creature spoke only once, in a nasal snarl, and they could not understand what it said, but they all knew that the baby born that night, the son of the great Ngangu Ankisi's third wife, would someday be very powerful, incredibly wise, and inevitably evil. They had seen the Nkuyu!

Antonio grew rapidly and became physically powerful, which is so typical of the African child with the opportunity for proper nutrition and health care. Antonio's father knew these things and Antonio had many brothers and sisters with whom to associate. As time passed, he developed a keen mind and physical dominance. It did not hurt that he was the favorite of his mother's brother who, in their clan, was the dominant force in young Antonio's life. As he grew, he knew that his uncle was a very important man in his village by the way others spoke of him. Even when they traveled to the large village of Bindu, the people knew him and spoke his name with great respect. He saw his father very little because he was not the first son, yet he knew that his father was a greatly revered and feared Ngangu. People came from long distances to gain knowledge from the celebrated man. The people knew he spoke with the ancestors, and he could cast dreadful spells. Also, he had the power to drive away the Ndoki, the awful entity that could *eat* people and cause their death.

Antonio's father died a full year before he was to reach the age of the pubertal rites and circumcision. The funeral was the largest ever seen in that region. His father had now joined the ancestors and was more in control of their lives than when he had been alive. They must never do anything that would anger him. How much this had influenced Antonio's future no one will ever know.

But in his youth, he longed to know his father, despite having many brothers and sisters and a very learned and patient uncle. A young boy can be barren from the lack of physical contact and love of a father. He did not know his father well in life, but in death he experienced far more of the great Ngangu. In life, he had been worshipped greatly, but now in death, his father's powers were much more dangerous and depraved. All the sons of this honored Ngangu grew up undisciplined and pampered, but they were also prepared and skilled by the very best of resources.

What might seem paradoxical was his early education in Catholic mission schools, where this strong, intelligent, and intense young boy was taught subjection and regulation from the stern Sisters. He learned to acknowledge their demands, but never capitulated to their strictness. And he learned his lessons well. In 1960, the year of Independence of the Congo from her harsh Belgium rulers, he was nineteen years old. That year, Kasavubu became the first president of their new country and news had spread from the east of the Congo that Lumumba had become what leaders called a Prime Minister. It was that year in which Antonio's family sent him to the Catholic secondary school at Kasuku; 150 kilometers (ninety miles) from his home. The small village of Kasuku was where two great rivers joined, helping form the vast Congo River begin its great excursion through the heart of their country. He learned basic information from the Sisters and advanced subjects from the Jesuit Fathers, who often were more immovable and querulous than the Sisters. But Antonio grasped well the Sciences, History, Geography, and the French language. As an energetic and prodigal student, he learned easily and was bored when the other students lagged behind. He was especially drawn to the study of government and politics that were being influenced by the turbulent times. By the time he had reached twenty-one years, he was tall and had an unmistakable aura that made him a natural leader. Yet, everyone knew there was something in his eyes and in his conduct that caused fear. What none of his family, classmates, nor the Priests knew—for Antonio guarded it well—was that the spirit of the Ngangu, his dead father, visited him on many nights while others slept in peace.

CHAPTER 5

Ben did not know what brought him from unconsciousness. Was it the angry voices, the horrible smells, or the intolerable pain in his head? Any movement resulted in severe pain in his temple and neck, momentarily expelling all other sensations. If he lay quiet, the raw, stinging pain diminished a little, and he sensed he was lying on a rank smelling dirt floor. Total darkness prevented seeing anything, but he began sensing the presence of other life. A viscous substance filled his right ear canal but by slowly and carefully turning his head to expose his good ear, he could hear the quiet breathing of someone else. As the senses gradually returned, he was overwhelmed by the odor of excrement. And he quickly discovered that any move created a horrible throbbing throughout his entire head. He lay back, holding his head between his hands, as if to squeeze the pain away. He tried to determine just how long he had laid here. The dried blood matting his hair gave little clue, for he knew that the coagulation of his blood was dependent on the severity of the wound. He could hear the respiration of others a little more clearly now and detected their guarded activities. Reaching out, he moved a hand over the dark mud floor that was hardened and smooth from many years of footsteps.

Suddenly, fear engulfed him and this emotion mingling with the pain of his shattered lips and lacerated scalp produced an unrestrained terror arising from some primitive center of his brain. Someone was approaching! He could smell the acrid odor of sweat and blood and felt someone near him. He had no way of knowing if this was a friend or the arm of death. Then a hand touched his arm and he recoiled instinctively.

"Monsieur Docteur Ben, c'est moi."

Ben's taut nerves suddenly relaxed and tense muscles released their spasm. Brackish tears welled forth, spilling down his cheeks.

"Joel, what are you doing here?" Ben's words were spoken and instantly recognized as inane. The here and why were not fathomable. The effort of just this brief question caused his head to explode and the cut lip to start bleeding again. He lay back on the dirt, exhausted by his efforts.

Joel Lusomba moved closer and took Ben's head in his hands and, with great gentleness, held the doctor's body against his in an attempt to counteract the hypothermia his training taught him was occurring from exposure and blood loss.

Ben had seldom seen the kind of devotion, consideration, and love that Joel had displayed over the past ten years. He had found this young African to be capable of extreme compassion, courage, and affection, especially to a mondele (white man) like he. Their relationship had not always been good, and in its first few months, it had been a turbulent one. Joel had just recently graduated from ITML (Institute Technique Medicale of Lubutu) when the association began. The Institute was a four-year nursing program run by the Belgium government and it had gained a reputation for quality students. But Joel had come to work at the Mission's one hundred and fifty bed hospital with an arrogance fed by conceit. Additionally, he was carrying a chip on his shoulder that could be measured in kilos. Ben seldom lost his temper even when fatigue, heat, and frustrations were at their highest. But this handsome and incredibly arrogant man of twenty-three years had tested his reserves beyond endurance.

It was several weeks after Joel had arrived when Ben's constraints had been reached. This young nurse had continually rebelled against authority, challenging all of Ben's attempts at harmony. It was late one morning, when events came to a breaking point. It had been an especially difficult one because the surgery schedule was severe. To make matters worse, Ben had already performed an emergency Cesarean Section and appendectomy during the night. He was fatigued and on edge. The generator had been down for two nights and it would be days before parts would arrive from Stanleyville. Exhaustion, frustration, and anger had boiled over as he opened his bureau window, hoping to catch a slight breeze, and discovered Joel leaning lazily against a tree, laughing and joking with a female student. He was in charge of the Operating Room, the garcon de salle d'op, and as the director, he was responsible to have it cleaned. Soiled and bloody linen were to be placed in one basket, surgical gloves soaked in an antiseptic solution—to be used again. The floors should have long ago been swept and mopped. But none of this had been even started and this blatant display of rebellion overflowed into Ben's icy anger. "Joel, get into my office, now!" Joel heard a voice filled with hardness and, even from the distance, could see in Dr. Ben's eyes a blaze he did not know existed. Joel suddenly felt fear.

As Joel entered the bureau, closing the door behind him, Ben took several slow deep breaths, attempting to diminish the anger that made him tremble inside. He tried to pray inwardly but couldn't, even though he knew he should. God's Word had much to say about the dangers of uncontrolled anger. But right now he wanted to be angry!

What followed was not so much an interchange as a tirade flung from pent up anger and now unleashed upon Joel. The young man stood back, startled, fearful, and not the least certain that he might be in physical danger. The words spoken during this incident, so many years ago, had been long forgotten. However, it had been a turning point in Joel's life and had opened the path to an association which developed into one of mutual respect, deep affection, and a true father-son relationship. Joel turned his attitude around and began to learn and work faithfully. Within a few months from that angry scene, Ben felt comfortable in allowing him to take greater and greater responsibility. He even became at ease when it was necessary for Joel to perform unsupervised surgical procedures. Once, when Ben had gone to Stanleyville for supplies, Joel had had to do a bowel resection because of a strangulated hernia. He obviously did it skillfully, for the man was eating and ambulating well when Ben returned.

But now Ben lay helpless, his head held firmly, but with great care. He was the powerless one and his protégé the counselor.

"Whe . . . where are we? How long have I been here?" The small effort to speak caused an exploding pain to radiate from behind his eyes and across his face and temple.

"Dr. Ben, you are in the jailhouse at the Collectivite' (the county seat). The soldiers brought you here only about thirty minutes ago. I thought you were dead because you made no sound when they threw you on the ground and kicked you. Only a few minutes ago, you made a noise and I realized that you were alive."

Ben and Joel could hear the sounds of voices drifting through the barred window above them; loud, drunken, and violent voices.

"We must speak very quietly or the soldiers will hear and come back and beat us," Joel's voice trembled with perceptible fear. They lay quietly with only sound being that of their breathing.

CHAPTER 6

A s the throbbing pain in his head began to dissipate, Ben became more aware of the pain in his ribs, legs, and arms. Pressing on his right ribs, he stifled a sudden desire to cry out. He felt the familiar crepitation, "like walking on eggshells" was how a professor had described it. He knew that he had a least one broken rib,

"Dr. Ben, please, I would like for us to pray together. I know God will protect us."

"Yes, Joel . . ." The effort was fiercely painful and his voice was harsh and raspy. The young African recognized this.

"I will pray for us." And so there on the dirt floor with the smell of excrement, blood, and sweat permeating their noses and the sound of drunken soldiers outside, Joel prayed. He asked the Lord Jesus Christ to give them strength in the face of this ugly situation. Joel pleaded with God to help them worship Him in this danger and pain, as they worship Him in the good times. He asked for protection and for relief to Dr. Ben's pain. In Joel's prayer there was no doubt of any kind that there was a supernatural power hearing it.

He seemed to have finished, and then added, "And Lord, forgive the soldiers. They are poor and hungry and they haven't been paid for many months and their minds are terribly distorted by the excess of palm wine and beer. In His name, Amen."

Ben must have slipped back into unconsciousness, for when he again opened his eyes, sunlight was streaming through the wooden bars of the jail window. Fear gripped him as he suddenly and illogically expected the blows of the soldiers again. But as his mind cleared its shrouds further, he realized that he was alone. Propping himself up against the mud wall, he gazed around the tiny room that was about twelve feet square. Joel was gone, as were the others! Or had there been others? Had his imagination played tricks on him? But small sacs, bits of clothes, and sandals lay on the floor, attesting to the fact that there had been others here at one time. Ben sat up a little straighter and experienced a sudden wave of nausea and vertigo, but the pain seemed less severe. His shoulders and arms throbbed with the movement. Someone, it must have been Joel, had wiped the dried blood from his face and neck. However, his thick gray hair was still caked with it. Outside the barred window, an early morning fog had moved in. Ben agonizingly pulled himself up to look out the window, clinging to the bars for support. Ghostly shadows moved along the path and at a distance, trees partially obscured by fog, appeared like multi-appendage creatures with tiny shadowy fingers vibrating rhythmically. Close to the window, a gnarled tree trunk extended upward about ten feet before branching. The bark was bulky and furrowed like thick weathered skin. In many places, green fungus obscured the bark. But bright red blooming flowers were placed deep within its gnarled branches, lessening their ugliness.

Ben reflected for a moment. We humans are so much like this tree—hideous and disfigured. Yet, there is something of beauty in all of us—if only we were searched deep enough. Ben stared for several more moments at the beautiful blossoms partially hidden within the deformed branches. He had no idea from where the ensuing thoughts came, a reaction to his pain, no doubt, but against his will horrible thoughts were rising in him. There had been times in his life when he had come close to hating, but never so overwhelmingly as he felt now. But Ben knew that the Lord Jesus Christ experienced the horrible torment and suffering on the cross, enduring the most malignant torture ever devised by the depraved mind of man. Yet, the Lord had actually prayed for His tormentors. Ben suddenly felt deep remorse for the cruelty he found inside. But yet, at that moment, he would have gladly strangled his tormentors. He fought back the nausea—and guilt.

A violent noise startled him from his thoughts, as a rotting door was shoved open. A soldier in a filthy uniform stood before him. He had double red cloth bars stitched on the right shoulder and an empty cartridge belt around his waist. Only his boots seemed new.

"Kwisa na mono!" he barked. "Come with me." He jerked Ben roughly forward and Ben again had to fight a surge of nausea. But he was pleased that his arms and legs obeyed the commands from his brain. The soldier partially dragged, but mostly shoved Ben toward a group of men sitting in the shade of a

Banyan tree. Ben immediately recognized the revolting face of Colonel Ching. Beyond him, on the ground in front of the mud walled jail laid Joel. His face was covered with dried blood and was battered almost beyond recognition. His right arm was twisted and deformed, obviously severely fractured.

Colonel Ching looked almost pleasant as he smiled at Ben. "I want to treat you to some entertainment." His French was excellent as he nodded to one of his soldiers who jerked Joel to his feet, causing him to cry out with pain. Ben moved instinctively to Joel's aid, but a soldier blocked his way. Helpless, he watched them push Joel up against a tree. He clung to the trunk for support. The soldiers moved away, and before Ben had time to even comprehend what was happening, the Colonel raised his pistol and fired twice at Joel's chest. There was only the nauseous sound of a high caliber bullet hitting flesh. Joel's body was jerked upright for split second and then soundlessly crumpled to the dirt. Ben started toward his young friend, but the butt of a soldier's rifle struck him on the back, driving him the ground. The blow must have made him lose consciousness because when he was able to raise himself up, Joel was gone.

"One of the things I learned from my teachers in the great land of China is that a visual lesson finds a more worthy audience than do words alone." The Colonel's voice was melodious and sounded almost sympathetic. "Come, we must talk." He put his arm around Ben's shoulder as if they were long lost friends. He continued in the benevolent manner. "We know that your friend worked for the CIA, and we know that you are a spy for the United States government." His voice remained calm, but when Ben looked up into the Colonel's eyes, what he saw was unrestrained hate.

Ben was completely taken back by this allegation. "How can you believe that?" Ben asked incredulously. "You know who I am and know that I have been a missionary doctor in this country for more than twenty years."

"Fermez la bouche!" the Colonel's voice had taken back its barbarity. "Shut up!" You will speak only when permitted to!" He turned to two of his soldiers, "Take him away!" These soldiers were grubby and wore tattered, filthy clothes. Their eyes were horridly bloodshot and they reeked of palm wine. But, surprisingly, they were gentle in their treatment of him, although he was so weak that they had to partially drag him. As the soldiers half carried him down the sandy trail, he was able to turn once and his eyes fixed on Ching. The Colonel's posture was erect and he stared at him with eyes that seemed to reflect that all the rage in him was totally concentrated on Ben. Ben's last image was a slight grin appearing at the corners of the Colonel's twisted mouth. It seemed again to come from the depths of hell.

CHAPTER 7

As Pascal Mutamaya left the emergency room, now a scene of silence, he was wondering about this exceptionally gifted young surgical resident, Zach Wylie. Pascal always exited the back entrance through the staff parking, although he chose not to own a vehicle. Dawn was well exposed now as he crossed the parking lot. He saw a few of the other physician's cars already in their marked places. The ever-present pigeons were actively involved in starting their day, doing whatever pigeons do. Pascal turned down Eden Avenue, sardonically called *Blood Alley* by the local residents. It took little imagination to realize the origin of the name. He had seen the blood from this district often flow in the ER. This was a part of town most people choose to avoid. By Midwest America's standards, the buildings here were old, mostly constructed in the early 1900's. They were small, one story brick structures, decent in their time but now decaying. For several blocks, these made a passageway of unpretentious cement cubes with inconsequential porches and even more trivial lawns. This was one portion of the "black ghetto" in the city.

"Hi, nigger," a young adolescent yelled.

"Hey, cool it man!" Pascal retorted using a phrase he had heard on the streets. The young man stared nastily at him for a few seconds and then turned and was gone.

These people were poor and a few could be very dangerous. Most of the inhabitants in these slums struggled to survive while loving their wives, their children, and their neighbors. But for a small number, drinking, copulating, and gang wars were the way of life; alcohol, heroin, and amphetamines drove their existence. They cursed and hated, sang and danced, loved and gave life and took life. They felt rejected by society and yet demanded from this same society huge amounts of things they felt were due them.

Pascal found himself in deep reflection. *Why do the Americans blame this subculture on Africa? These people are not my kinsmen. We have criminals and bad people, yes, does not every culture? To declare this offensive and distorted way of living on Africa is a gross injustice. I wished the Americans could know my people.* This was not the first time Pascal had entertained these thoughts.

However, in some way, Pascal had bonded with these people. A breakthrough had come early in his association when he had treated the leader of particularly violent gang who called themselves, "the Black Cross." Its leader, Moto, had sustained deep knife wounds to both his upper arms and abdomen. It was late at night when two ill-tempered young men burst into Pascal's apartment and ordered him to come with them. They led him down dark, filthy alleys into a dingy room lighted with a single bulb hanging from the ceiling. The place smelled of beer, marijuana, sweat, and old blood. Moto lay on a filthy rug that covered the floor. If he was in pain, the poor lighting did not reveal it in his face.

"You're going to help me, man. No cops, no questions, and no reports or you're dead meat, sucker, and I mean, like chopped meat, understand?"

"You do not threaten me or give me orders, young man! I am not your servant or your frightened *sujuet*—how do you say in English—your inferior!" Moto had backed off a little, probably more from pain, weakness, and his needs than from any particular fear caused him by this black doctor. Pascal had returned to the Hospital with a semi-concealed escort. He gathered a few things and returned to Moto's room. After assuring himself that the wounds were not too grave, particularly the abdominal wounds, he had cleaned and sutured all the lacerations. He injected the young tough with penicillin and anti-tetanus vaccine and left a prescription for some codeine, realizing that this gang leader would probably sell some of it for profit. He visited Moto several times after that, but at these times it had been in his home. He found that he had a wife and two small children, to whom he seemed exceedingly devoted. Moto recovered quickly and well. From that time on, the word was out, "Don't touch this black doctor with the funny way of talking."

All these reflections were going through Pascal's mind as he turned up the short sidewalk to his apartment and ascended the two steps to his door. The fat, toothless landlady stuck her head out of the house that abutted his.

"Hi, Doc, how was your night?"

"Magnificant, ma petite mademoiselle."

She giggled as she pulled her head back. She had no idea what he had said, but the words sounded so nice and clean. She wanted to believe they were good words.

His apartment was small, but clean and immaculately kept. His salary would permit much better, but this is what he preferred for now. It was enough to meet his needs. Pascal had no delusions, for he realized that by denying himself many comforts, he experienced less guilt when remembering the conditions in which his family had lived for so many years. Conditions in his African village had been pleasant during his early years. Although his house had dirt floor, walls of sticks and mud, and a grass roof, it was comfortable and tidy. It was during his teen years that conditions changed. This was the time when the Congo was gaining Independence and so much anarchy reigned. It was in the late 1950's when Moise Tshombe led the Shaba district in revolt against the new government of Patrice Lumumba. During these years, there were the massacres of several missionaries and many white people in his country. But the Congolese people themselves suffered the most. The memories of those years of cold, hunger, horror, and death were never far from his consciousness. He and his family had spent many months hidden in the forest to evade the rebel forces. He was eighteen when they heard that an unknown Colonel by the name of Mobutu was campaigning for the presidency. The colonel promised peace to the land, and meat, radios, and vehicles for all. And peace had come for a period. But to Pascal, to his family, and to his village, the lingering pain and terror of those years had seared scars into their memories. A sister and three brothers had died from malnutrition and disease. His older brother, Antonio Ansaka, had disappeared during their first year of hiding. The last information heard of this older brother was that he had been kidnapped by a rebel army lead by one man; although some said he was not a man, but a fiend. He was Chinese and had come to the Congo with a small army to spread, by force if necessary, the great Communist doctrine.

Dr. Pascal Mutamaya lay back on his small couch staring at the undecorated walls. How much he had loathed his older bother during the years before he disappeared. He remembered him as an intense and sullen boy, given to quick attacks of anger. But he knew him also to be quick to learn and had intelligence beyond his peers. Antonio could be very amicable at times, but more often callous and diabolical. Pascal remembered the occasions when he captured scorpions and placed them in his blanket at night. He could mimic the sounds of many animals and when he would find his younger brother alone in the dark, he could roar like the hideous lion or cough like the terrifying leopard. It brought him great ecstasy to see Pascal's fear. More than once he had held Pascal's hand close to the flame of their night fires until he would scream with pain. Often, he would go to bed with his hand blistered and raw, only to find a small viper slithering across the floor of his bedroom. After their father died, Antonio's grief had been unrestrained and far more severe than felt by any other of the family. During the ensuing months, his brother was gone more and more from their village. Then, when the soldiers came, he vanished completely.

Pascal suddenly shivered, as if something cold had passed through his body. Why were these memories coming back so strongly now after this many years? But, instinctively, he knew that in some way it had to do with this young resident, Zach Wylie. There was something in his demeanor and in his eyes. He sensed emotions in this young man akin to his own fears from the forest where he and his family had hidden for so many years. Yet, beyond his instincts, he had nothing from which to base these feelings. However, Pascal also knew to trust his instincts. Zach Wylie was being tortured and driven into an exile of his own forest, not by rebel soldiers, but by forces of which Pascal had no knowledge. He felt determined to know this young man better, and if he had a hiding place in the forest, he would try to bring him out of it. Would there be a way?

The sun was rising higher in the east and the temperature in Pascal's apartment was mounting in accord. He went to the refrigerator to find a cold drink, but there were neither soft drinks nor iced tea, so he opted for ice cubes and tap water. In his preoccupation, he had failed to see the letter placed on his small desk by the landlady. His heart leaped, as it always did, when he saw a postmark from the Congo. Excitement regarding news from home is a universal reaction. Letters from his family in Africa during the past two to three years had become fewer and fewer, as conditions in the Congo were again deteriorating. Even though excited, he calmly opened the mail with a knife. He was rarely pushed to unnecessary actions. Years of surgical training requiring calmness in the face of adversity and stress had made him react with composure.

The letter opened with, "Mon frere en Jesus Christ." It was from one of his best friends from childhood, Jeremiah Mabimbi. From the early years in their village through the years at the University in Leopoldville, they had remained close friends. The letter continued, "I wish you well and pray that God's grace is strong in your life. But I am writing because I must tell you that some rebel forces trying to depose the present government have captured our friend, our counselor, and our father in Christ, Dr. Ben Wells. No one has received news about him for several weeks and we fear him dead."

The letter went on to give news of family, mutual friends, and the conditions in the Congo. But Pascal was too dazed to be interested in the words. Tears flooded his eyes and a cold, oppressive anxiety gripped his body. For a few seconds, he felt as if the hand of death was crushing him.

"It cannot be, dear Jesus, it cannot be!" His small room seemed to become narrower and the air more stifling. Often in the past, when Pascal found himself in overwhelming and oppressive situations, he had learned to clear his mind by running. In moments he was changed into his jogging clothes and out in the street, oblivious of the shouted words and hostility. There were many people in their yards now, some sitting on steps or mowing lawns, others were cursing one another and scolding their active children. Pascal passed by without acknowledging them. For the next hour he ran through filthy streets, into a park where lovers were holding hands and people were walking their dogs. He moved along streets littered with paper, cigarette butts, and beer cans, then down an alley where dark-haired young people were shooting dice and doing drugs. They were startled and angered by his presence, but he ignored their swearing. He entered the Park View district, an area where even the police will not go without solid backup. After about an hour and a half of running, he finally began to experience fatigue. Sweat stung his eyes and his lungs burned; muscles were becoming taut. His lithe body was covered with perspiration, but his feverish thoughts were becoming composed. What he must do was frighteningly clear. He must return to the Congo. He must search for Dr. Ben . . . and he *would* find him! He had vacation time coming and in fact, Dr. Tharp had been encouraging him to take some time off. Pascal was walking now, making plans in his mind. He was completely oblivious of the angry stares and filthy words hurled at him. Suddenly, a large black man stood menacingly in his path. His legs were apart, arms folded across his chest. His eyes burned with hate. The odor of cheap booze extruded with each of his breaths.

"What ya' all doin' in these parts, black boy?" His right hand slipped into his pants pocket and there was no prelude to the appearance of a vicious knife. It was hardly out of his pocket when the blade flashed and locked itself into place with a sinister click.

Pascal's voice was calm, "I'm sorry, man. I didn't mean to be comin' to your part a town. Man, I was just runnin, you know, and I is kinda, like, you know, lost, man." He purposely had fallen into the vernacular of the streets he had heard so much. "I is goin' ta get my black butt outta here right now."

But as Pascal started to pass the hulking frame, the huge man brought the knife forward and struck toward his abdomen. What occurred next happened so quickly that there is no agreement among those who observed it. But the one thing they did agree on is that the large black man was suddenly lying on the ground, his right arm twisted at a grotesque angle. He was trying to scream out in pain, but could only emit a gurgling noise. The blow from the edge of Pascal's hand had found its mark on the man's trachea. That blow had fallen a split second before the arm holding the knife was twisted down and back. Even bystanders several feet away heard the cracking of bone. Pascal kicked the knife away and looked down at hoodlum. His demeanor was calm and his face showed real concern. Quickly, he removed his sweatshirt and rolled it into crude splint. He then secured it to the man's forearm with a couple of belts obtained from the crowd that had appeared around the scene. The forearm was now no longer at the ugly angle it had been. The man was quieter now and as Pascal looked more closely at his assailant, he saw that he was younger than he had realized—and very terrified. But he made no mistake; this could still be a very dangerous enemy.

"You get him down to County Hospital and ask for Dr. Setleff!" Pascal commanded, facing a couple of young men he was certain were friends to this man. "Dr. Setleff is a bone specialist and will take care of him."

His victim was regaining his voice enough for foul curses to burst out. He took a few raspy breaths and then said, "Hey, man, I ain't got no money for no bone specialist." Where you from man, you don't talk like no nigger I ever heard of."

Pascal ignored the question and turned back to the fallen man's friends. "You just see that he gets to the hospital. The rest will be taken care of." There would be no arguing from them after looking into Pascal's eyes. He gave them no room for any other decision as he turned and walked quietly away.

As Pascal was entering his apartment, the phone was ringing. He hesitated for a moment. He could not take calls now! He had to start making plans for a trip! But his training made him answer.

"What the heck did you do to this guy, my friend?" Joe Setleff said without preamble. His counterfeit gruffness always amused Pascal.

"I think he fell down, Joe."

"Sure, and I'm Marie Antoinette. Most people fracture the midshaft of the radius and ulna falling, and they also always wind up with an ugly bruise over the trachea. Bull, my friend. That's bull like in Brahma bull . . ."

"Never mind, Joe, I get your point. The man attacked me with a knife. It was some of my stupid training from the past. I did not mean to hurt him, just slow him down. How is he doing?"

"Oh, he'll be just fine, but if I have any troubles with little Lord Fauntleroy here and the two dwarfs with him, I'm calling you."

The line was dead before Pascal could thank him, but he had to smile to himself. Joe Setleff was one of the best orthopedic surgeons with whom he had ever worked and he really cared about his patients. This black street fighter would receive good care and it remained unsaid that there would be no charge. Besides, Pascal had never known anyone who mixed his stories as much as Joe. He could not help but chuckle, imagining two of the seven dwarfs and a little *lord* something or other. He returned to making his plans.

CHAPTER 8

A t the very moment that Pascal was jogging, fighting his fear for the one man he cherished more than any other human being, Zach was just leaving County Hospital. His mind was invaded with plans almost too bleak to think of on a conscious level. He had to see his daughter, hold her close to him, and feel her silken hair against his face. Just to hear her say "daddy" in her musical voice. He had to be with her, even if only for a few minutes. He knew that Susan would not allow it; she would resist and scream at him and the scene would become ugly. During the past several months, when he had tried to see Desiree, she had acted more and more mentally ill. Also, he had increasingly detected the odor and behavior of alcohol intoxication. On his last attempt to see his daughter, he was sure there was a man in the house. If he would insist on seeing Desiree on these occasions, it would be his daughter who would suffer the most afterward. The whole scenario was replayed again and again and he would have to leave, if for no other reason than to protect her. If only his plan now would work, he thought, and instinctively felt the small packet in his side coat pocket. He was not so worried about giving Susan the strong sedation, but he felt real self-contempt that he was drawn to this level. Yet, he could think of no other way. This was his only chance. Nearing the home, he once again began to suffer the gut rendering apprehension he experienced each time he approached Susan. If only he could only get her to stay calm for a few minutes and visit normally. Maybe, just maybe, he could convince Susan to make coffee. And conceivably, he could slip the sedative into her coffee without being seen. Susan would become formidably angry if she detected the taste but the drug should act so quickly that there would be little she could do. Apprehensions flooded in now. What if she would not even let him in, as so many times before? What if the dosage was too little—too much? His self-shame became stronger as he felt the familiar knot forming in his stomach and he noted a slight tremor of his hand—*not much of a man, are you, Zach?* he thought. As he pulled the car in front of her house, a sudden shiver shook him. A cold chill filled his body and he once more experienced an overwhelming feeling of a presence, so similar to the day at the hospital. Again, he shook it off. *Too little sleep*, he argued to himself. Yet, he couldn't completely rid himself of the feeling that there was something or someone wanting to contact him. Then, entirely unexpectedly, Zach felt peacefulness and assurance sweep over him, something he had not experienced for so very long. When he approached her door, he no longer felt the near panic he normally felt on her doorstep. He rang the bell with a steady hand, expecting Susan to open the door in her nasty way, but nothing occurred. Just silence. Zach then knocked and as he did, it caused the door to swing open, so he stepped in and quietly spoke her name. The room was a mess and smelled horrible. It was dark in the living room because the curtains were still drawn. Dirty dishes were on the table and two chairs were on the floor several feet from the table. He called again and there was still no response. Still, Zach still felt no apprehension. Susan's behavior had been so erratic during the past couple of years that nothing much amazed him. Thinking she might have been drinking and fallen asleep, he pushed open the door to the bedroom. The sight that confronted him was one the normal mind cannot visualize, even in its worst nightmare. The entire room had been devastated. The dressing table was wiped clean of all objects and the mirror shattered. Clothes lay strewn all over the floor and blood was splattered on the rug and walls like a scarlet Rorschach test. Zach was so overwhelmed by the condition of the room, he had failed to glance at the bed until now. Susan lay on her back, naked except for blue panties. Her arms and legs were dispersed at strange angles and she would have appeared like a discarded rag doll except for the hideous crimson wounds over her chest and abdomen. Blood was everywhere and even to a surgeon, familiar with blood and hideous wounds, this sight caused revulsion in him like nothing he had ever felt. He rushed to the bed, instinctively knowing nothing could be done. Feeling for her pulse and checking pupils were done mechanically. Her hand was still warm, and for a few seconds, his mind awkwardly traveled back in time to when they had held hands and loved one another so intimately. Suddenly, he dropped her hand and his whole being tensed, nerves strung in tight bands. "Oh, God, where is Desiree?" Vision of her limp, blood covered body flooded his brain. He rushed to her bedroom to find it neatly kept, quiet, and empty. Much calmer now, much surer that nothing so horrible had happened to her, he glanced in the bathroom. No human should ever have to encounter the terrible shock that once again met Zach. There was blood everywhere; on the walls, floor, and sink. The small, naked, twisted body of Desiree was in the bathtub, discarded as if she had been no more than a wet rag. He knew he had to exam her for any signs of life, but for a few seconds, he couldn't make himself touch her. The arms he had so much wanted to feel around his neck were now just soft flesh with multiple ugly cuts. Her golden hair was stained with blood. He gently lifted her out of her white porcelain coffin. There was no life in her and it only took seconds to know that she had not been dead long. Zach stood there, tears running down his face and sobbing uncontrollably. He had dreamed of her running through the doorway, blond hair bouncing up and down, little hands reaching up to him, and her child's voice repeating, "Daddy, Daddy."

Zach carried her limp body back into the living room, too engrossed and occupied with grief to see the woman standing in the front doorway. She screamed at him with foul and violent words, then turned and ran from the house. He thought he had seen her on one of his previous visits here. *A close neighbor*, he thought vacantly. Assuming she would be calling the police, he took Desiree's flaccid body over and laid it next to Susan's mutilated one and carefully placed a sheet over them. He knew he was messing with evidence but he couldn't just let their bodies lie there, twisted, torn, and naked for all to stare at. He pulled the bench from the dressing table next to the bed and took Desiree's tiny hand in his. He was there when the police arrived. He was shocked to see three uniformed officers coming at him with guns drawn. Before he could even speak, they were barking out orders. "Get your hands on top your head, spread your legs. You make one funny move, just one, and we start using you for target practice! Got it!"

Zach didn't have the strength or proclivity to say anything to dispute their orders. It would all be cleared up in a short time, he was certain. He felt detached and numb, all life drained from him. They could do to him anything they wanted. All he could feel was Desiree's limp, cool hand in his, and he didn't care any more.

CHAPTER 9

It took Pascal most of the remainder of the day to visit with the necessary individuals, in particular, Dr. Leadbetter, the Coordinator of Surgery and the ER, Also, he spoke with Dr. Tharp, the Chief of Surgery, and Mrs. O'Neal, the assistant administrator. They all agreed, although reluctantly, that he could take a three-month leave of absence. They would have to call a meeting with the Board of Directors, of course, but that this would only be a formality. It was early evening when he returned to his apartment, the congenial landlady, stuck her neck out the window.

"There was some people lookin' for you about an hour ago."

"Black or white folk, Mrs. Brown?"

"They was both white. A pretty young gal and a big tough looking man with a scar on his chin."

That would have been Joe Setleff, Pascal was sure, but of the young woman he could not imagine.

"Merci, madame. Vous étés encore mon petit papillon."

"Hey, Doc, ya quit givin' me your bull!" She withdrew her head, chuckling.

Pascal was naturally curious about Joe's visit. This was not an area that he was necessarily afraid of; it was just that socially and professionally, he had no contacts here.

The phone rang and Pascal sensed immediately that he would soon have the answer to his questions. Picking up the receiver, he answered, "Hi, Joe!"

"Hi, my friend, aren't you the mind reader. We've been looking for you. Glad you're home."

"We, Joe?

"Yeah, do you remember a small, brown-haired nurse from the ER. She wears her hair short; kind of a pixie style, I guess. She's no bigger than a minute and real cute."

It sounded as if Joe put his hand over the phone and Pascal assumed he was saying something to someone.

"She is staring daggers at me," he laughed, and continued, "She has worked with you many a shift, I think."

"Certainly, I know here. Her name is Miss Powell, Angela Powell, I believe. Was she with you this afternoon at my apartment?"

"Right! Let me explain." Joe sounded a little uneasy, and if Joe seemed even slightly disturbed, something was very wrong.

"She called me this afternoon and told me that Zach, Zach Wylie is in jail. She has worked with him in the ER and respects him a lot. Well, she has a close friend who is a cop down at the Mason Street Police Station. Apparently, Angela has spoken to her friend about Zach, and so when she was helping book him in, she thought she recognized the name and gave Angela a call. She said he looked a mess and appeared rather dazed. His hands, clothes, and shoes had blood on them. The officers that brought him in say that they found some kind of powder in his pocket, but no weapon of any kind. They arrested him on the spot for "possession" and *also* for possible murder of his ex-wife and his daughter. Pascal, it sounds like it must have been one gruesome sight. Their bodies were all naked and both the woman and the child had been stabbed multiple times. The cops said it looked like a slaughterhouse. Guess it was!"

"Has anyone gone down to talk to Zach yet?" Pascal asked.

"Nope! Not that we're aware of. That is why we have been trying to get a hold of you. We know you are his chief and I understand you've taken a little extra interest in this young resident. We thought you might want to go down there, Pascal. Besides, we didn't know whom else to call. His file doesn't list any family."

"Thank you, Joe. I am on my way." He started to hang up, but Joe said, "Hold it a sec, Pascal." A pause and then, "Angela wants to know if you would mind if she met you at the station?"

"Not at all. I will see her there."

The police station at Mason and Sixth Street was about two miles from Pascal's apartment and he would normally have walked, but time seemed to be too important, so he called a taxi. He arrived at the station within thirty minutes of Joe's call. Angela was already there, standing on the steps leading up to the old three-story Municipal Building. She appeared strained and tense, but stood erect and assured. She seemed smaller here on these step than in the ER, not more than five foot two with deep brown eyes, placed almond like on each side of a lilliputian nose. Her closely cut hair was brown, but by no means matched the dark abyss of her coffee colored eyes. Pascal could not help but notice that in her jeans and blouse, she had a very engaging figure. He had never seen her in anything but nurse's uniform or a scrub suit.

She really is a very pretty young woman, Pascal thought, *for a mondele anyway.* He smiled to himself, knowing that pretty is pretty, whether white or black.

Angela greeted him anxiously, but with a smile that transformed her face in an almost angelic vision and drew Pascal to her immediately.

"Thank you for coming. It is so kind of you. I just didn't know whom else to call when I got the news from Sara here at the station. I know you are his chief in the ER, so I tried to find you. They told me that you would be in meetings all day, so I got in touch with Dr. Setleff. He helped me find you."

Even though she was obviously distraught, her voice was calm with a low-pitched quality—quite resonant for such a diminutive young woman.

As they entered the building, she continued speaking, "I don't know Dr. Wylie except for working with him at the hospital. I have heard that he is going through an ugly marital situation and that he has been trying to find a way to spend some time with his daughter. Apparently, his ex-wife won't let him. I really do have a lot of respect for his medical and surgical abilities. He is one of the best residents I have worked with and one of the most competent surgeons I know."

"I must agree with your opinion. I feel very much the same."

"But Dr. Mutamaya, I must confess, I am drawn to him as a person. Sure, he is tall and good-looking. The nurses all call him a hunk. But that isn't the foremost issue. He isn't a content person—that is obvious. But I can understand that with his workload and the divorce situation. Yet, there is something else. Sometimes, for fleeting seconds, I have seen so much more in his eyes. I don't know if it is pain, a sense of defeat, or a deep urgency for something he doesn't understand himself."

"Or fears from the forest."

"I don't understand, Dr. Mutamaya."

"I am sorry, Angela, I will explain one day. For now, we shall go see Zach."

"Please don't say anything to Zach about what I have said. If the truth were known, I probably want to mother him."

"I promise!"

◇◇◇◇◇◇◇◇◇

"Can I help you?" The husky man dressed in blue behind the desk seemed cordial enough.

"Yes, please, we are looking for Dr. Zach Wylie," Pascal replied. He could not decipher the meaning of the inquiring look the policeman gave him. Was it the title *doctor* he had used for the prisoner? Or was it his accent or maybe the fact that he could not believe anyone would even be looking for this man?

"You his lawyer?"

"No, we are friends. May we see him?"

"You can, but only one at a time. Station rules."

Angela turned to Pascal. "Please, you go in and see him. I'll find a place out here and wait." *And pray hard*, she thought to herself.

"All right then, but I will let you know what is happening as soon as I can."

The sergeant led Pascal down a narrow hall lined on each side with barred cages. He stopped at the fourth enclosure from the entrance. Zach did not immediately look up. People had been coming and going during the hours he had been here. But then, sensing they had not passed by, he raised his face and found himself gazing into Dr. Mutamaya's dark face. Zack thought, *I've heard some of my religious friends speak of a savior. Well, this must be him!*

"Hello, Dr. Wylie." Once again, this man's presence brought him security. Even the fact that he called him Doctor brought back some confidence. In the lonely hours sitting here in this dingy cell, he had visualized his surgical training, the long hard hours of study, and his entire life all being destroyed by the events of the past few hours.

"I won't ask you right now how you heard about me. I am just thankful you are here. So far they haven't even given me the chance for that one phone call you always hear about. So I didn't think anyone knew about this. But, Dr. Mutamaya, I'm sorry to get you involved in this mess," Zack found himself speaking hurriedly.

"There is no problem. We just need to find out how to go about getting you out of here."

"Hey, Doc, they told me you were back here." There was no doubting the origin of this booming voice with strong Irish inflections. "What brings you to my little realm?"

Pascal and Captain O'Reilly had become fast friends over the last couple of years as a result of their paths mixing at that crossroads between the criminals and the wounded. What had solidified their friendship was when Dr. Mutamaya had testified in a case in which one of the captain's men had been accused of police brutality. Pascal had examined the injured man in the ER, and later testified that the wounds were not such to have been caused by a beating. Despite the demands and threats of an overzealous lawyer from the County Defender's office, he stuck to the facts and the officer was acquitted. The captain developed a deep respect for this African doctor's integrity, his grit and moral strength. The friendship had been strong from that time on.

"Doc, do you know this man we have here?"

"Yes, Sam, he is one of my best residents down at County." Then he added, "And also a friend."

"Good gosh, man, I didn't suppose this guy was any surgeon. From the looks of him when they brought him in, you'd think he worked in a slaughter house." Then he looked at Zach, "I'm sorry, young man, stupid statement!" Turning back to Pascal, "Anybody give you the details?"

"Not much, Sam, but we would like to know."

"We?"

"Yes, Dr. Wylie has another friend out in the waiting room. She is the one that brought this to my attention."

Zack was curious, but too exhausted to ask who was with Dr. Mutamaya.

"Yeah, well, we were called by a neighbor; a woman who lives next door. She called 911 and they put her call through to us. She was one frantic caller, I guess. She was crying and screaming about a neighbor being dead and all cut up and blood everywhere and the killer was still there! This didn't sound like any crank call, so we sent two patrol cars over there on the double."

The captain continued. "Your man here was in the house. He was just sitting and waiting, as if he were expecting my men to arrive."

"That sure doesn't sound like a guilty man, does it, Sam?"

"Hey, in my business, we don't take anything at face value. People have all kinds of ways of trying to look innocent. My men said that he appeared terribly hopeless, but he was cooperative, and he sure seemed to be in control of himself. I hope that my men didn't get too rough with him, but they were mighty shaken up when they saw that gruesome scene." Sam glanced at Zach, but found he could not read any expression in his eyes. He did, however, notice that he was involuntarily rubbing his wrist where handcuffs had been fastened tightly.

"Please, Sam, tell me what happened—as much as you are allowed to, anyway." Turning to Zach, "Would you rather we spoke elsewhere?"

"No. What you describe can't be any worse than I what already went through. I know what I saw, but I would like to know what the police found."

"Okay, then." Sam said. He turned to Pascal. "Doc, if you'll vouch for this man here, then that's good enough for me. We'll let him out and he can clean up a little, and then we'll go down and get a cup of coffee and talk things over."

"I'll take full responsibly for him, Sam."

"Alright." He turned back to Zack. "I'm going to let you out. You go down to the end of the hall. That's my office. Go wash the blood off yourself and comb that head of hair of yours. Oh, and grab one of my clean shirts out of the locker. We can't have you going out there to talk to that pretty little gal with blood all over your shirt."

As Zach went down the hall, he hardly heard the last comment because he was so absorbed with the fact that the captain of a major police force would let a possible cold blooded murderer walk away just on the basis of one man's say so—no further questions asked. *There is no way I will ever get that much admiration and respect in a life time*, he thought.

While he washed, he dimly tried to think of who the woman was in the waiting room. No one came to mind. The chance to clean up and get rid of the bloodstained shirt had a humanizing affect, even if the shirt was wildly flowered and hung on him. When he went back out into the hall, they were gone. A kind appearing white-haired gentleman was standing there.

"Come with me, son, they want you to join them down at the coffee lounge, but I use the term 'coffee' rather loosely."

Dr. Mutamaya, the captain, and the girl were in an active conversation when he entered. The young woman arose instantly and he recognized her, although he embarrassingly could not recall her name. He did remember his response to her in the ER.

Without any sense of shyness, she walked quickly to him, threw arms around his neck, and hugged him warmly. It seemed the most natural response in the world coming from her.

"Oh, Dr. Wylie, we've been so worried about you." She released her arms from around his neck and took his hands in hers and stared directly into his eyes.

"There is no way I can tell you how sorry I am, and I can't stand here and tell you that I know how you feel. There is no way anyone can know. But if you will permit, I would like to stay here while you talk." She also wanted to cry with him and pray with him, but did not feel this was the proper time or place.

Zach had to turn his head away. Tears were forming in his eyes, and he didn't want her to see them. Yet, he somehow sensed that he could have cried openly with this lovely woman and it would have been all right.

"Thank you, Miss . . ."

"Angela"

"Thanks." He looked straight at her, no longer troubled that she would see his tears. Maybe she would see more. Maybe she would see the crushing terror that was also there.

Zach joined the officer and Dr. Mutamaya at the table. Angela got them the coffee and joined them while they began talking. During the next hour, Sam did most of the questioning, and Zach the answering. They went back through the last stormy months with Susan and his overwhelming desire to be with his daughter. He did not try to gloss over the terrible scenes between Susan and himself, nor did he attempt to hide his irrational and immature reactions to her. He was totally ashamed of the fact that she could reduce him to childlike behavior, but he could not deny it to these people. He had often reflected how thin a veneer of stability can camouflage a mound of instability. Maturity and immaturity lay closely entangled in each other's arms, waiting only for one to act in order for the other to react.

When it came to the part of finding the mutilated bodies of his ex-wife and child, Dr. Mutamaya studied Zach's face intensely. Sam stared at something directly over Zach's head, and Angela's eyes filled with tears. She reached out and put her hand over his.

"I know that I messed with evidence when I carried her from the bathtub and laid her on the bed and covered her. I didn't care! I didn't want people staring at their naked, mutilated bodies. It seemed the right thing to do at the time." Then he added softly, "And I would do it over again." There was no defiance in his voice, just despair.

"I don't think that is going to be a problem, Doc. I'd probably have done the same thing under those circumstances." The manner in which Sam said *Doc* made Zack feel less wretched.

"But there is the matter of the sack of powder we found in your pocket. We're having it analyzed. It is some kind of drug, isn't it?"

This was the one subject that Zack had hoped to avoid, but it was out now and he met it head on. "It is a drug, but probably not the kind you're thinking. It is Doriden. Three tablets ground to a powder."

"You're out of my league, what is it?"

Pascal volunteered, "It is a sleeping pill, rather mild at that, although it would sure make someone sleepy."

"And Susan was always very sensitive to medicines," Zack said. He went on to describe his plans to have a little time with his daughter. He did not try to hide the self-contempt he felt for having allowed himself to be driven to such a point.

"I have to ask you to describe the scene as it was when you first arrived there. I know it is going to be hard, but I need you to begin right when you got to the house. For starters, was the door open, were the lights on, did you sense anyone else was there?"

Sam was trying to be considerate, but he needed as much information as he could get. "Oh, and I'm going to record what you say, if you don't mind." He placed a cassette tape recorder on the table between them.

For the next several minutes, Zack recounted the events. He tried to be rational and logical, but at times he couldn't keep his voice from breaking. When he said that all he had really hoped for was just feel Desiree's arms around his neck and hear her say, "Daddy," Angela had to excuse herself and leave the room. And Sam, a cop who had heard and seen it all, wasn't holding it together too well either.

Angela closed the door behind her. She wasn't sure if the agony could have been any greater if it had happened directly to her. She was fighting back tears, but at the same time, she was feeling strong admiration toward Zack. Through all his anguish, he was able to be so honest and forthright. Angela did, as she most often did in times of crisis, reflect on the Bible and pray. From somewhere, memorized verses from a Psalm came to her.

"Who, O God is like you? Though you have made me see troubles, many and bitter, you will restore my life again; from the depths of the earth you will bring me up. You will increase respect for me, and comfort me once again."

What kind of agony had the writer of that Psalm experienced? Could it have been anything like Zach is experiencing? No doubt it could have been, Angela reflected. *If only there was some way I could share these verses from the God's Word with Zach, just to let him realize that God does knows his troubles, many and bitter, and can bring him peace and encouragement.* She prayed quietly, not the least ashamed if people knew she was praying, although she did not want to make a display.

When she returned to the room, Zach turned and watched her. His silent green eyes searched her face intensely. She wished she could know what he was thinking.

"Well, Docs, I think I've got all the information that I need for now," Sam said, getting up from the table and stretching his big frame. "If you'll take full responsibility for this man, Doc, I'm going to take a chance and let him go. If he is guilty of killing his ex and his little girl, then I'm Cleopatra."

"Oh, thank God!" Angela said, and in her enthusiasm, she went to Zack and spontaneously hugged him again. Feeling Zach's uncertainty, she let go and said, "Oh, sorry about that; I get a little too excited sometimes."

Sam faced Zack, sensing that if it had been another time and place, he would have found humor in seeing this young surgeon's discomfort with the young woman.

"But you can't leave town 'cause I'm sure we are going to have to have you down here several times more for questioning."

"Hey, Captain, I'm going nowhere. I'll be available anytime you want me. Just say the word."

"Then get the heck out of here! And, son . . ." Zach turned back. "I'm really sorry about your little girl . . . and your ex-wife. We'll get the person who did it!"

"Thanks. Thank you very much."

They all three climbed into Angela's small Ford coup. Zach's legs hit the dash, even with the seat pushed back.

"Well, where to?" It was actually a perplexing question. They could not go to Pascal's ghetto apartment or to Zach's cubicle, so that left Angela's apartment, the most accommodating of the three places. They stopped by the hospital for a few minutes to let Zach run in to his room to shower, shave, and change clothes. While this transpired, Pascal shared his future plans with Angela, more to get their minds off the events of the past couple of hours than to inform her. But she proved to be greatly interested and asked many questions. It did not take Pascal long to realize that this young woman had a lot more knowledge of Africa than he could have expected. He soon found that she had actually been born in the Republic of the Congo, just across the Congo River from the Belgium Congo. Her parents had been missionaries in Brazzaville and surrounding areas. She had lived there and attended mission schools until it was time for college, and then she returned to the United States to attend Wesleyan University in Illinois, followed by nurses training for four years in Chicago. Because of the increasing unrest in that entire region of West Africa, her parents had left Brazzaville about a year after Angela had finished college.

Zach climbed back in. "Thanks for waiting so long, but the shower and cleanup really felt good." It had obviously performed a rejuvenating affect on him. Dressed in a light blue polo shirt and dark blue slacks, he appeared amazingly vigorous.

He has to be one of the best looking men I've ever seen, Angela thought to herself. Although Zach was oblivious, Pascal didn't miss the way she looked at him.

Angela's apartment reflected her excitable charm and outgoing personality. Although it was plainly furnished, it radiated affability and an instant feeling of a warm welcome.

"Please, make yourselves at home. You both must be very hungry. I don't have much to serve, but I'll try to get something together. Dr. Mutamaya, I wish I could cook you some luku (manioc flour) and chenni (dried caterpillars) but they aren't easy to find here."

Pascal caught Zach's quizzical look but thought best not to say anything. "Angela, why don't we call out and have some pizza delivered. That way we will have time to talk. If that would be all right with you and Zach?" he asked politely.

"Eating isn't one of my top priorities right now, but I know you guys must be hungry. I'll join you." Zach realized just how that must have sounded and added. "Forgive me. That sounded too much like a pity party!"

Zach's openness and frankness continued to impress both Angela and Pascal. When one considered the terrible anguish he was experiencing, he had a right to a *pity party*, as he had put it.

When the food arrived, they all went through the motions of eating and drinking, not saying much until finished. Pascal shared more of his plans about traveling back to the Congo. He told them a little about his friend, tutor, and spiritual father, Dr. Ben Wells. He spoke of him in such reverent terms that Zach began to think he was more of Dr. Mutamaya's imagination than, in fact, a man. But he knew the surgeon well enough now to dismiss such thinking. He and Angela persuaded him to continue to share with quests for more and more information. It was well past midnight before they realized the time. Zack and Angela were completely captivated by Pascal's recounting of life in the Congo. They learned that he had been educated at Catholic primary and secondary schools, and then went to a nursing institute run by Jesuits. Such schools were very difficult to find during those times because of war and poverty. The Catholic mission station had been left untouched for no explainable reason.

After graduation from the two-year program, he traveled several kilometers away to study further at the mission station of Kikungu, where Dr. Ben Wells was the physician and surgeon. This man had a reputation all over the Congo for doing excellent medical work and was known for his remarkable surgeries. This was one of the few places one could learn western medicine and, in particular, surgery. Friendship between Dr. Wells and Pascal developed almost immediately. Ben found this young man to possess a very intelligent and inquisitive mind. Also, he seemed so much more physically commanding than many of his fellow Congolese. Ben was surprised when he found out that he had suffered so much in order to pursue medicine at a higher level. With time, he became more and more amazed at just how capable this young man was, especially after learning about some of the horrors he had sustained while hiding in the forests. It was for these reasons he worked hard to get Pascal into a small, Baptist Church affiliated college in western Switzerland. It was Ben who encouraged Pascal to study the basic sciences, and Pascal excelled in all his courses. He was an amazing learner with a penchant for languages and science. He graduated in three years and from there went to Stanford University in the United States with a foreign student scholarship. By then, Pascal had decided unequivocally to pursue a surgical degree. So Ben encouraged him to obtain his surgical training at a university in Virginia under the tutelage of his mentor, Dr. Levi Uehling, whom Ben knew to be one of the truly great general surgeons of his day. But he was also a true man of God, who despite his great knowledge and skill, never lost sight of the One who is the true healer. "I sew them together, but God heals them," was one of his common clichés.

As for Zach, hearing Pascal's accounts of this missionary doctor, the conditions in Africa, and the lives of the people, he became more and more fascinated. As a youngster, he had read many accounts of the early African explorers. Names like Burton, Spike, and, of course, the Stanley and Livingston saga were familiar to him. At that time, Zach had imagined that a lot of the tales of these men had been enhanced by the passing of time. Now he wondered if the stories were actually more truthful than he realized. Also, he thought, for everyone he had read about, there were probably many who remained obscure.

Angela broke into his introspection, "Zach, you must be very tired. Actually, you look exhausted—no put down intended."

"I'll accept the comment like it was intended. Actually, it has been a long time since I have been supine."

"You doctors, why can't you such say that you need to sack out." Angela's voice contained slight jocularity. "Listen, the sofa in the other room is also a hide-a-bed and sleeps comfortably. Why don't you stay rather than go back to that closet you call home?"

"I'm too beat to argue with you, Angela, but I really feel that I'm imposing on you too much."

"Nonsense, it is absolutely no trouble. Really! I use the couch for friends and family who come all the time. It will just take a second to get it ready."

It took only a couple of minutes after lying down and Zach was asleep. He took the time only to remove his shoes for comfort. But his sleep was fitful, and he talked aloud a couple of times. Pascal and Angela could only wonder at what images might be racing through his subconscious mind.

Angela watched a sleeping Zach for few minutes, noting some relaxation of the tension around his eyes and corner of the lips, and then returned to Dr. Mutamaya.

"There isn't much of the night left. I will be happy to take you back to your apartment, but would you consider staying here until morning? I can give you my bed. I'm small; I can sleep in the chair very easily. Actually, it reclines . . ."

The offer to give up her bed was firmly, but politely refused. "I would have no problem sleeping in your lounge chair, but I cannot take your bed. But, yes, I will accept your offer for the night."

When she had found a light blanket she returned. "Dr. Mutamaya—"

Pascal interrupted, "Please, call me Pascal. We are friends, are we not? Also, I guess we are also countrymen, n'est ce pas?"

"Well, Dr. Muta—I mean, Pascal, I was planning to leave County next week. I have given my notice. My parents and sister live in Michigan, and I had planned to stay with them for a couple of weeks until I can get enrolled in the missions program at the Moody Bible Institute. I am planning to return to Africa as a nurse practitioner. Eventually, I would like to serve in a francophone country because of the advantage of speaking French. I know that this is on the spur of the moment, but Dr. Mut—Pascal, I'm wondering now about postponing these plans for a few weeks and going with you to the Congo? I have the money, and I wouldn't be a burden." As she continued, her excitement built. "It would be excellent preparation for me, and I could assist you in some of your medical work. Practicing medicine is not the reason you are going, I know, but when people find you are there, they will want much medical care."

Angela's excitement and animation were contagious, even to Pascal, who was normally reticent. How could one dampen this pretty young lady's enthusiasm? Besides, her ideas did have some merit.

"Could you be ready to leave in six or seven days?"

"I could," she replied with a great deal of certainty. "My immunizations are up to date and my passport is current. I can start on malaria prophylaxis right away. The only thing would be obtaining a visa. I am not sure if there is any way I can get one for the Congo on such short notice."

"If you will give me your passport, I believe I can get you a visa. I do not think there will be a problem."

Angela seemed to be in deep thought. She appeared to want to ask something, but was hesitant to do so.

Finally, Pascal spoke up, "Please, young lady, out with it. There is something on your mind."

"Yes, I am thinking of something, but am trying to decide if it is anything that I should bring up."

"Well, if it is going to curl your pretty face like it is now, you had better share it," Pascal said good-naturedly.

"Okay. I am thinking—would it make any sense asking Zach to go to the Congo with us? I know the hospital board will suspend him temporarily until this whole mess is cleared up. And we both know that he needs time off from his work, from surgery, from the ER, and even from this city. Right now, he might not even recognize the need."

Pascal smiled. "It seems we are often on the same path in our thinking. I have been deeply considering the same idea during the past few hours and partly for the same reasons. But there is another. Do you remember that I said I would explain my comment about Zach's fears of the forest? I think now would be a proper time, if you don't mind."

"Not at all, Pascal." It was becoming easier for her to use his Christian name. "In fact, I think it would be great if you would."

During the next several minutes, Pascal shared briefly and concisely some of his fears and the horrors that came from the years hiding in the forest. It was in the grisly years of the late 1950s and early 1960s. This was a time of tremendous turmoil in the Congo, a time when the eastern district of the country was rebelling against the Government in Kinshasa. Although the eastern region had many intelligent and judicious men, such as Patrice Lumumba, there were also malignant and cruel men who were driven by hatred—and evil forces. Many of these led the rebel troops. It was during these turbulent times that Pascal and his family hid in the forest for months that became years. But once the soldiers found them and he saw his sister and mother raped while others held him back. And he had watched as two younger brothers died slow, agonizing deaths from malnutrition, malaria, and intestinal parasites.

"The fears from the forest are still there and have changed me in so many ways that I cannot even begin to understand. The fears return often, especially at night, when I see the mutilated bodies of my mother and sister. It is then that demons rise up in me. I must tell you, Angela, it is only through the grace of God that I am able to deal with those events even now. For a long time, I was filled with fury and hatred. My days and nights were filled with the desire for revenge. And not just vengeance, but to torture and brutally slaughter these men! It was only after I went to Dr. Ben's mission and learned to know Jesus Christ in a personal way that I begin to accept and forgive. It is an ongoing process, even now, and God continues to be patient and forgiving of me. But I know this: God's power is always there!" Pascal spoke with composure and with absolute certainty in his voice.

Angela's heart went out to him in a way that she had never experienced for anyone before. Was it their common bond of faith in Jesus Christ that made his life so compelling? She did not know the answer, but did know that there had quickly developed a covenant between them that few people would ever experience.

"Maybe you will begin to understand what I am sensing about Zach. This young Dr. Wylie has something in his life and his experiences that seem to be causing him fears. Sometimes I see a fleeting look in his eyes, like he is seeing something very awful. He is an extremely capable and confident young man, yet there is something else, possibly his *demons* hidden away."

"And you are thinking that a trip to the Congo might give him time to face these *demons,* if they exist?" Angela inquired.

"At the pace one must go in a surgical residency, he has had no time for anything else. And besides, if he went to the Congo we might have some quality time together. I would like to know him better. Who knows what might happen to his *demons*? And now, Angela, the fact that you also are thinking of going, it could be even more beneficial for him. I must consider it even more." Then he smiled with a slight mischievous expression, "Of course, you wouldn't have any other reason for wanting him along on such a trip?"

Angela felt herself blushing. "You darn surgeons. You guys are too inquisitive. Or maybe I should say nosey." She spoke with a smile, "Yes, as I have said before, I can't deny that there is something drawing me to him. I can't explain it exactly." She glanced into the room where he was sleeping. "He is good looking, of course, and quite masculine, but as I tried to express to you, there is something more. I know you will understand, Pascal. It is as if something like an inner voice that keeps telling me I must somehow witness to this man. I must tell him about the Lord Jesus Christ. Often, I wish that God would just speak to me, right out, as He did to the ancient prophets. But He doesn't. Ever since I first worked with Zach in the ER, something has directed me to pray for him, and I have regularly."

"But you have not shared any of this with him?"

"No, not yet, but I have felt all along that the right time would come. But I will need God's direction. I sure don't want to drive him away. Pascal, I know it is very late and you must be very tired, but may I ask you one question?"

"Of course, by all means."

"After all the terrible things you experienced during those dreadful years of hiding, how have you really been able to forgive and forget?" Angela's voice trembled slightly. "How does one learn to forgive that much? I know you shared a little about the grace of God, but how did you reach that point?"

Pascal took her small hands in his and they sat down on the sofa. He looked directly into the depths of her dark brown eyes.

"Angela, I do not believe anyone can *learn* to forgive." He spoke softly, but his deep voice resonated. "Forgiving is nothing one can acquire, nor do I believe it can be taught by someone. I do not think that anyone has ever given a lecture on the 'seven steps of learning how to forgive.' If they have, I missed the course. I believe that in human terms, the only means by which we can come close to forgiving is attempting to forget; in other words, by suppressing it. But there it lies, feasting like a cancer. I found that I could not accomplish this toward the men that tortured, and raped my mother and sister. Tell me, Angela, do you know any way I could have in my human nature? How I could forgive these men?"

Angela was quiet for a long time before answering, "In human terms, I cannot think of a way to genuinely forgive the things done to your loved ones."

"I have so often wondered how it was possible for Jesus to sincerely say from the cross, '*Father, forgive them*,' at the time he was suffering from that most horrible and painful method of death ever devised. Yet, He was truly able to forgive! How?" This was really an rhetorical question because Pascal sensed that Angela had long ago found the answer.

"The Apostle Paul, two thousand years ago, wrote to the church at Colossi telling them that now as believers in Jesus Christ, they could be clothed with such traits as kindness, compassion, and love and they could forgive one another because all those gifts were cloaked with the knowledge that God had forgiven them. And He has forgiven me also. Good grief, how much God has forgiven me! Oh, I have never raped or killed, but in the eyes of God, I have done things just as bad, and Christ came to tell me that God would forgive me.

So forgiveness cannot be taught. It came for me, as it has for so many others, directly from God in a supernatural way through his Son, Jesus Christ. I am at peace with those men and what they did, Angela."

There was a long, almost serene silence, and then Pascal spoke, "I am sorry, Angela, for the dissertation. I know that you are a Christian. You know these things."

She smiled warmly. "But I don't believe that I've ever heard them said more beautifully or ever from someone whose life experiences are like yours."

He squeezed her hands and then tenderly wiped a tear from the corner of her eye. "Now, we have many plans to make and things to get done."

CHAPTER 10

At the moment that Pascal and Angela were making plans for their trip, heavy torrential rains were falling in the rebel army camp, turning the red dirt into a viscous, adhesive substance that was both slippery and gluey. At times, it pulled at one's boots, and other times made the footing so precarious, walking even short distances was both frustrating and exhausting. The roads were completely impassable, even for the soldiers' stolen Land Rover. A few seconds in the torrent of rain left the skin soaked and chilled to the bone, despite the tropical warmth. There were about two hundred soldiers in all and they had taken over the Methodist mission station of Kilundu that lay along the Kwilu River, about three hundred kilometers (one-hundred and eighty miles) inland from Leopoldville. It was a small station, consisting of a tiny medical clinic, a school building, and two unpretentious houses for the missionaries. It was difficult to determine with any certainty when the missionaries had left, but by the condition of things, it had probably been within the month. A few of the ranking soldiers were crowded into the small schoolhouse and others in the clinic building. The majority was left open to the storm and cold. The moods of these men were turning from festering anger to a virulent ugliness, assisted by their increasing state of intoxication from palm wine, beer, and hashish.

Colonel Ching was quite comfortable in the larger of the two mission homes he had taken to be his headquarters. He and his small group of trusted men were dry and warmed by fire they had started on the cement floor in the center of the living room. One of the men kept it going using pieces of broken furniture. Ching was a leader of men, and he was fully aware of the mood of the soldiers out in the raging gale, most of whom were untrained youth, many not more than fifteen years of age. He sensed that some were coming dangerously near mutiny. He also knew that these men had come to both despise him and fear him during the past several months. Their fears were very real. They knew he had great powers and could call down death with just his voice. They had watched the bullets from the guns of government soldiers go through his body, leaving no injury. They had also seen this man, with the powers of Nkuyu, cause people to die with his evil eye. Ching was staring out into the storm and contemplating action to take against these discontented and frightened soldiers. Deep in thought, he did not see a dimly lighted figure moving through the darkness, going from tent to tent. The shadow of a man was bent and had a faltering gait; whether as a result of the blowing rain or from a physical disability, one could not tell. Dr. Ben Wells entered the tent where eight men huddled together. On the oozing mud floor between them laid a youngster. He was probably no more than sixteen. The gaunt body was moaning softly. Ben sat his dim kerosene lantern as close to the young soldiers as the crowded tent would allow. Even in this gloomy light he could tell the man was critically ill. For the past several weeks he had been treating these men as best as his limited supplies permitted. When they would come near a larger village, he would ask some men to go for a few medical supplies such as quinine, chloroquine, penicillin, and anti-diarrheals. They also sought whatever medicine they could obtain for intestinal parasite and for packets of the precious electrolyte solutions needed for replacement in severe dysentery cases. He knew that Ching was aware he was doing this, for Ching was observant of all things. Ben shivered, but not just because of the chilly air.

Ben knew the youngster was dying, but was also convinced he could have done nothing more for him even if he had been back at his hospital. He was certain the man had far advanced typhoid fever with multiple perforations of his small bowel and colon. Peritonitis had started several hours ago. He could only try to make him comfortable and pray. He was very aware of many dark eyes on him as he bowed his head and prayed silently for this dying youth. As he left the tent, the wind and rain eased a little, but his gait was still excruciatingly deliberate and he remained bent and weak. During the weeks in captivity, Ben had become a mere specter of the vigorous and healthy man he had been. Even though the beatings had ceased, poor diet, bouts of dysentery, recurring malaria, and the harsh elements had taken their toll. As he finished his rounds and headed back to the small tent he shared with six other men, he glanced toward the house where Colonel Ching stayed. What he saw silhouetted in the window from the flickering light within was a sight that made his blood run cold. His first instinct was to turn away, but he could not. The image in the darkened house was far more visible than the murkiness should have permitted. What he saw framed in the window was the face of some hideous beast. The grotesque countenance had long, curved fangs covered with saliva and blood. As Ben stared, the horrible creature opened its mouth further, as if emitting a loud scream. Then it was gone. Only a faint flickering light from the lanterns within showed through the window. More shaken than he could ever remember, Ben turned and entered his tent. In the faint light of his kerosene lamp, he could see the young soldiers clinging together. The smell of unbridled fear was in the air. None of these men had been outside the tent, and yet Ben was sure that in some way they had also experienced that gruesome, fiend-ish creature. Ben knew not what they had experienced, but he had been in the Dark Continent long enough to never blindly disregard things not readily defined. Having no rational explanation for events does not mean that they do not exist. *We humans,* he thought, *believe we can control that which we can explain. Therefore, we attempt to convince ourselves that we can explain everything.* As Ben lay down and pulled the soggy blanket over him, his mind ran free. He was trained a scientist and he felt that he approached things analytically. All his life he had tried to find proof of things, but he had also learned that so many things accepted as being facts are in reality just theories based on mul-tiple observations. Few things in life and nature can be positively proven, only observed, and then calculated to occur or not occur. He had never observed the actual resurrection of the dead and yet believed with total certainty that Jesus Christ had done so.

He prayed briefly that the horrible sight he had seen would not enter his dreams, and quickly fell into a fitful sleep.

CHAPTER eleven

It was a few minutes after six in the morning when Angela's bedside phone rang, awakening her from an exhausted sleep. She and Pascal had talked and planned until well after two in the morning. When they finally stopped planning, they felt that most details of the trip had been covered.

"Hello," she answered the phone hoarsely.

"Good morning, Angela—this is Angela, isn't it?" It was the Irish brogue of Captain O'Reilly.

"I'm sorry to awaken you, Miss, but I have some news to share. Can I speak with Dr. Mutamaya, if he's around?"

Angela was wide awake now. Quickly, she got out of bed, threw on her robe, and went out to the living room. Pascal and Zach were shaved and dressed, sitting at the table drinking coffee and looking very fit. "Darn surgeons, they don't ever get tired or need sleep like we mere mortals," she said, feigning displeasure.

"Dr. Mutamaya," she said, slipping back into her old pattern, "Captain Sam is on the phone wanting to talk to you. He says that he has some news. You'll have to take it in the bedroom, I don't have an extension."

As Pascal went into the other room, Angela was suddenly aware that Zach was staring at her. She unexpectedly felt self-conscious.

"Sorry, I must look a mess," she said, impetuously brushing the short hair away from her face.

"I'm the one who should be sorry for staring. That was rude on my part. It is just that . . . well, I just didn't imagine that anyone could look so beautiful just getting out of bed in the morning."

He said it in such a simple and honest manner that Angela experienced no embarrassment. She only felt sincerely complimented. On Zack's part, he gave her no chance to say anything, nor did he want to place her in the position of having to reply.

"So, what do you think the Captain has found out? It is only a little after six. I'll bet the man never went home last night"

Sam's voice seemed animated when Pascal picked up the phone. "After you guys left, we put out the regular dragnet and rounded up all the known perverts; all the sex offenders, female abusers, and drug addicts. Well, the net caught a heroine user who is a notorious conman. He is particularly good with duping young widows and divorcees. We had been watching him for some time, but couldn't quite get enough on him. So, on a hunch, I sent a squad car over to his place about three this morning, and when they knocked on his door and identified themselves, a real mess broke loose. He started shooting through the door. Luckily those officers followed protocol and didn't stand directly in front of it. They are two tough, experienced men and it didn't take them long to break in and overpower this crazy. Man, I guess he was so high on something that they almost had to sweep him off the ceiling. Well, in this jerk's apartment, they found blood-spattered clothes in the closet, along with a bloodied switchblade. The guy hasn't confessed to anything and keeps demanding his rights, but I've one big hunch the blood on the knife and clothes is going to match the girl's and her mother's. We'll need you both to come down here a little later, but I wanted you to know now. We'll call you. And, hey, I'm really hoping this'll clear that young doc of yours!" He hung up before Pascal could reply.

Pascal returned to join Zach and Angela. "Zach, wonderful news! They think they have already found the man that murdered your daughter and her mother!"

"How . . . it's so soon!"

Pascal recounted the conversation with the captain. When he had finished, Angela was so excited and overcome with happiness that for the third time in less than twenty-four hours she hugged Zach in a spontaneous display of affection. "Oh, thank God, thank God!" The words flowed from a joyous heart.

Zach didn't seem quite so stiff or resist as much this time, and when she stood back, she said, "Now that wasn't so bad, was it? I guess if we are going to get to know each other better, you'll just have to know that I come from a whole family of huggers."

Zach smiled. "Thanks! I've always heard of the *healing touch*. Well, I'm beginning to grasp how real that may be."

They all had many questions about the details of the capture and even more about the man they had captured. They realized that after Zach was called to the station, they would learn many more details. Angela made some more coffee and warmed rolls in her tiny oven. While they were eating, Pascal related to Zach the forthcoming plans for travel to Africa. A part of Zach seemed very interested, but another appeared detached. Angela noticed and thought he was re-living the ghastly events of the past few hours.

Shortly before 9:00 a.m., the phone rang. A Sergeant Nelson said that they needed Dr. Wylie down at the station as soon as possible. Angela said it would probably take him about forty-five minutes, and the sergeant thought that would be all right. This gave her enough time to take Pascal to his apartment. As Pascal was getting out, he turned to Zach. "I am sure that until a lot of things are settled and all the publicity surrounding this whole thing has died down, the hospital board and Dr. Jansen are probably going to put you on a leave of absence. In case that happens, would you consider going to Africa with Angela and me?"

Both he and Angela were anticipating that Zach would be both astonished and resistant to such a plan, but amazingly he replied, "You know, guys, something inside me has been asking the same thing. I was thinking about just that last night and again this morning when you and Angela were talking. Give me time to think a little more about it and let's see what's going to happen here today."

Pascal got out of the car and leaned through the open window. "That is fair enough, Zack. Please let me know if I can help in any way." Before Zach could thank him, Pascal was springing up his steps, saying something to a heavy set black women leaning out her window.

As Angela was pulling away from Pascal's apartment, she reached over and squeezed Zack's hand.

"What was that for?" He smiled at her.

"Oh, nothing. I was just thinking how God works things out in so many special ways."

Zach sat back in the seat. He considered asking Angela what she meant, but then thought, *I best leave the religious things to people like Angela. I am a physician and scientist, and religion is full of so many unproved declarations and superstition.* Zack told himself that he needed facts—proof. Yet, how could he explain what was he seeing in this near-stranger next to him? She came from almost nowhere and for no apparent reason, and yet was filled with such warmth and sincere kindness towards him. Why? Coincidence?

The car stopped in front of the station, interrupting his thoughts. Zach insisted that Angela go on home, "You have many things to do and not much time to do them. I don't know how long this will take. I can grab a taxi back to the hospital when I'm done here."

"All right, but promise me that you'll let me know the news as soon as you can."

"I promise." Zach gazed into her dark eyes, so comforted by the depth of compassion he found there. He was trying to phrase correctly what he wanted to say. Finally, he said, "I always seem to be saying thank you, but again—thank you! Your presence . . . well, it has made things so much easier. Angela, you are quite a person. I've never known anyone like you." He seemed slightly uneasy for having expressed himself.

"Now it is my turn to say thanks."

As she drove away, she was considering his words. *But I'm not a special person. I'm just a girl trying to find her place in the world. If he sees anything special,, then it is Jesus in me, and for that I can take no credit—that is a gift from God.*

Captain O'Reilly was in his office when Zach inquired at the desk. The sergeant had orders to send him in as soon as he got there. Sam raised his large body from behind his desk when Zach entered. He met him with a warm smile and a strong handshake.

"Darn good news, Doc. I never doubted your innocence for a minute, but I didn't think we would be able to clear you this fast."

During the next several minutes, Sam told Zach some of the details. He had stayed at the station all night directing the investigation. "The best time for getting a killer is when the trail is fresh," he said, using a common hunting metaphor. It was when they started browsing through a list of men who had been arrested for beating up their women that they came across the name of

Nick Adams. It took little time to pull up his complete record. Twice he had been accused of physical violence against his girlfriends, but never convicted. Charges had been dropped at the last minute. But he is a well-known con-artist who likes to prey on young widows and divorcees. He is thirty-two and quite good looking, in a mean sort of way. And he is a really slick one. Also, he's had two arrests for possession of heroine, but not enough to get him on possession to sell. He has a long record as a teenager, reform school at fourteen and then two years in prison at age eighteen for car theft. At twenty-two he was again in prison, this time for manslaughter. He was drunk and drove his car off the road, killing his girlfriend. There was some question in the report that all the injuries to the girl were due to the accident, but nobody could prove anything. Then he dropped out of sight until two years ago when he reappeared in this area because a girlfriend filed an assault and battery charge against him. Those charges were also dropped because the woman changed her mind. There is also some evidence he's pushing drugs, but nothing proven."

The Captain paused, as if he were checking records on his desk, but was actually postponing something he had to say. "I hate like the devil telling you this, Doc, but we're sure he was . . . ah . . . seeing your ex-wife. We did some waking up of people during the night and I think we've found some witnesses who have seem him with her, several times at your . . . at her house."

Zach wondered if the presence of man he sensed that day was this killer. If he had said something to Susan then, could he have prevented these gruesome murders? He shared none of these thoughts with the officer.

"From here on, it is pretty much speculation on my part, but I think this guy probably found out your ex-wife had no money and told her he was dumping her. They probably started fighting and he lost it. He is a bad tempered creep anyway, and when the lab gave me the report on him this morning, it showed he had enough amphetamine in him to light up the Brooklyn Bridge. This scum was really strung out. I guess the rest you know better than any of us."

Zach could almost visualize the scene. Susan's sharp tongue and her capacity to degrade with looks and gestures would have produced a rage in this drugged-up excuse for a human being. He could sense, in a projected way, how she could have driven this man into a murderous rage. But then he thought, *why kill my little girl?*

Captain O'Reilly broke into his thoughts. "I've had my secretary type up our conversation from yesterday. Would you read through it, and if you if think it is okay, then I need you to sign it."

"I can do that, but first, can I see this guy?"

The captain thought for several seconds. "Look, Doc, you're going to have a lot of hate in you for a long time. Do you think you really want to know this guy? Do you think it's better to direct that hate on somebody you know, or direct it at something or someone more detached?'

Zach really gave the question some thought before answering. "Your point is well taken, Captain. Let me think about it. Where are those papers?"

As Zach was reading the report, he kept thinking about Sam's question. *Is it better to direct hatred at an obscure object or at a specific one? Would the mind process them differently?* He didn't know. When he finished reading the report, he had no problem signing it because it was completely accurate. When he went to Sam's office, he was told that the captain had left and wouldn't be back until early afternoon, but that if he needed anything to call him at about two that afternoon. He would be back in his office. *I hope the poor guy went to get a little sleep,* Zach thought to himself. His admiration for this police officer had developed to a high level in a short period of time.

The taxi let him off at the main entrance and he entered the hospital among dozens of patients checking in and paying bills. The first person he saw was Ms. Garfield, who was assistant administrator's secretary. He noticed her because she was actively trying to get his attention. There was no doubt in Zach's mind why the she wanted him in her office. His first impulse was to walk away, but then he decided that this was as good of time as any to get it over with. Mrs. O'Neal was not alone when he entered. Dr. Lowery, the administrator, and she had apparently been in conference. They greeted him cordially and with apparent sadness in their voices. If Zach was any good at reading body language, he felt certain that they were sincere in their expressions of sympathy for his loss. But after the condolences were extended, they quickly got down to the business at hand. Dr. Mutamaya had been prophetic in his evaluation of the situation. Actually, after they told him that they had to suspend him for an indefinite period of time, he felt relief more than resentment. He could actually empathize with their decision. If he had been in their place, he would have felt it to be the only responsible move to make. They were quite generous in their promise to continue his salary and to reinstate him as soon as the entire thing had passed over. The whole meeting took less than fifteen minutes, and Zack left their hideout of censure with much less dejection than he had anticipated. He crossed through the waiting room and down the corridor, hoping that he would not come in contact with any of his colleagues. He made it up the creaking stairs and down the hall to his room, passing only a couple of residents whom he did not know and seemed not to recognize him. He showered and shaved mechanically, trying not to focus for long on the image in the mirror. If he had, he would have noted new lines etched in his forehead and a lifeless refection of a once assured man. It took just minutes to randomly place his few clothes into a tattered Skyway suitcase. Then he sat on the edge of the small bed and stared around the small room and thought of the many grueling weeks and months he had spent at County. He was aware of the knowledge he had acquired, the surgical procedures he had performed and the experience gained. With sadness, he thought of the kinship with fellow residents who often connected to one another through their common needs. And yes, there had been lives he had saved and the pain he had relieved. Zack had always believed that when his time at County came to an end, a part of him would cease. He was feeling none of this. Strangely, he felt at peace about leaving, even though there was no certainty he would ever return. On the other hand, he was acutely aware of a feeling of security and a looming sense of certainty he could not explain. Although he was not sure where this conviction lay, he sensed it was because of the burgeoning relationship with Dr. Mutamaya and Angela.

Picking up the previously despised bedside phone, he dialed Angela's number. When she answered, he shared quickly what the police had found, a little about the murderer, and about his freedom from being a suspect. Then he spoke carefully, but with the assuredness of a decision well made.

"If your offer for the trip to Africa is still open, then I accept. How soon can we get together to make plans?" The anticipation of seeing Angela gave a glimmer of life back to his eyes. "This is all new to me, so I will need yours and Dr. Mut—Pascal's help for the travel plan."

Angela fought to conceal the excitement in her voice, but accomplished it poorly. "Zach, that is wonderful! We just need to meet and discuss the essential things like passport, immunizations, flight plans, and the gear to take."

During the next five days, Zach, Angela, and Pascal used her apartment as a center for the windstorm of activity. A passport for Zach was obtained with a minimum of difficulty, and Pascal assured him that the visa could be obtained easily after arriving in the Congo. Zach saw little of either of them. Angela was working the night shift in the E.R. until the day before they left for Europe, and Pascal spent his remaining time in surgery and the emergency room. Life as usual! In between the rush to obtain the necessary immunizations, with-draw his meager bank account, and complete the proper forms for his "leave of absence," there was little time left to Zack for thought and reflection. He deliberately tried to keep his thinking away from the terrible engraved images of Susan and Desiree. So he spent much of his free time reflecting on why he was so drawn to Angela. He tried to fit her into some type of standard in which he had subconsciously placed other women, whether friends, nurses, or lovers. But he had to acknowledge that since marrying Susan and starting his surgical residency, his experience with women had become totally impersonal—that of doctor-nurse or physician-colleague. The relationships were driven by patient histories, diagnoses, laboratory reports, and X-ray findings. He had detached personal relationships entirely void of social feelings. Yet, as he thought of past experiences, he could remember none like Angela. He had to admit that he was physically drawn to her. She was petite and very graceful, cute more than beautiful, but genuine warmth exuded from her. She seemed so honest and real—so secure and yet exposed. The old saying "what you see is what you get" was so appropriate for this gracious and sensitive young nurse. But he was puzzled about her openness about God and Jesus Christ. It had been so many years since he had entertained any thoughts of a religious nature. God seemed a vague conception that had no place in one's real existence. This philosophy lay in the realm of theologians and preachers who fought with science as to their importance to the origin of mankind. It was far away from the real world and had no affect on his life. Yet, Angela's effervescence reflected a relation-ship with God that he knew nothing about. Religion seemed so surreal and ineffectual for dealing with life's important issues. A man's destiny is up to his own incentive, strength, and abilities. God might be there, but how could such an impersonal force influence the direction of an individual's life? It makes no sense, and yet—the ringing phone interrupted his reflections. Pascal's normally calm voice held a slight excited edge.

"I believe that everything is in proper order for the flight to Brussels and from there on to Leopoldville. We will spend the night in Belgium before traveling on. When we arrive in the Congo, we must trust God and some of my friends there to get us through customs. Zack, I really believe everything will go well. Can you be ready?"

"Yes, by all means. All I must do is to notify Captain O'Reilly of my decision and talk to a few people at the hospital. I could be ready by this evening if needed."

Pascal's excitement was infectious to Zack. He asked eagerly, "What about Angela?"

"I have spoken to her and she is ready."

CHAPTER 12

The flight from Midwest International left nearly on time just as the sun was rising. Zack had seen many sunrises, but none like this one. The sun lighted the entire horizon with a blaze that colored it a bright scarlet, giving the skyline an awe-inspiring display of light. He had never believed in omens, and yet he could not help entertaining the thought that this was fanfare for them. He knew this to be ridiculous, but he could not quite disregard the imposing beauty of the brilliant horizon.

Pascal and Zack were seated next to each other, but Angela was placed further back in the plane, trapped against the window by a distraught mother and her crying infant. The two men spoke little, each appreciating the other's deep introspection. Pascal's fears for his lost friend and Zack's mind reliving the terror of his daughter's lacerated body. They had had only an hour of wait before the American Airline flight left for Brussels. Zack slept little after take-off. He tried to extort thoughts from his memory by pondering this jet airplane—a Boeing 707 is how they had described the plane. Flying at this high altitude, over the vast expanses of land and water below, he felt small and insignificant. Finally, he slept until a touch on his arm awakened him. He looked up to see Angela's smiling face.

"While you were dozing, the pilot informed us that we are about an hour out of Brussels, so I thought that I would talk to you for a few minutes before we land." She looked amazing, fresh, and rested. If she felt as fatigued as he, it didn't show.

"Thanks, Angela," he managed a smile and reached up and gently touched her arm. The way they looked at each other and the feeling between them did not go unnoticed by the middle-aged woman sitting in the seat to his right. Zack and the woman had spoken very little, just enough for Zack to learn that she was a Catholic nun headed back to some country in Africa about which he knew nothing. She was perceptive and felt more than observed the feelings between these two young people.

"Mademoiselle, I will be most pleased if we change the seats, you and I." Her voice was heavily accented.

"Thank you so much, Sister, you are so very kind. I would like to spend a little time speaking with my friend before we land."

Just Angela's presence had a way of clearing away his fatigue. She took his hand firmly in hers and neither spoke for some time, just enjoying each other's presence.

Finally, Zack broke the tranquility of their silence.

"Do you know anything about this Dr. Ben who Pascal so admires? From what I am hearing, he is a very brilliant and highly trained physician and surgeon. Why would someone like he become such an unimportant person in a totally unrecognized existence? It seems such a hopelessly insignificant life, especially with his apparent ability to be someone very prominent in his profession?"

Angela was quiet for a long time, to the point that Zack finally said, "Please forgive me. I didn't mean to place you on the spot or make you talk about something you don't want to."

"Oh no, it isn't that. I am trying to organize my thoughts so I can best share my feelings—there are so many emotions involved. As you know, I grew up with missionaries, many very wonderfully dedicated people, and others... well, less dedicated. Because my father was a medical missionary doctor, I want to be very careful not to project his reasons, his dedications, and his faith onto Dr. Ben. However, I would tend to believe that my father and he are very much alike."

"Please don't think that I am preaching at you when I say that in the book of Matthew it states that Jesus, the Son of God, came down to this earth to minister and to serve us and not to be ministered to. In a way, Jesus said that he came to be the 'doormat' for others. It is so difficult to even conceive that Jesus Christ, who I believe is the true Son of God, came and served us human beings, in all our sin and ugliness. Through many years of Bible study and fellowship with other Christians, my father—and I believe Dr. Ben—developed such an intimate relationship with Jesus that their love for Him drove them to serve Him completely. My father rarely, if ever, spoke about serving the African people or even healing the sick. He was motivated by his love for Jesus Christ."

Angela paused, gathering her thoughts, and then continued. "I read somewhere, I think in some writings of Oswald Chambers, that if people, even Christian, go out to just *serve* humanity they will soon be crushed and broken-hearted. They will be met with about the same gratitude from men as they would from a wild animal. They must go forth to be faithful to God; the desire to serve their fellow man will flow from that."

Suddenly, Angela had tears in her eyes, and she turned to look out the small window. A very pale, rose-colored light was appearing in the early evening sky.

Zack squeezed her hand tightly. "I'm sorry. Talking about your father must still be very painful."

She turned back to face him, wiping away the tears. "It is, I suppose, I loved him so much. But it is more than that right now. I am crying because I want so very much to share with you what I believe, but I feel like I'm coming across as a babbling idiot!"

With all his medical training and experience, Zack was at total loss to know how to reply. Never had he felt so inadequate to explain his feelings. He found himself caring and believing what she was and what she stood for, but was unable to process it.

He was saved from having to reply at all by the pilot's static announcement that they were to prepare for their landing in Brussels. within a few minutes. He conveyed the information in French and then in heavily accented English.

Deplaning and passing through customs were relatively uneventful, although he was separated from Angela and Pascal for a short time because of some questions about the dates on his visa. But the customs officials were mostly bored and went through the motions of checking the papers, and they were joined again within thirty minutes of landing. Pascal and Angela's knowledge of French enabled them greatly, so they had no difficulty getting to the center part of Brussels to the Metrople Hotel where they had reservations for separate rooms.

Zack's room was small, and being his first trip to Europe, he was especially cognizant of the high ceilings and walls covered by patterned wallpaper. An ancient radiator, covered with white paint, sat below the only window in the room. A large chair, looking like something out of Mount Vernon, sat in one corner, and a small bed with a colorful designed bedspread was placed near the middle of the room. A small, dimly lighted room to his right contained a small bathtub, sink, and toilet. Next to the toilet was another fixture that looked like a miniature bathtub. He was unable to fathom its purpose.

Zack walked to the window and looked down the four stories and found himself gazing upon a narrow cobblestone street. The local time was 10:00 p.m., but it was still light. He had only dozed a few times during the past twenty hours, but did not feel particularly tired. He considered going out for a walk. The night was warm and there seemed to be a lot of people on the streets below. As he was contemplating this, there was a very light knock on his door. Opening it, he found Angela standing there. She had changed into jeans and was wearing a light tan turtleneck sweater. Her short hair was combed lightly and she wore no makeup. Zack found himself once again thinking that this was the most radiantly attractive person he had ever known

"Hi! I saw your light on and I thought . . . actually, I hoped, that you might still be awake. I trust that I am not disturbing you?"

"Angela, there is no way you could bother me," Zack said with a sincere smile. "I was actually thinking of going for a walk. Would you want to go? I'm sure not too tired!"

They left their keys with the clerk and were surprised at how many people were in the lobby and on the streets at this time of night. They walked for a couple of blocks and suddenly found themselves at a large open plaza, maybe a block square, and surrounded by ancient buildings with beautifully carved sculptures and figurines. Angela revealed to him that this was called the Grande Plaza, and much of the architecture was seventeenth century. Most of the sidewalk tables and restaurants were occupied with people enjoying exotic food and fine wine. Other tables held couples just sipping coffee and taking pleasure in one another's presence. The air was gently warm, the surroundings tranquil and picturesque, creating a fanciful and warmly romantic scene. They walked for about twenty to thirty minutes, not able to find an empty table, but just enjoying each other's company. Both Zack and Angela were enchanted by the pristine surroundings, drawing them back to medieval Europe. Zack reached out and took Angela's hand in his. It seemed such a natural thing to do and neither felt any self-consciousness. Angela's hand was so small, soft, and warm, but for a moment, Zack was startled by the strength of her grip. They walked slowly around the plaza, gazing at the sculptured buildings, watching people and listening to the sounds, but mostly, enjoying the oneness of their enclosed hands.

Finally finding a vacant table, they quickly sat down, not having any definite plan in mind.

"Are you hungry, Angela?"

"Not really, but I would enjoy a cup of coffee and maybe a croissant."

"Sounds good to me. Coffee I know about, but the other I will just have to trust you," he said smiling.

A crisply dressed waiter suddenly appeared above them. He was dressed in a white shirt, black slacks, and bow tie.

"Bonsoir, mademoiselle et monsieur. Voulex-vous quelques choses?"

"Do you speak English?" Zack asked quickly, forgetting for the moment that Angela was fluent in French.

"Oh! Oui monsieur. I say very good English," he said with an almost undecipherable accent.

"Could we just have two coffees and a couple of those cwa—"

"Croissants," Angela interjected.

"Certainly, monsieur."

It was well after 1:00 a.m. by the time they arrived back at their hotel. The lobby was now empty. The pleasant clerk had a conspiratorial expression as they gathered their keys. Now walking hand in hand, they stopped outside Angela's room.

"Goodnight, Angela, thank you so much for going with me. Sincerely, it was a very . . . well, special time." She smiled that radiant smile of hers and he turned to leave. But then, probably as unexpectedly to him as to her, he suddenly turned and took her in his arms, pulling her close to him. The soft warmth of her of her body was magnificent. Her firm body pressed against him, and he thought that he could feel her heart beating against him. Lifting her blouse, his hand moved over the silken skin of her back. Reaching around her, he started to un-snap her bra, but as he did so, he felt her body tremble. Angela held him even more tightly. Misinterpreting her response, Zack continued to unfasten the strap, but as he did so, she gently pushed him away.

"No, Zack, no I can't!" She was flushed and obviously fighting for control. Trying hard to battle back tears, she spoke in a quiet, tremulous voice, "Zack, please . . . please understand, but I just can't let this happen."

As she spoke, she quickly arranged her blouse. She looked directly into his eyes as she started to share her thoughts and emotions. "Can we talk just for a moment? I want to try to explain."

"You don't have to explain anything, Angela." He felt foolish because he knew that his voice had to reveal his damaged ego.

"Yes, but I want to. I need to!" Her voice held so much emotion and determination he could not help but look down at her.

"Okay."

"Zack, I am a Christian, and I am constantly struggling so hard to follow Jesus' teachings. *And I mean really struggling* because it is so awfully difficult at times! But the Bible stresses so strongly the importance of purity and chastity. I must—I have to wait for the one man I love and marry." Her voice broke and she couldn't go on, so they silently walked back to her room. As they stood outside the door, she looked into his eyes and saw distress and uncertainty there, and she wanted him so badly to be loved completely by him. To be his! Her desire to hold and be held—to be never separated—was so powerful. She threw her arms around his neck and buried her face into his chest. He responded without reservation, and she felt his strong arms surrounding her.

"Oh, Zack, Zack, I never want to let you go!" Angela desired, with her whole being, to draw him completely into her as their bodies compressed. She felt no embarrassment or shame enjoying the strength and warmth of his body pressing against hers. She was so close to surrender, but was somehow able to kiss his neck and slip gently out of his grasp. Zack allowed her to go from his arms with a resigned acceptance.

He bent and very lightly touched her lips with his and then once again focused his eyes above her head. But now, he had a more composed expression.

"Well, I think I had better go take a very cold shower." He had no more than gotten the words out than he then felt stupid for his attempt at cavalier humor.

"I have driven you away, haven't I?" She stared up at him, her doe-like eyes filled with tears.

Zack couldn't make himself look into her face, nor confront the anguish in her eyes. He drew her to him once again, not with the previous urgency, but with gentleness he had never felt before. Placing his hand on the back of her head, he pressed her face tightly to his chest. He did so partly because he still wanted to hold her close, but also it was too painful to see her tears. For several moments, neither spoke. Finally, Zack took her shoulders and tenderly pushed her back. "Angela, you have done nothing to make me not care for you." He was grappling for the right words. "My feelings are so much different than you think. Angela, I have never known anyone like you." He paused again, obviously struggling within himself. "Angela, I think that I could very easily fall in love with you."

So startled by his words, a soft gasp left her throat. She wanted to shout to the whole world how much she loved him. She wanted so badly for him to know this. Yet, she remained quiet.

"Well, I still think that cold shower is in order," he spoke with great affection mixed with what now seemed like courteous humor.

"Goodnight, Angela." He kissed her lightly on her forehead and brushed his fingers casually through her hair.

Angela entered her room and leaned back against the closed door. Her heart was racing, and she was experiencing an unbelievably strong throbbing in her abdomen. Everything in her femininity was trying to force her to go to him and to be his completely.

Without warning, God's Word once again broke into her thoughts as it had so many other times when she found herself defenseless and confused.

"There is no temptation taken you but such as is common to man: but God is faithful, who will not suffer you to be tempted above that you are able; but will with the temptation also make a way to escape, that you may be able to bear it."[1]

Angela had memorized these verses from the book of Corinthians so many years ago, not knowing at that time just how powerfully they would come back for her. She had never experienced temptation this dominating before! But God was giving her His strength to overcome what she, in her humanness, could not.

Thank you, Lord, for being so faithful to your promises. She prayed these words gently and exquisitely, inwardly praising such a wonderful God. Then she smiled because of thoughts that intruded into her mind. *God's Word is so wonderful, yet . . . Zack's practical idea of a cold shower ain't all that bad.*

---

1   King James Version

CHAPTER 13

The soldiers dragged Joel's body behind the decaying jailhouse and left it. There was no reason to check him. Colonel Ching's bullets always caused fatal wounds. But if they had bothered to do a cursory exam, they would have noted shallow respiration and a very faint heartbeat. Joel lay there for possibly an hour before he regained some semblance of consciousness. He had just enough strength to straighten his crumpled body. As his mind began to clear, recent events began coming back. He remembered Colonel Ching firing his pistol and remembered the explosions and terrifying impact to his chest. Joel knew he had been shot. He had felt two bullets enter his body, and now wondered why he was not having more pain. Then cold fear struck him. Was the lack of pain because the bullets had torn through his spinal cord, leaving him paralyzed? He experienced intense relief when he found that he could move his arms and legs, although even insignificant movements exhausted him. As a result of his brief effort, he breathed deeply, and this in turn resulted in severe searing pain across his chest and back. Although he almost lost consciousness as the result of the furious pain, he felt a wave of comfort because the pain was there. He realized he had not opened his eyes yet, and when he did, he was totally disoriented by his surroundings. He saw that it was near dusk, and he tried to make a mental note of the direction of the setting sun. He slipped back into an unconscious state. When he regained consciousness, it was totally dark, and he stared upward at the blaze of stars so prominent in his part of the world. Yet, despite the many stars, total blackness surrounded him; blackness that one cannot describe without having been in Africa. The pain in his chest was even more hideous now, but he made himself ignore it and found that he could turn to his side. Having accomplished this gigantic feat, he lay back and quietly prayed to his Lord. His prayer was simple, but earnest. He thanked God that his life had been spared. He prayed for Dr. Ben, and he prayed that somehow God would send him some help. Exhaustion overwhelmed him again, but this time he fell into a more natural sleep. He had no way of knowing how much time had passed, but when he awakened, darkness and obscurity still surrounded him. Suddenly, he sensed there was someone or something near him. He could feel its presence and hear its breathing. Terror gripped him; his first thought was that the soldiers had returned. But then the apparition spoke in Kilunda, his native tongue. It was a woman's voice, soft and melodic.

"You are safe. I will help you, not harm you." It was a young woman speaking. "I was returning to my village. I followed this path because it is the shortest way, and at night I can hide from the soldiers. I examined you as best as I could in the darkness while you were unconscious. I am afraid to light my lantern here because of the soldiers." She spoke in a whisper, "You have been shot, have you not?"

"Yes." This was the first he had spoken since the colonel had wounded him. He found his voice to sound rasping and harsh. "By the soldiers. I do not know if any remain in this area or not." He had great difficulty getting these few words out and the woman recognized this.

"Please, don't talk now, you may explain later. Now I will help you."

Joel had prayed to Jesus for help. Now he felt that the woman must be an angel. Of this he was not certain, but he had no doubt that God had sent him the help for which he had prayed.

The human being, or angel, touched his forehead gently. "I will go to my village and return with help. It is not far, and I should be back in the time it will take to walk about one kilometer and return. Joel remembered her covering his body with her cloak and knew that her torso and legs would be exposed to the chill of the night. He lapsed into a restless sleep filled with dreams of a sinister monster burning his body with hot coals. He did not know when the woman returned with her two brothers, nor was he aware that they carried him to her hut on a bamboo stretcher. When he opened his eyes, he found himself on a mat woven of grass that covered a wood frame bed. There was a small, glassless window carved into the wall of mud and sticks. Sunlight entered the room, and he felt warm for the first time in many hours.

As Joel absorbed the warmth and light, a faint shadow fell over him. Looking up, he gazed into a youthful face, and instinct told him this was the *angel*. She wore a short-sleeved white blouse and had a decorative orange sarong wrapped around her waist. Her hair was braided into long thin strands that radiated from her head like sunrays. The dark eyes spoke of intelligence. Even in his disordered state, he found her to be more attractive than he had imagined. But mostly, he was taken by the kindness in her dark African countenance. As the braids of hair radiated toward the heavens, her face diffused a small amount of an angelic Being to him. Pain induced delirious thoughts, he knew, but he nonetheless wanted to hold on to them because of the strength and peace they gave him.

"You are finally awake." He appreciated again the soft tone of her voice as much as he did hearing his mother tongue being spoken.

"How long have I been here?" He hardly recognized his own voice.

She sat down on the edge of his wooden cot and gazed directly in to his face.

"You have been here for two days and nights. A few times you have spoken to me, but I do not think you knew what you were saying, nor could I understand most of your words. Please, do not speak much now. You must rest to gain strength. I have come to change the dressings on your wounds."   •

As she removed the blood stained dressings from his chest and back, she spoke so softly he had to strain to discern the words.

"My name is Rachael, Rachael Nzinga. I am the third child of my father, who is the grand chief of this region." Unexpectedly, Joel found her to be now speaking French. During the time it took to change his bandages, he discovered she was a student at the missionary school of nursing at Lualuba and was home for the holidays. Her touch was gentle and professional. She had torn strips of cloth from her only white nursing uniform to make the bandages, cutting some into ribbons and others into squares. She had then boiled them for several minutes before squeezing and drying them.

Just the act of moving onto his side to permit access to the damaged areas of his back caused such agonizing pain that reflexes closed his eyes. This was just as well because he did not see the ugly wound in his left chest. The bullet from Ching's pistol had struck his third rib, and then the flattened lead missile had deviated upward, shattering his collarbone before leaving a gaping hole in border of his trapezius muscle and the overlying skin. Rachael had carefully extracted several pieces of bone and lead fragments from this lacerated area when she had first cleaned and dressed the wounds. Joel's other injury was in the right chest where the colonel's second bullet had torn a ragged canal from the skin and pectoral muscle. The bullet had then torn a path through tissue from about the middle of his chest to his armpit, forming a channel that exposed muscle, grayish tendons, and white ribs. It was much later that Joel learned that the colonel's shot had not penetrated his heart and lungs because of the well-worn Bible he always carried in his shirt pocket. The Bible that had slowed the bullet's force enough to divert it along its more superficial path through skin and muscle.

When Rachael had finished her work, Joel opened his eyes. He did not know her, but thought he read deep worry in her face.

"Your injuries are becoming badly infected and you have a high temperature. You must receive some antibiotics. We have none here in the village. I must go to the mission hospital. I think I can get you some penicillin and pain medicine there. But the trip is long. If I leave now and walk without stopping, I can return by tomorrow before late afternoon. My brothers are gone. They are hunting the meat of antelope for us to eat. I believe they will return before dark to care for you."

Rachael stood close to him and reached down, and for just a brief moment, touched the back of her hand to his cheek. Joel found the fleeting gesture to be one of great comfort.

Joel slept restlessly again, for how long he did not know. When he awakened, the shadows seen through the window were now in the opposite direction. The early morning must have spent itself into afternoon. He shivered despite the heat inside the hut. He sensed more than heard someone enter the room, but was unable to turn to see who was there. It seemed like an eternity during which he heard not a sound of movement or breathing, but he knew that someone was there. Joel shuddered again. Then without warning, a man stood over him—Joel had heard nothing. The man was tall and painfully thin. His graying hair was short and his large forehead was deeply marked, not by age, but by disfiguring scars that ran parallel to one another across his high forehead. He had a short, pointed goatee of an ashen color that made his face appear even gaunter. A decaying black wool suit coat covered bony, hunched shoulders. Beneath the jacket, he wore a filthy white high-neck shirt. By pure resolve, Joel turned just a little and was able to see the man more completely. A scrawny hand grasped a wooden staff upon which he leaned. His appearance, more of an apparition, was made further imposing by his right eye, or rather, where an eye should have been. Its lid hung loosely, covering a gray disc of dead tissue, sightless, yet somehow piercing. The tattered black coat hung well below his waist. His lower body, from the waist to his gnarled, callused feet, was wrapped in dark patterned cloth. His only visible ornament was a necklace of animal teeth. Joel could not see the bracelets around his wrist, for the sleeves of the black coat hid them. But if had been able to, he would have noted them to be woven of many human teeth.

Joel knew instinctively that this dark specter was the guérisseur, the traditional medicine man. And even with Joel's education and intense Bible knowledge, this ominous presence at his bedside filled him with apprehension bordering on terror. The presence brought back childhood fears that years before had been woven, compressed, and then entrapped into a child's fertile mind, there to be subconsciously nurtured and never completely conquered by maturing to manhood. Maturity and knowledge do not easily defeat experiences undergone when young. Joel had first come into contact with a guérisseur when he was a five year old boy. The old medicine man had been requested to their village home to treat his older brother. The single memory that Joel had of the episode was one of lasting fear. He could remember that his brother had been very ill, but was soon well after the shaman's visit—but his brother was never the same after that.

The dark shadow spoke some words that reverberated in the silent air, sounding harsh and guttural. Joel could not understand the words, but was startled by them. In the presence of this healer he did not feel the horror he had when young, but rather now it was the overwhelming sense of evil. For just a moment, the scared and twisted face seemed like that of a child's except for the one good eye, which shown like the flames that leaped from their night fires. His lips were large and twisted into a repulsive grin. Unconsciousness was again overcoming Joel, but before it did, he wondered if he was hallucinating because of fever. *Is there ever a time when our fears leave and evil is allowed into the life of a believer in God?* In the last moments of awareness, he knew the answer.

During the ensuing time, Joel experienced a sense of being apart from his body and was able to observe the healer lift his body off the cot with ease. The bent old man now moved with the strength and suppleness of a young warrior. He laid Joel on the hard dirt floor next to a small fire that was surrounded by fétiches. Through a fog-like state, Joel recognized some of the objects. The teeth of crocodile, the rhinoceros horn, and the ears of a goat he could identify. But there were powders, potions, and other items he did not know. The old man spoke again, but his voice was no longer crackled and harsh, but feminine and comforting. The voice was chanting more than speaking. The following minutes, or hours, were filled with vagueness and shadowy figures. Joel felt searing pain in his wounds, but also gentle release from his feverish injuries. At times, it seemed that flames from the fire reached out and licked his hideous wounds, but at other times, his damaged tissue was covered by a gentle coolness that soothed and seemed to heal. There was one time he seemed to be staring into the hot embers of the fire. No flames were present, and deep within the coals he saw a face. It was that of a wise, gray-haired man with a furrowed brow. Joel knew the face to be that of his dead grandfather, and he appeared to be angry with him. Joel's whole life, until learning of Christ, had been filled with the *knowledge* that bad things happen to people because of angering their ancestors. Since this horror had all begun, these beliefs had continued to enter his thoughts, despite knowing them to be false. Childhood fears, his constant pain, and septic delusions all mixed once more in his unsettled mind. Once again, he wondered what the truth was.

Joel had no idea how long he remained in this state of semi-consciousness, but when he opened his eyes, it was dark except for the dying flames of the fire in the center of the room. He had an awareness of strength he had not experienced for many days. His mind was alert, and when attempting to move, he found that he felt very little pain. The medicine man sat behind the flames, his silhouette flickering on the wall behind him. He was old and bent again, but in the flickering darkness, Joel could see his face well enough to see a smile forming on his lips. It no longer had the totally sinister features. But his lips seemed woven into a menacing grin. He arose slowly and with some difficulty, like one who was physically spent. However, he spoke clearly and in Joel's native tongue. The voice was once again coarse and parched.

"There are many gods, my garçon. Some that offer evil and some that bring good. Do not think that your God is the only one. There are many life forms you do not know or understand."

He left the hut quietly, leaving Joel with the terrifying and plummeting feeling that this healer had taken some of his soul with him. He turned back to gaze at the embers. His grandfather's image still appeared in the dying coals.

But the vision was no longer angry with him. From the embers, Joel heard sounds like a man speaking. The voice was that of his deceased grandfather: *Joel, do not seek the dead on behalf of the living!*

Joel sat up from his cot. The guérisseur must have lifted him back to the bed before he left. He was startled by the fact that he could sit with such ease and so little pain. While pondering this strange phenomenon, there was a stirring outside the hut. His first thought was that the old medicine man was returning. When the curtain was pulled back, however, Rachael stood there, her expression one of a mixture of concern, astonishment, and fatigue.

She apologized profusely, "I am so sorry that my trip took so long. I was sick inside thinking that you might be dying from your wounds." It was now fairly dark in the hut, yet she could see strength and alertness in his face. For a moment, emotions overcame Rachael and she started to cry softly and for just a few seconds she turned her face away. When she turned back, she was again composed, but still appeared exhausted and lines of concern remained etched into her face.

"Oh, Joel, the hospital had no penicillin. They have had a recent outbreak of diphtheria and had used their entire supply. My friend, Ruth, told me there have been at least thirty deaths in the past week and that many more were going to die. I thought my heart would be torn apart because so many people have died—mostly children. But also I feared so much for you. I did not know if you would be alive or dead when I returned."

Rachael's words flowed quickly, "I stopped at my cousin's village for a brief rest, but found the village deserted. It was so eerie! There was no sound of children, no dogs barked, and the fires were cold. Yet, cooking utensils, chairs, and mats were arranged outside the huts, and clothes dried on the lines. There were still some stands with manioc drying. I became very frightened and left quickly. Then, just as I reached the edge of the forest, some village people came out to meet me. One of whom was my cousin, Jonah. They were hiding from les soldats—the soldiers. The people were very terrified. They told countless stories of the soldiers who killed many of our tribe. They were stealing, burning our homes, raping the women, and murdering the men. It is so awful to see the people like this! The women were crying, many children were hysterical, and the men appeared so defenseless. They cannot fight the soldiers with theirs guns and large knives. These men are farmers and gatherers. And they became the most frightened when they were told of the leader of these renegade soldiers. Jonah shook with fear when he told me his name. They call him *Le Diable Noire*. Others say his name is Ching. I don't believe I have ever seen such fear as I saw in these people."

All the time Rachael spoke, she was actively building up the fire and lighting the kerosene lantern. She stopped and studied Joel for a long time.

"Joel, has the guérisseur treated you? You look so much better." She touched his forehead. His fever was gone, and he revealed vigor in his eyes.

In the next few minutes, as Rachael examined his wounds and changed his soiled dressing, Joel tried to relate what had transpired during the old healer's visit. As he told of the strange visions, the sinister apparitions, and the return of strength into his body, Rachael listened intently. She saw that a great deal of healing in Joel's wounds had occurred. Much of the angry redness and swelling of injured flesh had resolved. A few hours ago, she had left a man not knowing if he would be dead or alive when she returned. Now, his injuries were still tender and far from completely healed, yet something incredible had happened during her absence.

Joel had been sitting for several minutes and was experiencing some vertigo. When he leaned back, the movement caused discomfort, but not the excruciating pain as before.

"Rachael, how does one explain what has happened to me? I don't believe in witchcraft. I believe in God! But these things I experienced were not in my imagination. And look at my wounds; they are almost healed. Most of the infection is gone, and a lot of my strength has returned." Joel searched her face in the dim light, expecting to find distrust in his words, but he could find none.

Her words were careful and precise as she spoke, "When I was a child, I saw many things the sorcerers did in our village. I saw some good things happen, but mostly, they were evil. Most often the medicine men were associated with pain and suffering and even death. As I studied the Bible, I began to believe that even though the sorcerers communicate with evil forces, God **can** use them to do good if he so desires. I cannot disregard all the powers they have. But I believe these powers are from Satan. My grandfather was a very wise man. He once said to me, 'The white missionaries say that sorcery does not exist, but they reveal their ignorance by saying this.' I feel he was right."

For a while, they spoke of familiar things. She shared of seeing her friends at the mission, the diphtheria epidemic, and of her family. He talked also of his mission station and the hospital. Her background was Catholic and he related to her that his was Protestant, but many of their beliefs seemed the same. When he spoke of Dr. Ben, Rachael let out a small gasp.

"Oh, my dear God! Jonah and others spoke of a white man among the soldiers. They said he was their prisoner, but that he treats their illnesses. They spoke as if he is a doctor. He apparently is just the ghost of a man. He is dirty, very emaciated, and looks extremely ill. They could not see his face well because of a long beard. Could it be your Dr. Ben?"

"It is possible. Did they tell you from where the rebel soldiers came?"

"I know some of the villages. Jonah and some other men said that they had been avoiding the larger cities, such as Bumbi, and had attacked Mwambo and Tshivumba during the last few weeks."

Joel was familiar with these towns and knew them to be to the northeast. His home and Mission Station were about two hundred kilometers (one hundred and twenty miles) to the southwest. He wondered if these rebel soldiers were making a circle and returning to where he and Dr. Ben had been attacked. Possibly, they thought there might be some plunder and medicines they had missed.

CHAPTER *fourteen* 14

Joel had no way of knowing that two of the finest trauma surgeons in the world had landed at the Leopoldville airport. At the very time he and Rachael were discussing the recent events in their lives, Pascal, Zack, and Angela were experiencing the mayhem of entry into an African country. The only way Zack could find of describing the total bedlam besieging them was like being inside an anthill after someone had kicked it. When they stepped off the plane, the heat and humidity had assaulted them with the force of a sauna bath out of control. Africans were everywhere, pushing, jostling, and clutching at his hand luggage. He found himself surrounded by inquisitive and begging faces chattering incoherently. He had never experienced such total chaos, and yet, next to him, Pascal and Angela stood calmly and seemed unaffected by the mayhem around them. During the next hour or so, Zack stood back and watched Pascal and Angela argue, demand, plead, and intimidate various individuals. The heat and foulness of the air in the airport created waves of weakness and nausea. Sweat caused Zack's shirt to fuse to his body. The muscles of his arms cramped from fiercely grasping the handles of his suitcases to keep them from being jerked away. But finally, they had collected all their baggage and exited the building where the air was a few degrees cooler. A slight breeze evaporated some of the sweat from their clothes. But even in the parking lot there were hordes imploring them for the opportunity to load their baggage into the dilapidated van that awaited them. Cash was placed into the appropriate hands, orders were shouted, and a path was cleared through the mass of humanity. Finally, the decrepit Volkswagen bus entered the main route toward the city. Talking was made nearly impossible by the constant racket of auto horns, verbal outbursts from their driver, motor noise, and the clatter of old metal parts. So Zack spent the time viewing the activities around them as they traveled. He smiled to himself when he found he could look down and observe the road beneath them through rusted out places in the floorboard. The traffic was intense, and there was a constant flow of people on both sides of the road. For the first few miles, there were many small open shops and wooden tables stocked with bars of soap, canned goods, and various other merchandises. After a few miles, the route brought them to compact buildings and for the next forty minutes or so, Zack stared with fascination and astonishment at the small cement structures and open ditches carrying water and refuge along both sides of the road. He saw that many of these structures were lived in. The doorways and windows were mostly open, but some had old rags covering them. Many people were talking, and some old men sat at small wooden tables, apparently playing games. Children of varied ages moved in all directions, mostly naked, but some with cloth around their loins. Women, both young and old, were carrying buckets of water, scrubbing clothes on slabs of rocks, or sitting and staring with vacant eyes. Even here, as at the airport, there seemed to be total disorder and purposeless activities. But Zack sensed that this was probably not accurate. He had never encountered anything like this, not even in the slums of Los Angeles or those near his hospital. He was perceptive enough to realize that he was within a culture so different from his own that there would be no way to make sense of it with his limited knowledge. But where were the masses of people going? What were they doing? Was there a purpose in their activities? His mind drifted. *How can one live, or eat, or make love and have babies surrounded by foul smelling sewage and oppressive heat?* As they approached the center of the city, conditions improved. There were broad-leaved trees, great flowering bushes, and larger buildings. But the heat and humidity were no better and the road still contained large craters preventing any kind of speed. All the stores had large, steel bars on doors and windows. As their road began to climb, conditions improved some. The air was cleaner and slightly cooler. Dusk was advancing, and with the dimmer light, the shrubbery seemed greener, the streets less formable, and the air less stifling. Behind massive stonewalls he glimpsed vast houses. One almost had the impression of southern plantations except for huge pieces of broken glass cemented along the tops of the walls, jutting up to form deadly knives.

Zack's deep thoughts were broken by Angela's hand on his shoulder. He turned toward her and even in the grime and lack of sleep she was still quite lovely. But he saw sadness and pain in her eyes.

"Do you ever get over the impact of this squalor and these dreadful conditions?" Zack asked, but did not wait for her reply. "From the sorrow I see in your eyes, you have not, have you, Angela?"

"I have driven through this area and many like it numerous times, and it doesn't ever get any easier. Yet, Zack, I honestly pray that it doesn't ever stop affecting me this way. I do not ever want to reach a point that I can look upon starvation, disease, filth, and human humiliation and feel nothing. I have seen this happen to others, and I realize that sometimes it is a defense mechanism to protect from being overwhelmed by the awfulness of what one experiences. God forbid that will happen to me. I would rather feel the pain than cold indifference!" she spoke with deep conviction.

This brief conservation was suspended as their van pulled into a short drive that faced a large iron gate. A few honks by their driver brought a small, wiry man to the inside of the entrance. He unhooked a heavy chain and one half of the large metal doorway swung open, allowing them to pass through, but only after the driver and sentry had exchanged several moments of friendly greetings.

Pascal turned from the front seat to face them. Zack thought he saw a lack of tension lines in his face that had been there for so many days.

"Welcome to the Mission complex. This compound used to belong to a wealthy Belgium family who left during the early rebellion years. The Mission purchased it for the staff working in Leopoldville and to be used as a guesthouse for visitors and workers who travel to and from the interior."

It felt so good to climb out of the cramped van where they had been packed for the past one and one half hours. At first glance around, Zack thought he was in a scenic park. The compound was at least a full block long and wide and contained many bushes and trees, most of which had colorful blooms. Tall palm trees were loaded with clumps of dates. Many rose bushes and flowering shrubs flourished along the base of the bulky cement wall that enclosed the complex. To his left stood a large two-story house in front of which was a huge tree with its limbs hanging low with heavy fruit—the first avacado Zack had ever seen. The house itself was stone with a large porch along the entire front—curved steps lead to the doorway. The roof was made of green colored tiles, many of which were missing or broken. Zack estimated the wall enclosing the compound to be eight feet tall. It also had large pieces of broken glass protruding upwards from is crest, spoiling the aura of a garden paradise. Zack was to learn that all the homes of any substance had to be protected from thieves. Heavy iron gates, treacherous barricades, and armed sentries were the norm.

Pascal broke into Zack's thoughts. "This will be home for the next four or five days while we verify your visas and make the necessary arrangements for the trip to the interior."

Several workers appeared from almost nowhere to take their baggage and Pascal gave them directions in Kituba, a common language of western Congo.

To the right of the main house, separated by about thirty yards of lawn, was a small, low-lying building where the workers took Pascal and his luggage. Others took Angela's baggage to the large stone house. She noted Zack's puzzlement, and responded by a small gesture. With her palms up and a sprite smile, she said, "Some of us are more important than others." She quickly turned before Zack could reply, but he heard her chuckle.

The small accommodations that he and Pascal were to share were more like a cement bunker than an apartment. There was a small room with sink, stove, and refrigerator. This room connected to a living room that contained two uncomfortable appearing chairs made of bamboo—a small wooden coffee table was wedged between them. To their right was a short hall leading to two rooms that served as the sleeping quarters, each containing antiquated dressers and narrow beds.

The remainder of the evening went quickly. Night plummeted with the quick shroud of darkness as one experiences only near the equator. The exhaustion from traveling and the ten-hour time change made this small group of dog-tired travelers mechanically eat beans, thick rice, and a variety of fruit. Each disintegrated into their separate beds and slept the sleep of total exhaustion.

Zack was awakened by the sound of birds and the smell of his own sweat. It was light, but he could not determine the time of day. Unintentionally he dozed again and was abruptly awakened by the strange feeling of someone near him. He sat up hastily and found that he was totally alone in his small concrete room. He was acutely aware that his heart was hammering, and he was breathing rapidly. It was not the sensation of fear so much as a presence that seemed to be evoking his feelings. Suddenly, he knew this experience. It was the same as had visited him in the call room at hospital in what seemed like another era. The difference this time was that he perceived the *being* was there to somehow be helpful. In some way it was trying to reach him. But Zack knew that these things do not happen—it had to be his imagination or a weary subconscious mind playing tricks on him.

Zack took his watch from the dresser and found it was 0700 hour (7:00 am)—he was beginning to think in universal time. The stiffness in his muscles confirmed that he had slept for many hours. He slipped into his slacks and went into the kitchen where Pascal sat at the small table sipping coffee and writing what appeared to be a list of both names and items. His demeanor was polite, but Zack could not remember ever seeing him appear so intense.

"Bon jour, Zack. J'espère que vous vous étés dormi bien?" Pascal was returning to his former life and languages.

Zack did not know why Pascal was so intense, but he had to assume that it was from all the responsibilities on him. However, he had to wonder if he might have received some distressing news about Dr. Ben that he was not comfortable sharing at this time. During the ensuing two days he saw very little of Pascal and Angela. Both took separate vehicles and chauffeurs to the trade areas in order to purchase food, cooking utensils, insect repellants, and other staples needed for life in the *interior*. Pascal had full days making arrangements for visas, travel permits, immunization records, and maps. He also tried to gather information about the rebels, their leaders, and their whereabouts, and also to learn as much as he could about their organization, communications, and methods.

It was not quite light the following morning when they arose to leave. All their supplies had been packed into the Land Rover the evening before, except for the few items needed for the morning's necessities. Dawn was breaking with the orange-red sphere rising between the large palm trees that stood guard on each side of the heavy metal gate. The air was cool and serene. The ever-present rooster kept up his incessant crowing. In addition to the three in their team, there was the chauffer and two other men who were there to assist with the supplies, deal with the dangers of the route, and to repair the inevitable breakdowns.

Before starting the engine, Pascal, Angela, and the three men bowed their heads and prayed. Although Zack could not understand their words, he was strongly moved by being involved with them—a white woman, four Africans of which one was highly educated and sophisticated; three timid young men wearing tattered clothes who were obviously impoverished. Zack experienced a curious comfort and peace being with them. In addition, there was again the sense of a wonderful, unseen presence. When their prayer ended, Angela turned from the front seat to smile at him. Zack was again totally amazed at serenity in her face. He reached forward and took her hand—its soft warmth made him feel very close to her. It was impossible to talk over the clamor of the diesel motor, but their communication at this moment needed no verbalization.

By mid-morning they had traveled about one hundred kilometers (sixty miles). The first twenty-five kilometers (fifteen miles) that took them past the airport was paved, but now the road became sandy in places and in other areas there was red adhesive mud—and the constant cavernous ruts and washouts. In all of the Congo there was only one asphalt road, a stretch that wound its way east of Kikwit to where the Palmolive Company had planted a huge forest of palm trees. The company shipped out large amounts of palm oil for the consumers in Europe and the United States. During the Belgium rule the roads in many areas had been maintained by the local villagers who dug trenches to prevent washouts and firmed the soft soil with elephant grass. Now, with the wide-spread anarchy in the country, the devastation to transportation was reaching horrific levels. To travel an average of twenty miles per hour in the interior was extraordinary.

Angela, Zack, and Pascal had very little time to talk. Even during the many times their four-wheel vehicle was being dug out of the sand, they had very few opportunities to converse. If they weren't shoveling the Land Rover free, they were clearing the road of fallen debris. As the tropical sun was mercifully setting, Zack noted there were more African people along the road. Most were women carrying large jars or bundles of wood on their heads, some with small babies in slings on their backs. Also, many children darted playfully around them. The adults seemed to take little notice of their convoy, but the children waved and ran dangerously close to their vehicle. A few of the children would scurry in front of their truck and then jump out of the way at the last second. Over most of the last twenty miles, the terrain had been flat and monotonous. The land was covered with dwarfed trees, no taller than scrub pine back home. They suddenly broke into an open area that contained tall grass and numerous thatched roof huts. Their path was lined with mud walled homes. Many villagers stood by the entrances of their houses. Smoke rose from open cooking fires, and many dogs sounded their resentment at the intruders. A few persons waved, but to Zack many appeared hostile and irritated. He discovered very quickly that if you smiled and gestured to them, their faces would glow with beautiful smiles. Zack was to learn that most of these village dwellers, despite their fears and superstitions, could be demonstrative and affectionate people.

The tired voyagers stopped their overloaded Land Rover in front of a somewhat larger dwelling that stood out from the others by the presence of its metal roof. Even if they had not seen the large jagged cross on its roof, it would have been identified as a place of importance.

This village was apparently where they were to spend the night. At first, Zack experienced feelings of apprehension, but they were quickly defeated by a sense of wonderment. He had been abruptly thrown into the natural environment of the African with their cramped huts, dirt floors, windowless rooms and the smell of decaying grass roofs and crudely made dirt walls. Most of the people, especially the children, wore tattered clothes. The odor of sweat and smoke permeated the air and merged with the laughter of the children at play.

CHAPTER 15

At about the same time these travelers were eating their village meal of luku, rice, and boiled manioc leaves, Ben was huddled near the evening fire. The soldiers no longer tied him to a tree or locked him into a hut at night. During the weeks of captivity, many of the soldiers had become kinder to him, and with a few he had even been able to converse. There was one young soldier with whom he communicated with often. His name was Maludi, and he seemed very old for his twenty years. Several evenings while the other soldiers sat by the fire and became drunk, he and Maludi talked about many things. In time, the young man sneaked him Quinine for his malaria, Paracetamol for his fevers, and shared portions of his own food. Maludi seemed fascinated by the fact that a white man, who must be rich, was living in the villages with people like himself—poor and unskilled. He comprehended little of America or its people. He knew of the great city called New York and also *knew* that all Americans were very wealthy. Ben was very kind to the young man and grew to appreciate his inquisitive mind. He tried to share American culture with him as best he could, but some technology was beyond the young man's comprehension. How could he explain airplanes, subways, escalators, or pop machines? How could this young African grasp the fact of eating three hot meals a day or to drive one's own vehicle?

When Maludi started to press him about why he gave up all the great wealth to come to the Congo, Ben found the discussion easier. He had no trouble sharing his faith with this young soldier. Ben spoke slowly and gathered his thoughts as he spoke. The young man's mother tongue was not Kicongo, although he seemed to understand it well. This gave them a common language in which to converse. However, Ben also knew that he must start with the very basics of his faith.

A gentle warm rain began to fall as lightening flashed across the eastern sky and thunder reverberated through the valley below. The two men moved back under a large twisted tree, the leaves of which kept them reasonably dry. Ben prayed silently, asking God for the right words.

"Two thousand rainy seasons ago a man was born in a far away place called Israel. When he had become an adult, there was a short three-year period in his life that he spoke to large crowds. But he was not just an ordinary wise man because he performed many miracles: he healed the sick, destroyed many evils spirits, and even brought the dead back to life. But most of all, his life was one of love. He loved both those who were his friends but also those who hated him. This man was the Son of God, the same God that your people recognize. Over and over again he told the people that he had come so they could follow him along the direct path that led to God. He taught that *all* men are full of sin: the sins of hate, jealousy, anger, selfishness, and lust. He told the people that it was because of sin that all men's live were filled with fear, pain, and torment by the spirits. In your country, Maludi, the spirits are always surrounding you; the spirits of dead ancestors, the spirits of the forest and streams, and the spirit of the Ndoki. In my culture in the United States, we fight the spirits of lust, greed, and selfishness." Ben paused for moment; these were difficult words to find equivalents. But he found that by using many words, he was able to communicate them. "The words from God that we call the Bible, teaches we are all doomed to death. Then, after death there is eternity without Tata Nzambi (Father God). We will be forever surrounded by terrible evil spirits." Ben searched his friends face for signs of recognition. He saw what he hoped for.

"This man, the Son of God, was named Jesus. Many of the village wise men and tribal chiefs hated him because the people were following him and not them. So they schemed to kill him, although he was guilty of no wrongs. But they could not kill him themselves because a foreign tribe ruled them, so they convinced their conquerors to kill him. They did not just kill him, they tortured him until he was disfigured beyond recognition, and then they nailed his hands and feet to a tree and left him hanging there to die. This man, Jesus, was guilty of no crimes! He loved the people, and he taught them many wonderful things. This Jesus performed many marvelous miracles and made many sick village people healthy."

Ben suddenly realized he had been speaking more quickly than he had intended. He paused to see if Maludi was still listening. When he looked into the young man's face, he found tears flowing from his eyes—streaking the dusty face. For a few seconds Ben stared into the deep brown eyes, knowing that the African was not embarrassed by a display of feelings. When he started to speak again, his voice was trembling with emotion—but he had to continue.

"This man died there, nailed to the tree. But that does not end the story, Maludi. His body was prepared for burial, much like your people do, and he was placed in a cave with a heavy stone blocking the entrance. But three days later he came back from the dead. The stone was rolled away, and he came out of the cave and was seen by hundreds of people. For a short while he taught his close followers many things, and then they watched as he was taken up into the sky to join Tata Nzambi."

He again prayed silently for the appropriate words.

"This man, who is the God's *only* son, can set us free from the punishment for all our terrible sins. We do not have to hate, to kill, and to lie to each other. Nor do we have to become drunk and desire the bodies of shameful women. We do not have to be afraid of the ghosts of dead ancestors or other evil spirits. God sent his son to show us he loves us. His son Jesus came to earth two thousand dry seasons ago in order to give everlasting life if we believe in Him. God will forgive all our sins, and we can live beyond death because He became the perfect sacrifice to the great Nzambi."

Ben was amazed at the changes that come over Maludi's face. His eyes were brighter than he had ever seen them, and there was a faint smile on his lips. Tensions, angers, and fears seemed to have vanished from him.

"How can I do this? How can I meet this Jesus?"

Ben and Maludi had been so engrossed in their discussion that they had not heard the soldiers coming until the branches were swept back with great force. Two vicious appearing men glowered at them. Both had rifles and cartridges belts thrown over their shoulders and they reeked of palm wine.

"You are plotting against us," the older of the two soldiers growled. "Are you planning an escape? We will take you before the *great one.*"

The colonel had not slept well for many nights. His nerves were raw and anger burned within him. He had been drinking heavily and eating poorly.

Headaches, abdominal pains, and the spirits had plagued him. Evil feasts on evil and can increase monstrously—but will eventually devour itself. The spirits that now visited the Colonel no longer beguiled him and he no longer completely controlled them. Inevitably, as his fears increased, his wickedness swelled to unrestrained proportions. He had come to believe that the spirits were now tormenting him because of the presence of the white doctor. He knew that he should kill him, but an unexplained fear held him back. But now he was certain the mondele must die to stop the voices from tormenting him. The forces that had always responded to him now assaulted him at night. Their eyes were like burning coals and voices eerie echoes. Dreadful images in the twilight gloom! The headaches and terrifying dreams had to stop!

"Apportez le medecin a moi! (Bring the doctor to me)," he screamed at the guards standing at the doorway. The frightened sentries left immediately with trembling legs, fearing the Colonel's rage.

Ben and Maludi were wrenched viciously to their feet. Despite no resistance on their part, the men repeatedly struck them with their rifle butts, cursed, and spat at them. It was raining hard now and their clothes were drenched. Ben noticed that there was blood soaking through the shirt on Maludi's back. He wondered how deep the rifle stock had torn his flesh. They were shoved and beaten until they stood in front of a hut in the center of the tiny village. It was the largest and obviously the most important dwelling. Two more dangerous and well-armed soldiers flanked its doorway. One of their captors spoke to the guards. Ben did not understand their language, but the man on the right of the entrance knocked on the roughly hewn door and waited. After several seconds, they heard a guttural command, and the guards pushed open the door and entered. Ben could hear voices in conversation and his blood ran cold. After all these weeks of captivity, he had only seen Colonel Ching one time since the initial confrontation—it was in the terrifying vision that occurred on a wet night much like this. However, he had almost always sensed his existence, and now he heard that terrifying voice again. He trembled despite himself. He was once more to meet le Diable Noire face to face. The soldier pulled the wooden door further back and motioned them to enter.

Ben felt the young soldier at his side shake with fear from being in such close proximity to this terrifying chief. Ben's eyes became rapidly accustomed to the darkness of the room. Colonel Ching was in uniform much the same as on their first meeting. Even more than on their first encounter, Ben felt evilness radiating from this man—if he were a man. Ben wondered at his own irrational thoughts.

"Bonjour, monsieur Docteur. Nge kele imbote?" He mixed French and Kituba with a soft voice that carried no threat—his fierce look conveyed the opposite. The eyes that were twisted apart by his scarred face burned with cruelty. Hatred and possible insanity emanated from those eyes that seemed to glow like burning embers.

"Colonel, it is not true that we are . . ." A hard strike from the butt of a rifle took the remainder of Ben's words away. The soldier screamed at him, "Nege tuba ve!" Obviously one did not speak unless the colonel allowed it.

Colonel Ching confirmed this, "You may speak when I say so! Why are you plotting against me? Have I not treated you well? Have I not spared your life and given you shelter and food?" He paused and then said, "You may speak."

"What you say is true, monsieur Colonel, but we have not plotted against you. This young soldier, who is loyal to you, shared his food with me, and we talked about life in the Congo and spoke of my country."

"You work for the CIA! You were getting information from my soldiers!" Ben's body felt weak with fear, but his mind was unyielding. The colonel spoke in French, and he knew the young man at his side could not understand his words. The inferno radiating from Ching's eyes was even more horrifying, and the man seemed to have grown in size, towering over them like a monstrous statue.

"I do not work for the CIA or any government. My work is for God and the Congolese people. But even if I were an agent, how can you believe that this young soldier has any information that would be important to me? He follows your commands only."

This man, *le Diable Noire,* stood quietly for several minutes, his intense gaze fixed on something above Ben's head. His scarred face and brutal expression created dread and apprehension in not only Ben and the young soldier but also within the others in the room. This was a tormented, volatile force that seemed more animal than human.

Ben continued but only after saying a silent prayer, "We talked about God and about Jesus Christ, the Savior of the world."

"Faissez-vous! Ferme la bouche!" Colonel Ching's voice was a snarling bellow. "Kill him!" Pointing at the young soldier, "And take this mondele to the jail. I will deal with him later!"

"Please, monsieur Colonel, there is no reason to kill this man. He is a mere boy and he is of no danger to you."

"Then let your Jesus save him!" Ching was obviously beyond any reasoning. Ben had no time to speak further because he was grasped tightly, twisted around, and shoved out of the hut. He heard Colonel Ching already speaking with his men, and his voice now carried authority. "We will march tomorrow! Helo, you will take your two units to the southwest to Kangola, Lasaku, and Kiluka. Destroy those villages and seize what you can. By the second full moon we will meet at Kikungu—that mondele's village!"

Ben heard no more because the distance was now too great, and he was being pushed and battered by the soldiers. He was shoved viciously down the trail, wrists tied behind him. Just ahead he could see the other two soldiers sadistically dragging Maludi between them. The soldiers that held him were filthy and smelled of sweat and stale beer. They were violent and sadistic. For no reason they continued to brutalize Ben and Maludi despite the fact that they offered no struggle. The two captives were taken to the edge of the forest where a large game trail broke into the clearing. There, Maludi was forced to start digging a hole. The soil was soft from the rains, and he had dug down about four feet in a short time. Ben did not realize immediately what they were doing, but it was obvious the young man knew—his body trembled with every shovel full of dirt. His eyes were filled with terror and his mind screamed as he dug his own grave. When it was done to their satisfaction, the soldiers stripped Maludi to the waist and began cutting his torso with their knives. The incisions were deep enough to bleed profusely but would not be immediately fatal. Maludi made no sound, even when they threw him into the pit he had excavated. The drunken men then began to push the ground around him, pinning his arms to his sides. When they finished tamping the dirt around Maludi, only his head, neck and the flesh of his shoulders were exposed. The wounds on his shoulder had been pulled open by his effort, exposing the fatty tissue beneath. Some of the cuts continued to ooze blood. Night would fall soon and the nocturnal animals would investigate the scent of blood. As Ben watched in increasing revulsion and helplessness he remembered how the *army* ants had devoured his penned rabbits, leaving nothing but bones. Many times he had seen the vultures pick the flesh from dying animals. His young friend's fate was too horrible to think about. Ben prayed that his death would be rapid and the pain not too terrible. The guards, however, were laughing as they turned away from the hideous scene. They roughly pushed Ben ahead of them. He tried to speak to his tormented friend but was not allowed to so. Only their eyes met briefly, and Ben thought he saw acceptance in them.

As they were forcing Ben back to his jail the guards were too intoxicated and much too immersed in their riotous behavior to notice another pair of eyes watching from the forest edge. From the darkness, Joel watched the repulsive scene. As much revulsion as he had for the soldiers, he knew in his heart that he could not allow a fellow human being die like that!

CHAPTER *sixteen* 16

Completely unknown to Zack and at almost the exact time he and the others were preparing another full evening with village people, a young soldier was barely clinging to existence and was pleading silently, not for life, but for death. His pain and fear had become too much to bear. He was unable to move anything but his eyes and facial muscles. Thirst, heat, and the biting flies were tormenting him unmercifully. Now the *army* ants *had* found him. In a matter of minutes they would destroy his eyes and feast on the skin, muscles, and mucous membranes of his face. They would leave nothing but skull and teeth. He screamed out once more, knowing that nobody would come. He squeezed his eyes tightly to prolong the inevitable. The bites were piercing and fierce. Suddenly the torment ceased. He thought, *I am dead and now the torture is finished.* Yet he could still feel a cool night breeze on his face and hear someone digging. He tried to open his eyes but could not. *The ants have taken my eyes*, he thought and a tremor shook his entrapped body. He breathed as deeply as his tomb permitted. He had space to breathe only because he had filled his lungs and held it while they shoveled the dirt around his chest. The movements near him continued, and he felt some pressure being taken away from his neck and shoulders. Someone was freeing him! Had the guards returned to torture him more? Suddenly He could breathe deeper. If only his eyes were not gone. Then a soft voice spoke.

"You are alive, my friend. Please be very quiet because we do not want the soldiers to return."

It was a deep voice. A man's voice. Or was it a man? Was it now dead ancestors come to torment him? He had no friends! He had only comrades with whom he had raped and murdered.

"I have driven the ants away." Joel smiled to himself. He had taken branches and beaten the marching ants, turning the tens of thousand biting insects toward the military encampment. The soldiers might have a very challenging and sleepless night.

Joel now had to literally drag the young man from his death trap, again cautioning him to silence. It took Joel about twenty minutes to pull the young soldier to the forest edge. He then gave the soldier some water but did not allow him to drink too fast for fear he might vomit.

"I cannot see! Did the ants take my eyes?"

"No, but they are swollen badly. When the swelling goes away, you will see again."

"Who are you?"

"I am Joel. You do not know me, but I am your friend. I was shot by your soldiers, by your colonel actually. I am searching for the white doctor they took with them."

"You cannot be a friend. We tried to kill you!"

"You are right. You are not my friend, and I should hate you. But my chief is Jesus Christ, and he loves you, and because he loves you, I love you also. Therefore, you are my friend."

Joel knew that this young soldier was too weak from his beatings to be moved far. For now they were safe at the edge of the forest. He had gone back to the pit and made tracks leading in the opposite direction. He had wiped away all of theirs. During the ensuing hours of the night Maludi slept fitfully. When he would awaken and start to cry out, Joel would cover his mouth and speak softly to him. When he began to shiver, he covered him with large palm leaves, and when they no longer gave him enough warmth, he removed his shirt and wrapped him as best he could.

Joel slept very little that night. He was afraid that the sick soldier might cry out and the soldiers would come. The young rebel awakened just as a small amount of light streamed onto the forest floor and the treetop animals began to tune their voices into a raucous symphony. The young man had recuperated immensely as the result of the night's rest. The swelling of his eyes had gone down a great deal, leaving slightly opened slits. He could now see a little and that raised his mood immensely. The fluids and fruit that Joel had given him through the night made him feel reasonably strong. Few people have the recuperative powers of the African.

Joel had formed many plans in his mind to rescue Dr. Ben from the hands of Colonel Ching and his gang of murders. He resented the time this young soldier was taking from his plan, but he could not leave him. He was still too weak. So he and the young man marched deep into the forest, covering their trail as they went. They were still afraid that if the soldiers did return and find Maludi gone, they would start a massive search. For three days, Joel and Maludi hid in the forest, eating wild fruit and fish from the small river. Finally, they decided that Colonel Ching's men would not come.

As the days passed, Joel considered sharing some of his plans with Maludi but he still did not trust him enough to do so. On his part, the young soldier seemed to be genuinely grateful and eagerly did everything he could to be cooperative. The two men began to share a little about their family background. Joel learned that Maludi's parents had died when he was twelve years old and an elder brother had become the head of the family. But the brother was addicted to beer and alcohol and did little to help the other children. When Maludi was sixteen, he went to Kisangani to find work to help feed his younger brother and sisters. He soon discovered that there were no jobs, and he had to search in the garbage dump and sometimes steal to make the hunger go away. One day a unit of soldiers came to Kisangani and their uniforms and treacherous looking guns excited him. They seemed to be vigorous and adventurous, and they told exciting stories. However, most appealing to Maludi was when he learned that they ate regular meals. When the soldiers left the city, he went with them.

After many more conversations with Maludi, Joel began to feel safe enough to share with him some of his plans to rescue Dr. Ben. But he did not disclose all the details because there would be great dangers that he did not want Maludi to know about yet.

CHAPTER 17

Pascal, Angela, and Zack slept in separate huts. Zack was so exhausted from traveling that he did nothing more than take off his boots and quickly fall into a profound sleep on a woven grass mat stretched out on the hard mud floor. He must have started to dream immediately. It was again a dream of Desiree that he both hated and cherished. He hated them because of the anguish they caused but cherished them for the brief visit from his beautiful daughter. The dream this night was vibrant. Desiree was running along a forest path; despite the heavy foliage, the trail was bathed in golden sunlight. She was laughing and singing as she ran with light steps, feet barely touching the ground. Suddenly, she was in a clearing. The forest was gone and all around the small meadow were flowers blooming with a kaleidoscope of colors. She was playing a game with six other children. It was a strange game in which two at a time faced one another, moving their feet and clapping their hands over some squares drawn in the dirt. Then one girl would slip away, as if she had lost, and another would take her place. Suddenly, Desiree turned and seemed to be looking up at him. He blue eyes glistened like cut diamonds and her soft blond hair flowed around her cheeks and neck. She was smiling. "Hi, Daddy. Have you come to help my friends? Please come to help my friends. I love you, Daddy!"

Zack awakened with a start. There was light entering the latticed window. His watch revealed that he had slept more than seven hours. His body was stiff and sore from the hard ground. However, he felt rested. For several minutes he lay still, noting only the coolness of the dirt floor through the blanket on which he lay. Suddenly, he felt incredible warmth and peace all around him—and something else. What was it? It seemed familiar—he had felt it before. Yet, this time it was somehow different. There was a calmness and tranquility that far surpassed anything before! The dream was coming back to him. He wanted so badly to have Desiree close to him—and not just her, but all her friends.

The memory of the dream began fading quickly, as dreams always do, but the last thing he remembered was all of Desiree's friends looking up at him. Their bodies were now emaciated and there was no smile on their lips. Their dark, gaunt faces stared at him through vacant eyes.

He pulled back the heavy animal skin that served as a door and stepped out in to the early morning mist. Dawn was breaking as the sunlight expanded between two huge trees. The air was cool and very refreshing. Somewhere a monkey kept up an incessant chatter. Three small pigs were rooting a few feet away, but otherwise there was very little activity. Suddenly, a man stepped from his hut and began to sweep the dirt in front of his home with a broom made of woven grass. The orange sun changed to a radiant silver line as it rose behind clouds. From where he stood, the light silhouetted the grass tops of the small huts, giving one the impression of viewing antiquity. A pleasant breeze moved the palm branches with the grace and elegance of a ballet.

The serenity allowed Zack's mind to roam. He was thinking that life is so filled with contradictions: success and failure, hate and love, terror and caress. Very often there was no delineation between them. When does an embrace become pain or love degenerate to hate? When is success a failure and failure a success? Zack's thoughts continued to wander as he enjoyed the early morning air. This very dawn was driving away the fearful darkness for so many here in the Congo. He was slowly learning that with the coming of light came the fading of spirits and demons. But they would always return! Despite these thoughts, Zack was feeling more tranquility than he could ever remember. At this moment the peace within him seemed to be coming from the certainty that he would be with Desiree again. He did not know how he knew this and did not want to question it. The assurance was enough. These thoughts went against everything that he thought to be *true*. Science says that people die; life is transient and then over. Belief in a life after death is permissible for those who cannot face reality. All that Zack had known to be the *truth* was becoming far less certain than it had once been. *Man! This isolation is getting to me, or I must be coming down with some tropical disease*, Zack spoke to himself, but could have been speaking aloud. Even if these experiences seemed strange, he could not explain the strength and conviction that came with them.

This was the second day in this village of Kiyongo. The town was larger than others in which they had stayed—maybe six to ten thousand people.

There was a central water supply and a reasonably well-stocked market. He had barely seen Angela, for she had been busy treating, teaching, and encouraging the woman of the village. There was a great need for medical care here, but they had very little with which to diagnose and treat. With them, they had a few meager surgical instruments and some basic medicines. Pascal had left the morning before with some of the leaders of this and other nearby villages. The last Zack saw of him, he was walking down a narrow trail surrounded by tall trees. He moved rapidly and with sinuous grace.

Angela suddenly interrupted his revelry. She had come up behind him noiselessly. Her voice was so soft and pleasant that her sudden appearance did not startle as much as it might have.

Angela had her brown hair pulled back in a small spiral behind her head and was dressed in a pale yellow blouse and blue jeans. She wore no makeup and had on a heavy brown jacket. Zack thought her to be the most magnificent vision he had ever seen.

"You slept well, I hope." She took his hands in hers and looked into his face with sincerity. This was not an idle question. Angela was truly interested. For a few moments they talked about sleeping in an African hut, she on a bamboo mat spread on a wooden frame and he on a hard mud floor. It was almost an hour before some women of the village had gathered wood and built the fires to boil water for a hot drink. He thought it was coffee, or at least the grounds in the bottom of his cup appeared to be. Angela seemed more relaxed and at peace than he had ever seen her. Her features were tranquil and serene. Zack wondered if it was because she was home. She had known this life all of her earlier years. These were her people, her language, and her culture. There was pensiveness in her voice as she spoke. "You seem have become very philosophical toward these people and this land, Zack, or am I reading something that is not there?" Her expressed thoughts were more perceptive than even she realized. Zack was once again astonished by her insightfulness.

"I've been in Africa only a few days, but it all seems so overpowering. The mass of people in Leopoldville, with its refuse, garbage, and poverty, is beyond description. Now, out in the rural area, we find people living as if in the Stone Age. So many of these people are sick and aged well beyond their years. There is child after child with ulcers on their legs, distended bellies, and draining eyes fed on by flies. Yet, they seem cheerful and so well adjusted to their environment. Why do we white people want to change their way of existence? We could assist them with the problems of health, education, and with their infrastructure, such as roads, communication, and water supplies without trying to turn them into *little* Americans. Why do we try to force our lifestyles, morals, and religion onto them?"

This was an age-old question, and Angela had been approached with it many times. She herself had wrestled with it. But she responded to Zack as if this were the first time she had ever heard it. The answer was too important to do otherwise.

"That is a terribly difficult question, Zack. I am not sure that I can answer it correctly. Nevertheless, there is one thing I do want to say. I don't know how much one can improve a society without changing the focal point around which the people exist. We can construct magnificent buildings with big rooms and beautiful furnishings and call it a home. But it isn't a home until one puts into the depths of that building a loving family. A *home* must have a man and woman and the joy of new life. It requires the laughter of children and the tears of death. In the same way, can one truly change a culture by creating structures without altering the very hearts of the people? You cannot make the fear of angry ancestors and evil spirits vanish with road construction. Water supplies do not diminish the anguish you experience from the death of your child because you enraged the Ndoki—the evil one."

Angela was speaking from depths of her heart and Zack knew it. He sincerely wanted her to continue, but they were interrupted by a group of excited women. After a few minutes of conversation, of which Zack understood nothing, Angela explained to him that a mother had just brought two young children from the fields. Both were very sick and they were asking Angela to come. She gathered a few medicines and instruments and hurried way with the mamas.

Zack did not see her again until late afternoon when she explained that the mother was from a nearby village and had fed her family mushrooms the evening before. Her husband and two older children were sick with intense stomach pains and vomiting. However, the two youngest were unconscious and had died shortly after she had gotten to them. They obviously had eaten poisonous mushrooms. Angela gave the father two surviving children promethazine injections for nausea and atropine for the abdominal cramps. They needed intravenous fluids, but they had none. She did instruct a couple of mamas to give them frequent sips of a mixture of water, salt, sugar, and lemon juice. From there they were taken to another hut that served as a meager dispensary.

A little later in the day, Angela went to get Zack, and they returned to the small dispensary together. The four beds were filled with patients and the room smelled of disease and filth. A small boy lay in one bed, a huge wound on his leg was draining pus. White bone was visible in the wound. On another bed sat a girl, possibly three years old. Her face was swollen and her hair was gray like that of an old man. Her body was painfully thin except for a protruding stomach. She was dying from Kwashiorkor, a protein deficiency form of malnutrition. The other two beds were occupied by adults. One was in an apparent coma, the other coughed bloody sputum. Zack and Angela spent the next thirty minutes examining and touching these wretched human beings. They were both painfully aware there was nothing they could do for them.

Angela was tired, sad, and feeling defeated when she returned to their camp. She and Zack spoke very little that evening, both were absorbed with fatigue and their own thoughts. Zack anticipated the return of dreams that night but actually slept a dreamless night. It was dark when he awakened. Inside the small hut the temperature remained quite chilly. The red dirt floor emitted a damp, musty odor. Thunder reverberated in the distance, and as he peered through the slatted window, he could see a near full moon behind storm clouds. The pre-dawn sky was bright enough to see the adjacent mud walled huts silhouetted in antiquity against the gray skyline. Tall elephant grass swayed in the morning breeze, and he could hear voices in the distance. Memories of the afternoon before flooded back. How long would it take to become used to the sights and smells of incurable disease, infected wounds, starving children, and emaciated mamas. How many thousands were out there? How can one person make a bit of difference? So many lives born of passion, nurtured at young breasts, only to die before reaching puberty. The survivors could look forward to suffering incredible pain and diseases and then dying horrible deaths. Why? What is the use? What is it all about? Angela had spoken of a "loving God." What is *loving* about a God who created these horrors? To Zack, it all seemed to be embodied in one recent sight. It was that of a gaunt young woman, too weak to stand alone, holding in her arms the lifeless body of her emaciated infant. *Where is the love? Where is the sense of it?*

Exiting the hut, he first looked for Angela but did not see her. Dawn was breaking across the horizon with its dark blood-red glow. This awe-inspiring display seemed to partially cleanse the demoralizing feelings from his mind. He knew that it would be at least an hour before the mamas would start their fires, heat water, and begin to boil the manioc flour they had ground the evening before. It would be even longer before they brought him the gritty liquid they called coffee. Oddly, he craved the *coffee* and a piece of dry bread and the usual banana. Zack propped his mirror up on the hood of the Land Rover. He decided to go ahead and settle for cold water to shave with. Just then, a mama appeared with heated water and a basin. She sat them down in front of him, kept her head bowed, and never looked up. Her hands were clasped in front of her as she backed away in the submissive manner of the tribal women.

"I wish they wouldn't do that!" he cursed under his breath. Their subservient manner made him uncomfortable.

After so many days of rough, difficult travel, Zack was not sure what he expected to see reflected in his mirror. He knew that he felt filthy, like some empty flour sac, crumpled and tossed into the corner full of dirt and spider webs. *Some analogy*, he thought, *but I do feel like something discarded after hard abuse.* Before looking into his mirror, he anticipated seeing the reflection of a depraved derelict and was startled at the mirror's image. His beard was dark and grubby, but the eyes staring back at him were relaxed, and the deep lines at the corners of his eyes were hardly noticeable. One cannot judge accurately their own appearance, but still he saw enough to see a transformation. He was at loss to know how this could happen. He was too absorbed in his thoughts to notice Angela behind him. It was not until she put her small hand on his shoulder that he was startled out of his reverie.

"You don't exactly look like Tarzan," she laughed. "More like his chimpanzee."

He put his arms around her and drew her close, forgetting his grimy exterior. The hug began as one of friendship but quickly became an embrace that lasted several seconds longer than either had intended. Angela was as radiant as ever. She had again drawn her hair back and tied it into a minute ponytail.

This made her face seem thinner and almond eyes wider. The sun had caressed her skin to a golden glow.

"Either I am going to have to go further up wind or come back after you have had time to bathe. But hurry, I have a lot of things to tell you." Her exuberance for life never seemed to change.

Zack shaved quickly and then took his basin of water into the small circular enclosure made of bamboo poles and woven grass. This enclosure served as his *private* shower. In a short time, he had conquered the method of pouring just enough water to lather and leaving the rest for rinsing. With a touch of deodorant, a slash of aftershave, and clean clothes, he felt vaguely human. Yet, he knew it was not just the bath and clean clothes that made him feel so alive. Angela seemed to transform and invigorate everyone she came near.

They had eaten some bread and bananas and were sipping their second cup of impotent coffee before either spoke. Angela broke the silence. "Zack, the mamas here are so excited to learn about health and hygiene. A few weeks ago they had an outbreak of a disease that I am sure was typhoid fever. More than one hundred people died in a period of about a month. The government finally came and traced the source of infection to their central well—the one near the market. The government officials closed the well and told the village leaders that it was *germs* in the water that killed the people. The officials left saying that they would send teachers back to teach them more about these *germs*. That was over two months ago and none have come. Now they are asking me about these tiny things in the water that kill their children. They do not want any more loved ones to die."

"But how can you help them?"

"In simple ways, or at least in ways that seem simple to us." Angela's mood seemed very reflective—even disheartened. She drank the last of her coffee, avoiding the grounds.

"Angela, what is it? You don't often look dejected?"

"Oh, I was just thinking how often people must suffer and die when it can be so easily prevented. It is so unfair." Zack wanted to hold her close but instead allowed her to be silent. The shrill shriek of a parrot penetrated the silence.

"I have asked God so many times why suffering is so inequitable. I know, multitudes of people have asked this question through the centuries. But I don't have an answer. God seems to say, 'Some things are not for you to know right now. But while you wait to learn, let me use you to help the sick and suffering. Go, I will be with you."

Zack seem to reach a point of overload. He knew that what she was saying had to have merit, but bitterness suddenly gripped him. "But I have helped the sick and many were poor. That is why I became a doctor."

Angela realized how poorly she had chosen her words and how they had obviously offended Zack. She held his face between her hands and looked deeply into his eyes. "Forgive me, Zack, I didn't mean to hurt you. My words came out wrong." The softness in her eyes quickly tempered his injured ego. "When we were at County Hospital, I was attracted strongly to you because of your sincere attention toward your patients. You seemed to care more than any of the others physicians there. You never seemed to treat the wealthy any better than the worst derelicts. I saw in you the gift of real caring. If anyone is a complete humanitarian, it is you, Zack." She bit her lip, took a deep breath, and continued. "Zack, I cannot always tell the difference between Christian and humanitarian motivated acts. They are much the same, and I believe that they are both from God. One difference, and maybe the only difference—Christians also care deeply for the soul of the person. We care that their spiritual light should never go out." Angela did not know how to explain to Zack that God's Spirit empowered Christians to do things that can only be performed with His strength. She felt that she could sometimes recognize the difference. Their dialogue was abruptly interrupted.

"Mademoiselle, kwisa na mono, kwisa na mono." The man running toward them was very agitated. The African man and Angela exchanged several words and then she turned to Zack. "They have an emergency and want us to come quickly." Without waiting for a response, she turned and followed the man down the sandy path. Zack followed. He had no idea what was taking place but could feel the tension. He caught up with her quickly and took her hand.

"What's going on?"

"They brought a woman in from a village about twenty miles from here. She has been in labor for at least two days and now they say she is near death. They don't know if the baby still lives or not."

There was an agitated crowd outside of the chief's house, but they quickly parted to allow Angela and Zack to pass between them. Before them lay a woman on a crudely made stretcher. Her eyes were closed and mouth gaping in a silent scream. Angela knelt and quickly examined her. "She is alive!" She quickly pulled back the wrap revealing a swollen abdomen. She placed ear firm against it, listening for life within. Angela paused and listened again. "I think the baby is alive!"

Zack knelt down and placed his ear below a swollen breast. He could hear the woman's heart beat, rapid and faint, but definitely present. The sun was getting hot now but there was no moisture on the woman's skin. Her lips were parched and cracked. "She is very dehydrated and obviously in shock."

"I'll have them bring our supplies from the truck. We can at least get a blood pressure and get some fluids in her." Angela stood and began giving quick and concise orders. One man was assigned to get their supplies from the truck. Another was instructed to try giving the patient sips of water. She told another to boil water and another to get soap. Then, she told two men to carry the woman out of the sun and apply wet cloths her skin.

Zack was amazed watching her. Angela had obviously done this before. She was efficient, decisive, and completely in control. Was this the same person who had thoughtfully and compassionately shared her deepest feelings such a short time ago?

"Zack, we might have a chance to save the mother and baby if we act quickly. How would you like to do a C-section, right here and now?"

For a few moments everything within him revolted at the idea—but only briefly. "Let's go!"

An eruption of activity began. First, they opened the wooden shutters and door of the hut to give them as much light as possible. The critical woman moaned faintly, but was beyond feeling any labor contractions, although they were still taking place. Angela's swift exam had revealed the infant's head to be low in the birth canal with a lot of molding. The head was clearly turned wrong. Their meager surgical instruments were dropped into a pot of boiling water while a woman vigorously scrubbed the protruding belly with soap and water. Zack and Angela kneeled down on each side of the patient, facing one another. Their instruments were now arranged on a large banana leaf. Their eyes met momentarily, but they did not speak. There was no need for conversation. Without delay, Zack took the scalpel from her hand and rapidly made an incision through the skin and subcutaneous tissue. The incision extended from just below the umbilicus to just above the pubic bone.

"There is almost no bleeding. Her pressure must be nil!" He cut through the tough fibrous tissue exposing the rectus muscles and manually separated these muscles exposing the transparent peritoneum. Beneath this tissue lay the gravid uterus. This peritoneum was quickly opened with scissors. There was no catheter, as there would have been in a hospital. He took extra care not to damage her bladder. The huge uterus stood out before them, appearing surprisingly healthy. In a brief second, he had made an incision through the anterior wall of the uterus, and when amniotic fluid burst forth, he extended the incision in the uterine wall with bandage scissors. There was the baby! But was it alive? He and Angela spread the uterus as he reached in to grasp the infant's head.

"Oh, man! I don't think I can get the baby's head up out of the pelvis!"

The many hours of intense labor had wedged the fetus's head into the birth canal. Angela prayed silently. A brief moment later, the head was free, if in fact it was the head. It seemed more like a distorted glob of dough. After the head, the shoulders and arms and legs followed. The baby was completely flaccid in his hands; its arms and legs dangled lifelessly. Angela, ignoring the meconium and vernix covering the baby, breathed directly into the tiny mouth and nose—once, twice, three times. A brief wait and then again—still nothing. She repeated this several times, forcing air into the tiny lungs. It seemed hopeless. Suddenly, a feeble cry was heard. An arm moved and then a leg. There was another peculiar whimpering sound and then a cry—a real cry! The baby was alive!

"Oh! How stupid of me," Angela's voice seemed totally calm, as if nothing of any significance had happened. "I forgot the cord tie. You don't mind parting with one of your shoestrings, do you, Zack?" Before he could answer, she instructed one of the ladies to remove them. It was with them she double tied the cord and cut it. The baby was crying vigorously when she handed him to one of the women.

They had only two kinds of suture with which to work, 2–0 chromic catgut and 3–0 silk. They closed the wide incision in the uterus with the chromic and then sutured the peritoneum, fascia, and muscle with the same suture. The skin was closed with the silk suture. They covered the wound incompletely with some gauze. They would search for better dressings later.

As Zach and Angela washed the blood from their hands in the same basin, their eyes again met, silently exchanging feelings that few would ever know and even fewer could understand.

"Good work, Doc." Angela smiled pleasantly, like someone who had just performed a miracle—in a sense, they had!

Angela gave the new mother a large injection of penicillin and the baby a smaller dose.

"Remind me to repeat the injections in about four hours." Zack knew she would not forget. Angela stood before him as he finished drying his hands. Suddenly, she put her arms around his neck, stood on her tiptoes, and she kissed him warmly—her lips lingering on his for a long time.

"You are really something else, monsieur!" she said as she removed her arms from around his neck. Self-consciously, he looked beyond her. The surrounding mamas all quickly looked down, as if they were invading a realm in which they should not be; but he saw some were smiling and the younger women seemed to be chuckling.

Zack and Angela had a few minutes to visit after the evening meal, but then Angela left with some of the women. He sat staring at the fire, feeling as if saving this underprivileged woman was the most meaningful medical act he had ever performed. A thought entered his mind. He imagined he was at an elite hospital and was saying, "Sorry, Mr. President, but I can't see to your medical needs, I have a much more important patient right now." He smiled to himself, enjoying the paradox.

CHAPTER 18

The sun was just beginning to disappear beyond the large Achaia trees. Zack and the village chief were trying to communicate with the help of their driver, Kintambi. It was then that Pascal unexpectedly appeared jogging down the path. He covered the distance quickly and stopped abruptly in front of them. He obviously had been running for quite some time. He was shirtless, and perspiration covered his slender torso. It took him a few seconds to catch his breath. He appeared troubled, but when he spoke, his voice was composed.

"There are rebel soldiers coming our way. In the forest this morning, I met a man from the village of Kahila about sixty kilometers (thirty-six miles) north. He told me that there is a small force of about thirty men who have captured their village. They have taken over of their homes, enslaved the older women to cook and clean, and are raping the young girls. Some of his people escaped into the forest, but many of the men were killed—some cruelly tortured. The men have no way to fight back against the soldiers." Pascal paused for a moment, obviously trying to organize his thoughts. He continued. "We must pack up and leave quickly. I learned from this man that this small band of soldiers is going to head northward to join the main body of the army led by the man they call a Colonel—*le Diable Noire*. Apparently, his force numbers over one hundred soldiers. They are very well armed and trained. It seems that after the two forces join, they plan to march westward to vandalize several villages. But ultimately, their plan is to circle back toward our Mission Station.

Pascal had a defiant look in his eyes as he spoke, "If they carry out these plans, we have about two weeks before they arrive at our Station. If we travel fast we can be in Kikungu in about two days; barring any major breakdown.

That should give us the time we need to visit with the people, gather information, and try to save anything of worth that has not already been destroyed."

"Are there any other groups of soldiers near?" Zack asked.

"None that I know of. There is a lot of fighting in the southeastern area of our country, near Liksa and Bukavu. Also, straight north of us, near Stanleyville, there are many rebel soldiers. Some professional militias have joined the rebels in the east. These mercenaries are from Belgium, France, South Africa, and probably some from America. I learned that Belgium is considering sending help for the Congo Government to fight the rebel armies. People all over the Congo, from Matadi in the west to Rwanda in the east, are living in constant fear. In many areas of the country, people are deserting their villages and hiding in the forests. Many young men have been slaughtered and their wives raped."

Zack so greatly admired Pascal's composure. He had seen it all—felt it all! How could he describe all this horror and seem so unattached. It took an incredible strength to restrain his fears—his demons from the forest! He listened intently as Pascal continued.

"In addition, many missionaries have had to escape before their homes were destroyed. There was a very skillful American surgeon about one hundred kilometers (sixty miles) north of us who was killed, along with his wife and children. He had given many years of his life to help the people. I also received news that some at the American Baptist mission near Matadi had to be liberated by the Marines. Most of the missionaries from our Mission Station of Kikungu were able to escape into Angola, but Dr. Ben would not go with them. He stayed behind, but no one knows the reasons why."

"Did you learn any more about Dr. Ben, sir?"

"In fact I have. The people have seen him. He is a captive by the vicious band of soldiers lead by a colonel. As I told you, he is called *le Diable Noire*—the Black Devil. He seems to be a particular horror story unto himself. They say he has great powers. He communicates with the dead and can cause death just by glazing at someone. It is said that bullets go through him and do no harm. He is apparently the personification of evil and has great power over a group of soldiers that may number several hundred—if they would all band together."

"Pascal, you are certain that he is the one who has Dr. Ben?"

"Exactement! Je pense que le Diable Noire vient encore à Kikungu. We seem to be on a collision course with this Colonel. And another interesting fact I discovered. There is a young man who worked with Dr. Ben who is somehow involved in this whole matter. This colonel shot him at the time they took Ben prisoner. The people say he has recovered and now is following the group of soldiers that hold Ben prisoner."

"Good grief, this sounds like something right out of my Special Forces training!" Zack had not meant to say anything about his past. He had spoken on impulse. He had no intention for them to ever know this about him.

"You were in the Special Forces, Zack?" Pascal asked the question pensively.

"When was that?" Angela inquired. She had quietly returned unnoticed by the group.

Zack answered very tentatively, "Many years ago I was in the Marines. It was during the Korean War mess. I have tried to forget it." Zack was uncomfortable, obviously hoping to be able to change the subject.

"How long?"

"Two and one half years total in the Korea and Indo-china region. I caught a bullet and spent six months recuperating in Okinawa and at the Oakland Naval Hospital—then the Corps decided I was damaged merchandise."

Pascal recognized the discussion was making Zack terribly uneasy.

"Sometime in the near future you can share some of your experiences with us. We would like to learn more about your life, but right now we have to start making plans to move out of here very soon."

"Right, someday down the road." Zack felt tremendous gratitude to Pascal for giving him the reprieve.

Pascal quickly and concisely outlined plans that he had been formulating in his mind during his return travels. His demeanor was not dictatorial, but neither did his manner leave the liberty of discussion.

They all slept fitfully that night, each with their own thoughts and feelings. Within thirty minutes of sunrise, the Land Rover was packed and they were leaving the village, surrounded by waving men and women and the playful pursuit of laughing children. Before departing, Zack and Angela had checked on the mother and baby. The infant was crying lustily in the hands of the midwife. Nika, the baby's mother, appeared weak and had a slight fever, but the surgical wound looked good. The uterus was firm and there was minimal postpartum flow—and there was no odor of infection. Nika smiled radiantly at them. "Mbote, Mbote, Mbote," she exclaimed and reached for her baby with both arms. She held the infant close and rocked him, showing them how much she loved her new son. Then she lifted the baby up toward Zack. She spoke rapidly, though weakly.

"She wants you to take the baby and bless him," Angela explained. "She wants you to touch her baby so he will grow up to be a brave and powerful man like you." Angela smiled at Zack's embarrassment as he took the infant and kissed his forehead and held him close to his chest for a few seconds. He then gently handed the infant back to his mother. The mother smiled and again animatedly thanked him. The mamas around them clapped and began singing.

"What are they singing, Angela?"

"I don't understand all because they are speaking Kilunda. But I know they are praising God that the boy will someday be a mighty chief and will possess great strength and wisdom."

Zack and Angela bowed to them in their traditional manner.

"You have not asked what they have named him.

"It is alright, I would not understand it anyway."

Angela smiled. "This time you would. His name is Zack."

Their route was through savannah and the Land Rover made good time. Zack calculated that by late afternoon they had maintained an extremely good average of almost twenty miles an hour. They had passed a few small villages with unknown names, but otherwise they saw very little activity. It was late afternoon when the group began encountering woman and children along the road. They were obviously coming back from their fields. Many had bundles of chopped wood, others with baskets of manioc on their heads. Several of the younger women had infants strapped to their backs. Many of the children stopped their play to stare in astonishment at the strange convoy as it passed.

A few minutes later the road broke into a wide opening leading into the village of Mwadi-Mulumba. The community consisted of about two hundred huts in close proximity; a few more homes could be seen in the distance. The children were both excited and wary. The adults were extremely friendly and demonstrative. Their small group was extended great hospitality. It was only after they had eaten luku, rice, and beans, that Zack, Angela, and Pascal had time together. They sat on wooden chairs with a small table between them––it held a kerosene lantern. The light from the lamp gave the trio an almost ghostly appearance. The chief of the village sat with them. He was a small, graying man who appeared to be in his seventies, but they were to learn later he was in his early fifties. He spoke of his village, of his people, and of the increasing struggle their hunters had in finding meat. Many of the animals had been driven further and further away, and the men had to travel many days to find the antelope, the zebra, and even the large rodents. Pascal translated for them and the time went by very quickly. It was almost midnight before the chief left them.

Several hours had passed since most of the villagers had taken the coals from their fires into their huts to ward off the chill of the advancing night. Pascal, Zack, and Angela were quiet, enjoying the sounds of the darkness. Far in the distance they heard a coughing sound that Pascal informed them was a hunting lion. The bird sounds had been quieted for several hours now, but there was just enough breeze rustling the palm leaves to serenade them. Then, faintly in the distance, they heard the sound of drums.

"What do they mean?" Zack asked with amazement.

"The drums at night usually mean a death in their village. Sometimes they announce the arrival of an important visitor or the birth of a child. There are times that the drums warn of danger." Pascal breathed deeply and listened more intently.

Angela reached to her side and took Zack's hand in hers. There was no moon tonight, and he could see only her silhouette in the flickering light. But he could feel her warmth and sensed that she was experiencing some very deep feelings even before she spoke.

"The nights in Africa are so extraordinary. I believe they are made so by the primitiveness and simplicity all around us—life dating back to antiquity. This gives nights the sounds that are haunting and yet have a captive quality. There are sounds and sensations that find their way deep into one's heart and soul. One has the impression that if our ears were sensitive enough, we could hear the gentle wind carry with it the echoes from those far away villages; the wailings of death, the cries of a woman in childbirth, the strangling cough of a child's body shaken with whooping cough. Sometimes I believe I have heard the agonizing screams of a man dying from a bowel obstruction while being treated with herbs and sorcery. From other villages you might hear the sounds of drunken revelry or of lovemaking. Eventually, you will hear the sounds of bitter domestic fights as a man beats his wife into unconsciousness. In the hut a few yards away, you might hear the rattling cough from an emaciated body devastated with tuberculosis. These are just a few of the sounds that give the night air in Africa the winsome, lonely, frightening, and haunting quality. The night brings the knowledge that out there in the darkness there is the constant life and death struggle of man and nature, much as it has been occurring since the dawn of man. This, to me, is the wonder and awe that is the *call* of the African night."

Angela's voice trailed off. She realized she had been talking from the depths of her heart as she shared from her life experiences in the Dark Continent. However, even she had not realized how deeply they were imprinted on her very soul. No one spoke for a long time. The silence was profound but not uncomfortable. Each of them was groping with thoughts determined by their individual existence and experiences.

Pascal was the first to break the stillness. He stood and placed his hands on each side of Angela's face. There might have been a hint of moisture in his eyes. "What an honor to know you, young lady." His touch was as brief as his words, but the impact was enormous. "I will sleep now, for we have to leave early tomorrow."

Zack pulled her toward him, an arm around her back, and they sat quietly, shoulder to shoulder. Neither felt they had to speak because the silence between them was more insightful than words. Zack felt the anguish intensifying within him was building toward a breaking point. He recognized that the talk of life and death, cruelty and pain, had forced images out of the recesses of his mind that he was subconsciously trying to suppress. He thought of his beautiful daughter's body torn and shattered by evil. He actually trembled lightly as he tried to fight back his emotions. Angela placed her hand on his shoulder, and when she spoke, she confirmed that she knew he was in great turmoil. Through tears, her voice was passionate.

"I have always thought that sorrow can help mold us. But I think that it can only do so if we can consciously face it and try not to deny its impact."

Zack's voice broke, "But how can one face some horrors and anguish without using a type of psychological denial? We can only take so much pain and then something has to break."

"I can't speak for others, but I know that I cannot without God's help." She pulled him into her arms and held him close, his sturdy body and his innate strength seemed to have dissolved. Zack, the all-American football player, self-made man, and extraordinary surgeon sobbed softly in her arms.

"All men can break, Zack; that is universal. But not all can be reshaped—and even if they are, they not always whole again. I believe with all my heart that only God can carry us through the most awful things in life and then use these to mold us into stronger people."

Somewhere in the far distance of the night they both thought they heard the cry of a newborn baby. There was new life out there, bringing love and unity. They both heard the crying again but said nothing.

Completely unknown to Angela, vast and complex memories unrelated to the slaughter of his wife and baby were deluging Zack's mind. For years these memories had been too painful, too horrible, to reach the surface. Zack thought that he had successfully buried them, but now he wondered if they ever had been. He knew intuitively that someday he would have to share them with Angela.

◇◇◇◇◇◇◇◇◇

After a short night of sleep and a grueling twenty-four hours of driving, they arrived at the small village of Kabwati. They were now about 250 kilometer (one-hundred and fifty miles)) from the Mission Station. The roads had improved and the temperature had cooled. But Pascal had alerted them to what the drivers had told him. They were expecting heavy rains very soon, making travel much more difficult. So they continued to drive all night, more safely now because the chauffeurs were familiar with the terrain. In various positions of contorted pain, Angela and Zack slept erratically. If Pascal ever slept, it was difficult to determine. He sat firmly in his seat and stared into the darkness. Sometimes his eyes would close, but one could not ascertain if he was sleeping or thinking. Sometime during the night the landscape had changed from forest to savanna. There were now broad plains studded with stumpy trees, thorn bushes, and grassland. The road had become firmer, and easier to traverse. Occasionally they saw enormous herds of zebra, wildebeest and gazelle. Just as the sun was completely driving away the delicate light of dawn, the driver stopped their Land Rover and shouted excitedly. About sixty meters ahead, two large elephant strolled across the road, trunks swaying, and eyes straight-ahead. They were completely indifferent to this group of travelers. The group watched in fascination until the huge animals disappeared into the bush.

Their route remained reasonably wide and two vehicles could pass if necessary. Twice in a period of two hours, their Land Rover had become buried, requiring precious time and strong shoveling to free it from a sandy grave.

It was late afternoon when the driver abruptly turned north onto a narrow path. Actually, it consisted of two ruts, wider than their wheelbase. The path was probably a long ago used truck route. Their travel was grueling, but only for a mile, and then they stopped and got out. As they did, Pascal pointed toward two human skulls on poles bordering each side of the road. A few paces beyond these menacing objects was a wooden sign on which several words were carved. Pascal spoke quietly. "It is a warning that essentially states: 'Beware, you are ` entering a place of roving spirits of the dead and the remains of the tortured." Angela trembled imperceptible as she stared at the terrible skulls and heard the words. Her feelings were intensified by the fact that she knew of this place.

"We are a few kilometers out of our way," Pascal explained, "but I want to share this with you." Pascal started to say more—then shrugged lightly. "Seeing will mean far more than my words. We will walk from here."

In just a few minutes, the small group rounded a bend in the road and entered a clearing in which stood dozens of huts, no different than the many other villages they had visited. As they approached the nearest house, someone, or something, slowly emerged. The *thing* seemed obviously human but was extremely stooped and twisted. It made deliberate and agonizing steps forward, not on feet but on gnarled, grotesque stumps. This *thing* slowly raised it head and faced them. But there was no face except for barren eyes and a gaping cavern where the nose might have been. Where there should have been a chin, forehead, and ears, there existed nothing but twisted masses that looked like kneaded dough. Suddenly, the disfigured lips pulled back from amazingly white teeth and it raised a fingerless hand. It was greeting them!

"Mbote na beno!" The voice was rasping and nasal. The words were barely distinguishable. It could be the voice of a woman—they could not be certain.

"Mbote mingi, madame!" As he spoke, Pascal walked to this deformed creature and gently took the stump of its hand in his. Then he took it into his arms. Destroyed eye glands did not permit tears to accompany the deep sobs that burst from the body.

"This is my aunt, my mother's youngest sister. She has been a leper for the past twenty-five years. Her Christian name is Tabitha."

The Congolese men with them moved away. Entrenched fear and preconception were too deeply ingrained. Pascal continued to hold her and spoke with fervor, "C'est merveilleux vous encore rencontrer!" The distorted lips again retracted from her teeth. Zack was amazed that this *creature* would understand French.

While they were greeting, more skeletal and misshapen *bodies* appeared. Some walked alone, some with crutches, and others supporting one another. They all seemed to have some degree of tissue destruction and malformations. To their left about thirty yards away, Zack noted a sizeable building. It seemed large enough to encompass a dozen huts. On the ground in front of the building lay several objects, presumably human beings. Suddenly, at the doorway, a gaunt frame appeared—just bones with dark skin stretched over them. The *being* glared at them with sunken eyes, and then *it* was shaken with a horrible rattling cough. It would have collapsed if not firmly gripping the doorway. Seconds later *it* retreated inside.

"Zack and Angela, this is where the sicker of the tuberculosis and leprosy patients are sent by the village elders." Pascal explained further, "Once they become too sick to care for themselves or by their families, they are sent here for supervision. The people have learned that to isolate them reduces new cases in their villages. Volunteers come from time to time to help the ill, but mostly they care for each other. The stronger of them work the gardens, cook, bathe, and feed the weaker. They have really developed a system of nurturing that reflects a devotion which is difficult for us to grasp."

"How many people are there here?" Zack asked.

"I am not certain. It has been a long time since I have been here. But if it is as it was, there may be well over two hundred people here."

"Why isn't something being done for them?" Zack sounded angry.

"My dear friend, this is in the heart of central Africa. There are no physicians and no western medicines available. Even our own healers will seldom come here because of fear. I believe if you look around, you can understand that."

Zack stood motionless and could say nothing. It was as if his heart and mind were paralyzed. For a few brief moments, he was totally overwhelmed by the desperation of these neglected and tormented souls. Zack thought that if a person could be overcome to near death, then it was here. There was no way he could interpret or process his feelings. He did not try to. Angela moved to his side. Her instincts sensed the turmoil in this man she loved. Tears filled her eyes, but she chose not to speak. She put her arm around his waist and gazed with him at the torment and affliction before them.

For the next two hours the three of them moved among the small houses, talking, listening, and touching many of the inhabitants. A few had minor skin discoloration and some displayed disfiguring nodules. Others had bodies that were misshapen and emaciated. Many lay like cadavers on mats to be cared for by the humanity of others. A few appeared rather healthy until suddenly wracked with a coughing spell and then expectorating bloody mucous. All of the visitors, even Zack, being the novice, could feel how much excitement and happiness their visit was bringing to these people. To be treated as human beings, to be spoken to and to be touched, was something they had not experienced for years. Nor had they ever thought they would again!

Pascal and Angela knew what it might take Zack a few months to discover. Their visit to this place of horror, ever so brief, would impart strength, happiness, and an incredible sense of hope to these destitute people. Their stopover would encourage them for months. To these suffering and dying human beings, the three visitors reflected love and acceptance—they cared for the grotesque as if they were beautiful. These acts of love are a fraction of the powerful attributes of God, but when shared by men, they form a mighty shroud of strength and serenity over the tormented.

It was becoming dark before they made their way back to their Land Rover. Incredibly, Tabitha was there, holding herself up by the hood of the vehicle. How she had dragged her tortured body that far, only God could know. In her croaking voice, she told Pascal that they could not leave because many of the villagers had prepared three small huts for them to stay the night; others were preparing a meal for them. Despite their challenging schedule, Pascal and Angela gratefully accepted. Zack said nothing and hoped that his real feelings did not show. He was thinking, *I don't want to become sick. I don't want to look like these people.* These thoughts, he tried to rationalize, were totally understandable and normal. Then he looked at Angela and Pascal. They were confidant and so much at peace. There was no fear or apprehension in them. They knew so much more about these diseased people than he, and yet had such great assurance and security. But why? How?

Even as he asked himself these questions, he was beginning to grasp the answer. Their inner strength must have something to do with their relationship with Jesus Christ. If Angela and Pascal did not fear, he would not!

Early the next morning they said their good-byes to these tormented but affectionate human beings. They traveled all that day and night, stopping only to eat bread and banana and to take brief stretches. On some occasions they would fill the Land Rover's gas tank from large containers they carried with them. Only twice did they have to dig out. Dawn brought cloudless skies and a vindictive sun. By near noon the road narrowed as it entered the grounds of the Mission Station They drove under a canopy of mango trees that formed about one-quarter mile of a green umbrella. To their left was a large stone building with a corrugated metal roof and square openings in the walls; the sound of drums came from inside. People began to gather along the road and the children were shouting and clapping hands. As they pulled to a stop, Pascal got out and began talking with someone who appeared to be in authority. Zack and Angela also exited their mobile tomb, stretched, and rubbed their arms in an attempt to get the circulation going again—and quiet their screaming muscles. They were surrounded by dozens of inquisitive children. Behind them stood several adults who, if looked at, responded with cordial smiles. They had at last arrived at Kikungu! Each was experiencing varied feelings, as they finally arrived at their destination. They had reached their objective but *now* none knew their fate!

Angela left Zack to his stretching movements and joined Pascal and the others, anxious to learn as much as she could. Understanding nothing that was being said, Zack walked around the stone house to find they were on a huge plateau. About thirty yards behind the back patio, the land abruptly descended into a vast valley. In the distance, there stood a broad range of hills. The air was dry and the temperature pleasing. A slight breeze brought him the sweet fragrance of bougainvillea. As he strolled, the children followed at a safe distance. They were obviously fascinated by his appearance; but they were always ready to quickly retreat at the slightest hint of danger. Palm trees lined the edge of the canyon. On his left and right were several large trees, their branches hanging low with green fruit—Zack's first encounter with mangoes.

What a beautiful area, Zack thought. *Maybe this is one of the reasons that Dr. Ben didn't want to leave.*

"I thought you had deserted us or maybe jumped off a cliff . . . Beautiful, isn't it." Absorbed in thought, once again Zack had failed to detect Angela approach.

"It is quite incredible and certainly does not fit my preconceived image of Africa."

"We can see more later, but now the hospital administrator, the head nurse, and the village chief want us to join them for a meal."

Suddenly, Zack realized that they had not eaten for several hours. They entered the house into a rather spacious family room decorated with cushionless wooden furniture. The walls and floor were made of cement and above them was a high ceiling of synthetic tiles. Greetings and introductions were warmly made. Zack understood a few of their French words, but for the most part was left to his own thoughts. They were served, what he had learned would always be the same: manioc, rice, beans, and boiled cassava leaves prepared in palm oil and a hot pepper sauce that burned the mouth. Zack watched Angela and Pascal for clues of when to eat.

After feasting, Zack and Angela sat on the steps of the terrace overlooking the huge expanse of valley. White clouds floated down the valley below them and a few huge eagles glided by silently, searching for prey through breaks in the billowing clouds.

"The largest mountain to the southeast is called the *Haunted Mountain.* It is said that spirits inhabit all areas of the mountain. Near its foot, the great chief Nfulu lives. He is the ruler of most all the region you can see in every direction. It is said that he is very wealthy with many cattle, an enormous number servants, and it is claimed that he has over a hundred wives."

"He must be quite a glutton for punishment."

"Hey, cut it out!' Angela nudged him good-naturedly.

They both laughed, and their mirth seemed alien. They could not remember the last time there had been even a minute for happiness.

"It seems such a long time since we have had even a moment of time together." Angela spoke with remorse in her voice.

"It has been rather hectic, hasn't it?"

"Yes, and it may become much worse before it gets better."

For several moments, neither spoke, just enjoying the fragrance of the bougainvillea and the panorama before them. There was a mist forming in the air. The distant hills became faded silhouettes, like poorly developed black and white photos.

"I really love this area." Angela's voice was reflective. "Sometimes I have thought that God decided that this land was so harsh and the living so demanding that He placed the Mission Station here for brief tranquility."

"How do you know this area so well?"

"There used to be a school here for missionary kids. I attended high school at Kikungu for three years. We missionary kids lived here for nine months out of the year. I have some very warm memories of my times here. The old school is about a kilometer from here. I hope we can visit it later."

Zack put his arm around her and held her close, his thoughts totally occupied by her closeness, the fragrance of her hair, and the softness of her body. An inward clamor cried out to hold her more tightly. Their bodies should be totally intertwined. The struggle within him was tremendous. But ironically, he was totally unaware that it was the same for Angela. She turned and pressed herself into his arms and kissed him, softly at first, and then more deeply and passionately. When their lips parted, both were breathless.

"Oh Zack, Zack, I do love you so!" She rose quickly. "A bientot, Zack. Je vous aminez avec toute ma cour!" She left quickly, thinking that she wished there was a place for a cold shower.

Most of his life Zack had just acted on his emotions and passions, never considering that they should be brought under control. As long as he believed that he was hurting no one, he never gave it thought. But now, despite the powerful desires within him, he doubted that anything could cause him to hurt Angela, no matter how much he physically wanted her. He realized that for the first time in his life, he was experiencing what true, selfless love meant. It was an emotion that was not at all unpleasant.

For the first time in days, they all slept in beds. The following morning the three arose more rested than they could remember. Thunder had awakened Zack, and he opened his eyes to observe sheets of rain hitting the side of the house. They congregated in Dr. Ben's dining room, and after breakfast of bread, coffee, and bananas they made a more complete tour of the doctor's home. It still obviously had a woman's touch, and Angela wondered just how long Ben had lived alone. She made a mental note to ask Pascal when Ben's wife had died. The kitchen was primitive with a wood burning stove, kerosene refrigerator, and cement sinks. The three bedrooms revealed that there must have been children here at one time. The room of most interest to the three of them was Ben's bureau. The workers and nurses had obviously spent several hours cleaning up the destruction left by the soldiers. The exception, however, was Ben's office that was still in total disarray. File cabinets were turned over, drawers wrenched from the desk and emptied on the floor. Someone had maliciously turned over bookcases. Manuscripts, books, and reports were scattered everywhere. The padding of the small desk chair had been ripped open in several places, apparently by a soldier searching for something. To call it total mayhem was describing it lightly.

"They must have been looking for money," Pascal said. "I wonder if they found anything of any worth. I would guess they did not because Ben had very little. I never knew him to keep any funds for himself. If he did get some finances, he spent it on the hospital or the villagers."

As he was speaking, a metal object in the corner of the room caught his attention. It was a small lock box that someone had tossed there. The container was closed, but as he picked it up, the broken lid fell open. If there had been money, it was gone.

Pascal said, "I would very much like to try to put things back into some degree of order, but I think that we should not. When the soldiers return and see that the doctor's private papers have been restored, they might become suspicious that someone other than the workers have been here. Our culture makes us afraid to handle the very private possessions of a great chief. The workers cleaned the house but are afraid to touch Ben's private books and papers. These contain too much magic."

Later that morning, the three of them walked the distance of about three blocks from the house to the hospital. The main part was made of two barracks, one behind the other. Entering the first, they found themselves in a large, bare room with only benches along three walls. Down the hall on their right, they looked into what appeared to be a laboratory. They could see microscopes and what seemed to be a centrifuge. To their left, the door opened to a moderate-sized office containing a heavy desk. Along the wall behind the desk were bookshelves made of concrete blocks upon which had been layered crude wooden planks. On them was a mixture of new and molding text books. A tattered examining table was against the other wall. The room was well lit by large windows at their left.

"Welcome to the doctor's bureau," Pascal said. "Please, Angela, take the doctor's chair."

It was a straight back wooden chair with a piece of foam on the seat. The padding was a primitive attempt at comfort. Pascal turned and said something to the two men who had accompanied them. In minutes, they returned with some other chairs.

"Please, we must stay here a few minutes. The nursing staff wants to serve us some refreshments."

Pascal's words were barely spoken when two young men entered with tea, bread, and peanuts. All of a sudden, an enormous explosion shook the windows, shattering their few moments of calm! The tray containing hot tea and peanuts was torn out of one man's hands and scattered across the floor! Fragments of glass and wood were thrown across the room!

"Get down now! Stay there until we know what is happening!" Pascal's voice was hard and determined. The silence was eerie and menacing. The sounds of birds and the voices outside the window could no longer be heard. Aggressive fear gripped each of them, and each was responding internally in their own way.

Had the soldiers returned sooner than they had anticipated?

◇◇◇◇◇◇◇◇◇

The blast that shattered the windows and sprayed glass across the room left fragments of glass imbedded into the ceiling and walls. But none of the occupants had been injured. The worst was that their ears screamed from the explosion.

"Please, stay here and keep down. I will go out and try to discover what happened."

Pascal remained low until he entered the ampoule of the operating room, and then he straightened and was gone.

Every fiber in Zack's body was trying to propel him into action. Adrenaline was surging through his body, but his mind was taking over and common sense was winning. He knew nothing of the building, the adjoining quarters, or the grounds. Logic made him realize that aimless action on his part could do more harm than good.

"That was close!" Angela exclaimed in an amazingly composed voice. "Are you hurt?"

"No problems that I am aware of, except my ears are ringing. What about you? Are you all right? Do you have any injuries?"

"No. I am fine, just a little scared."

Zack crawled on his belly to her side and took her hand. Her grip was firm and her palm dry, but he could feel just a hint of a tremor. He again found it incomprehensible that the touch of a person's hand could evoke such great feelings, particularly in such a menacing situation.

"To tell you the truth, Angela, I have never been so terrified in my life. But not for me but fear that you were hurt or even . . . dead." His voice choked and he was trying to fight back emotions. He was stymied and embarrassed once again by his own inaptitude. He escaped his obvious clumsiness when Pascal burst into the room.

"Everything is alright. There are no soldiers. It seems that a young man found a hand grenade in the forest. He was showing it to a couple of his friends outside our window. Apparently, one of them inadvertently pulled its pin, having no idea what he was doing"

"Oh! Dear God! Angela exclaimed. "Were they killed?"

Just as she asked the question, two men entered the bureau carrying a stretcher upon which lay a man. The man's clothes were torn and bloodied, but he seemed to be alive. They moved on to the operating room, to be followed by a second stretcher. The third did not come. There was no need!

Cursory exams of both men, along with information from observers, disclosed that the man who had pulled the pin was the most severely injured. He was alive but with deep lacerations in his neck, face, and chest. These wounds did not seem life threatening, but most of his right hand was gone except for the thumb. The blast had destroyed a large portion of the palm along with the four fingers. Portions of shredded tendon and bone were exposed. Amazingly, there was little bleeding. Quietly, four of the hospital nurses gathered to help them. Pascal and Zack learned quickly they were the operating room staff.

"Angela, would you please go back to the house and talk with the chief and others. Explain to them the situation here. Would you also try to find out what information you can about their plans for dealing with the advancing rebels? We are going to be here for a while, so could you also examine some of Dr. Ben's papers. Maybe we can find out something about what he was thinking of the rebels. Also, you might learn something about his health. If you could do this, it sure would be a great help."

"You bet," Angela replied with a good Midwestern idiom. She went to the two wounded men, put her hands on each, and prayed quietly for both in their native tongue. The gratitude was vivid in their eyes.

"See you soon." Her clear eyes fixed mostly on Zack as she spoke.

Almost an hour passed by the time the operating room and instruments were prepared. Intravenous anesthetic was administered to the first man and his various wounds were scrubbed with an antiseptic solution. Pascal and Zack worked in synchrony, rapidly suturing the deepest lacerations of this face, neck, and chest. They then turned their attention to the frayed hand. Fragments of bone, muscle, and tendon were removed. The thumb was intact with the flexor tendons attached. During the next hour, they reconstructed the hand and reflected the skin so that it covered the proximal one third of the carpal bones. When finished, there remained the stump of a hand with a thumb. The strange appearing appendage would have some function.

The second man required a lot of debridement of foreign bodies that came from within the hand grenade itself. In addition, the explosion had taken away a great portion of his right pectoral muscle. They had to cut away a lot of lacerated tissue before swinging a large flap of skin from his side to cover the huge defect. By the time they had finished surgery on the second man, the sun was an enormous reddish sphere on the western horizon. As they had done at the hospital in the United States, Pascal and Zack had worked together resourcefully and in effortless harmony

"Donnez les malades 600,000 unité de Pénicilline Procaine IM et répéter en douze heures, si vous plait," Pascal spoke to the nurses who were in obvious awe of him.

"We will give them penicillin now and repeat in twelve hours and then see how they are doing."

"What about tetanus vaccine?" Zack inquired.

"I will have to check to see if any is available."

After thanking the nursing staff, they walked down the sandy path toward Dr. Ben's house. There remained a furnace-like glow across the valley, silhouetting the distant peaks. The one-quarter mile distance from the hospital to the house was not lengthy, but as the sun set, darkness descended rapidly. Once again Zack was astonished by the lack of any twilight here on the equator. He and Pascal were discussing the two patients, but Zack's thoughts were racing ahead in anticipation of seeing Angela. They found her in Ben's cluttered bureau, sitting at his desk. She looked up as they entered, and even with the dim light they detected a few tears in her brown eyes.

"Is something wrong, Angela?" Zack inquired.

"No, Zack, I was just reading some of Dr. Ben's journaling. I feel like I am invading his privacy, but also am sure he would not mind that we are reading them. Would you care if I read a certain portion of this to you?"

"Not at all." Zack pulled a chair over to her side. Pascal lighted the kerosene lantern and placed it by her. He stood silently at her side. She read an insert in the journal dated June 12.

As I walked up the path to the Pediatric Pavilion of our hospital, there was a sense of dread, a fear of the words, which in fact were to be spoken. Two days earlier a family had carried a girl to our hospital.

She was nearly dead on arrival, so the words that morning were not unexpected, but the detachment and finality with which they were spoken had their impact.

"How is the little girl?"

"Oh, elle est décède; elle est morte hier soir. (Oh, she is dead; she died last night.)

An event so expected and unremarkable that it seemed to evoke little emotion. But the following is an excerpt from my spiritual journal. I include it here because it bridges some thought basic to the Christian life.

She is dead; she died sometime during the darkness of an African night. She was about nine years old, emaciated, and bony. He shoulders protruded like the arms of an old rocking chair, her ribs as prominent as the rungs of a crib. Her thighs no larger than an infant's wrist.

"How is the little girl with the distorted face?"

"Oh, she died last night."

I am often awakened at night, seeing the face of the sick, the suffering, the starving, and the dying, and maybe this is necessary. Lord, help me never to become so calloused that the faces do not appear, but at the same time help me to have a concern that produces actions directed toward bringing glory to your name. There is sometimes a tightrope here. Help me, Father, to gird the distance over the abyss of torn emotions.

How did Jesus deal with the awesome demands from the crippled, the lepers, the diseased and dying whom he must have encountered daily? Our Lord suffered and struggled over the abyss of emotions torn asunder but was never overpowered by such forces. How did he deal with these potentially destructive situations? By prayer, close fellowship with the Father, and through the power of the Holy Spirit.

It is possible that Jesus' resilience, even while constantly meeting the diseased, the hopeless, and the dying, was due to his ability to focus beyond the physical to the eternal. Humanly we are greatly affected by images of starving children with distended bellies and haunted eyes; by the emaciated body of tuberculosis and by the distorted hands of the leper. And all our senses should be stretched to the limits. But do we experience the revulsions, apprehensions, and anguish when we see a friend, a neighbor, or a family member who is spiritually disfigured and dying? For most of us, it does not have the same intense effect. Yet it was for the lost souls that Christ offered the greatest emotions and tears. In the mission field of the Third World, where disease and poverty exist in such great numbers, one can easily fall prey to the subtle snare of shifting all time, energies, and efforts toward the temporal and fail to adequately share the good news of Jesus Christ. In doing so, the believer can lose the true purpose of the Christian life and the boundless joy it brings.

It is not just from serving God that we gain our greatest joy and fulfillment, rather from the knowledge that our holy, omnipotent God has chosen us to share in

His divine plan for the universe. This understanding helps keep efforts in proper perspective. We should never be overwhelmed by the task, whether it is evangelizing the masses; fighting death and poverty; witnessing to our neighbor; or sharing Christ with an unbelieving family member. God chooses us for a task because He feels us worthy. Tomorrow we may walk up a sandy path and inquire, "How is my neighbor, my loved one, my fellow worker? And we may hear those ominous words. "Oh, elle est décède."

Yes, she died last night, but she can be in eternity because God chose us to be witnesses of the free gift of salvation through his son, Jesus our Lord.

While reading, Angela's voice had broken several times. And twice she stopped altogether to gather herself. It was so real to her. When she had finished, Zack placed his hand on her shoulder, pressing it tenderly—neither spoke. Zack was glad the dim light in the room hid the moisture in his eyes. If he had tried to speak right then, his voice might have failed him. Zack could not grasp the full depth and meaning of the words he had just heard—but he found himself wishing that he could. He understood enough to know they were painful.

The following day Pascal and Zack spent time planning with some of the leaders of the Mission Station and village. Pascal included him in the discussions because they had become more than a medical team now. He needed Zack's skills from the Marine Corps. He needed him as a warrior.

They sat in a small, dingy room made of plaster walls. The area was about the size of a one-car garage. Cobwebs hung from the corners of the ceiling and dark stains in the walls reminded Zack of the Rorschach tests they used in the psychiatry classes.

"We are trying to determine how best to get near the colonel without detection. Some village people have told us that he has many guards around him at all times, particularly at night." Pascal paused briefly. "There are a few of his soldiers who will talk with the people. There are many of them who do not even like the colonel."

"Why don't they leave him?" Zack inquired.

"First of all, it is a matter of fear. Many believe he can kill them with demons even from far distances. Nowhere is one safe from him. Secondly, many of the soldiers are young, poor, and have no family and nowhere to go." His explanation was brief but needed no further clarification. Throughout the day they met numerous times, discussing plans, exchanging ideas, and studying some very flawed maps. It was late in the evening before they broke up the conferences.

CHAPTER 19

The darkness that descended upon Kikungu was the same as that surrounding Ben's prison conclave. He could hear the shrieking voice of the colonel. This was a man who Ben was increasingly convinced was totally insane. He knew that the guards would be coming for him very soon. The sky was darker than at Kikungu because the sky here had captured dark, angry rain clouds. Vigorous flashes of lightning kept the eastern sky almost perpetually alive with fiery swords. The guards arrived outside the hut as it started raining. At first, there were a few wet globules, followed almost at once with torrents of water. Lightning exploded even more, resulting in a strobe light effect. A sudden wind shook the walls. Ben felt the same oppressive fear that he had experienced several months ago during a storm much like this. Totally apart from the storm, evil was being discharged with incredible force, destroying everything in its path. Ben shivered, and not just from the wet, chilly air. When the soldiers finally entered his prison room, they carried with them the aroma of terror and madness.

"Kwisa na beno!" The guard's voice trembled and Ben sensed the man spoke with sadness more than anger. They took him toward the large hut that he knew the colonel used for special meetings. They were drenched instantly from the torrents of rain, and the darkness was now overpowering. *Le Diable Noire* sat alone in the middle of the room. There was nothing in the hut save a small table on which stood a kerosene lantern. It cast eerie shadows on the walls. The colonel was naked except for a loincloth. The most gruesome mask Ben had ever seen concealed his face. A small fire burned on the ground before him and a strong medicinal aroma permeated the air. As Ben's eyes adapted to the dimness, he saw a necklace made of various size teeth. It dangled on the Devil's neck in such a way as to create a grotesque grin.

"Asseyez-vous ici!" His voice was low and guttural as he indicated to Ben to sit on the small mat placed in front of him.

Ben said a silent prayer for strength as he sat before this fiendish creature.

"You know that you must die!" His voice was now almost conversational. Ben might have thought they were to have afternoon tea except for the maniacal eyes glowing from behind the mask and the human skulls on the ground beside him! The aromatic odor continued to ascend from the flames. Ben sat down cross-legged in front of the demon. Unexplainably, he no longer had any fear. He was completely certain that the God's protection was far more powerful than any evil forces the *Diable Noire* could call forth. His voice was calm and composed when he spoke. "If I must die, then I will do so. I have no fear of you, because the God I follow is so much mightier than all the spirits you serve. But before you murder me, I want you to know that the same God, the Lord Jesus Christ, loves you and will forgive you if you repent of your life of sin."

The colonel was stunned by Ben's steady voice. He had expected to create uncontrollable terror in this man—as with all the others.

"Fermez la bouche!" The colonel snarled. "You will soon fear me because the spirits of my ancestors are more powerful than your Jesus. I know of him. He was a man who was killed by his own tribal people. They nailed him to a wooden cross and he died. But where is he now? Do you hear him speak, or can you see him like this?"

With a motion of his outstretched arms, the scented smoke rose more thickly and broadened out, making it difficult for Ben to see through. Now, only an image, a vague silhouette of the colonel was visible. Lightning flared constantly outside, creating moving shadows on the walls, accentuating the uncanny scene. Rain was striking the grass roof with even greater force.

In the middle of the smoke a hideous face appeared. Ben recalled it from another rainy night many nightmares ago. The countenance came closer to him. Blood trickle from fangs that were prepared to slash, tear, and destroy him. Ben knew inherently that this was either a created vision or a demon that the colonel had called forth from the depths of hell. Whether this was a satanic force or trickery, he could not be certain. But one cannot deny that evil does exist, and sometimes there is a fine line between unadulterated evilness and pure satanic power. This maniac sitting there before him may well have broken through that line.

Ben knew that satanic images cannot kill, and the Ndoki cannot *eat* humans—but authentic evilness can. Of that Ben was certain! He felt no need at this time to demonstrate the power of God. He knew without doubt that His forces will always prevail over one who has given himself over to the sinister powers of Satan. Ben stared directly at the drooling face and experienced no fear. When it spoke, the furnace red eyes glared at him. Hideous shrieks came from all around him and a foul, putrid stench came from the menacing mouth. Despite all his faith, Ben was abruptly gripped by a numbing fear. Nausea started in the center of his stomach and foul juices rose to his mouth. His head hurt like tiny explosions were occurring in his brain. The shrieks were becoming higher pitched and penetrating. Ben again prayed to his Lord and prepared for death.

CHAPTER 20

Zack went to bed again that night. A *real* bed that he had always taken for granted, but now appreciated as he might a rare emerald. He ached all over and waves of nausea spread through him, although not quite to the point of vomiting. He did not bother to undress. He removed his boots and fell onto the mattress. His last waking thought was that it sure was hot. He then slipped into a cavernous and dreamless sleep. About midnight he awakened with an intense, unrelenting pain across his low back. It felt like someone had hit him with a plank. He began to shiver and pulled the light covers around him. But the shaking became worse, and his teeth began to chatter. A fire burned behind his eyes and a ruthless force was crushing his skull.

Later he was to remember very little of the ensuing four days as his body oscillated between high fevers and chills, driven by delirium and furious dreams. There were brutal periods of sweating and uncontrollable trembling. He faintly remembered an angelic visitation a few times—a tender voice and touch that were cool and comforting. He remembered the vision giving him drinks of cold liquid and sometimes medicine upon which he choked. On the fourth day the fever left him. The head and back pain began to diminish, but he found that just lifting an arm was exhausting. He felt sweaty and grimy, and the taste in his mouth was like something rotting. He attempted to sit up but decided that effort was not worth it. Bright light was coming in the window, but he had no idea if it was morning or evening. He must have slept again because when he awakened he felt totally disoriented. He could hear no activity and irrationally wondered if everyone had left him. He was debating whether to attempt at rising again when Angela quietly entered the room. Her hair was swept back in a bun and she wore a brightly colored Congolese dress. She had an apprehensive expression that changed quickly to a bright smile when she found Zack awake. She moved swiftly to his bedside.

"Good morning, Monsieur Zack. It is good to have you back with us. You have been a little sick the past few days."

"Sorry, I must have really overslept. I do not know what hit me. I didn't feel very well last night when I went to bed but just thought I was over tired."

Angela put her hand on his cheek, partly to determine whether he had a fever, but mostly just to touch him.

"Dear, dear Zack, that was three nights ago. As I said, you have been quite sick. Malaria attacks that way."

Zack wanted to argue, but when he placed his hand over her hand on his face, he felt a growth of beard. When he tried to sit up, Angela gently pushed him back.

"Please, don't rush things. We have to get some fluids in you and then some food when you are ready."

Zack realized her voice sounded muffled, and he became aware of a loud ringing in his ears. "Does malaria affect your hearing?"

"No, Zack, that's the effect of the quinine we have been giving you. The ringing will stop as soon as we discontinue it. The first two days we had to give it to you intravenously, but by the third day you were swallowing well enough to take it orally."

"You have been through this then?"

Angela smiled. "A time or two."

Zack attempted to sit up again, and this time Angela did not try to prevent him. He was suddenly concerned. "When I fell asleep, I was still completely dressed. Did . . . did you remove my clothes and put the . . . ah . . . this gown on me?"

Angela grinned mischievously, "Well, let's put it this way. I do know a little more about you than I did."

Zack suddenly did something that he never remembered doing before. He blushed!

After falling back into a short sleep, Zack awakened and drank some tea and a broth that was flavored something like chicken. It tasted good, and he actually felt hungry. He slept for another two hours, and this time, when he awakened, he felt almost normal. He was weak, thirsty, and hungry, but had no backache or head pain. He made his way to the shower with minimal effort, and after the shower and a shave, he felt even stronger. He found Angela in Ben's office examining some of his writings.

"Hi, Zack. You are beginning to look like yourself again. Usually, a bout of malaria will do that. It attacks very quickly and intensely, but when it is over, it usually leaves one weak for a few of days, but otherwise not with much aftermath."

"How often does one have go through this?"

"Maybe again in a few weeks or possibly several months. Maybe never. One does build up some partial immunity to malaria."

Satisfied with the information, Zack asked, "Where is Pascal?"

"While you were sick, he and a group of his most trusted men left to find more news about the rebel soldiers. They indicated that it was to be a scouting trip—to gather as much information as they could. They want to avoid any type of encounter if possible. The word is that Dr. Ben is still alive, but they keep a guard with him at all times, and at night they tie him so he cannot escape. Some of the village people tell us that *le Diable* has stopped his beatings. This was after Dr. Ben began treating some of his sick soldiers. At first, the colonel prevented him but then relented and has permitted him to treat his men. But he still does not trust him, and I think it is probably because Ben is known throughout the entire region to have very strong powers. What we think of as traditional medicine, the people here view as very strong magic."

Zack suddenly recalled Ben's article that they had read just before he became ill.

"Angela, can you tell me something? I am thinking of the article you read from Dr. Ben's diary. How does one develop sensitivity like that? He saw much more than a very sick little girl. He saw that neglected child as someone unique and special. That doesn't make sense to me."

Angela's insights glanced beyond just the question itself. "Zack, I know how much compassion you have. I saw it in the emergency room and on the wards. You have this very special quality. I told you it was one of the first things to attract me to you. You care for patients in a much deeper way than do most of the other physicians I know. But Ben walks to a different drummer—so to speak. He is a very committed Christian with a tremendously deep faith. God gives individuals like him a love for people that is of a supernatural nature. Ben did not work for it and did not earn it. It is a gift from God. God gives individuals this selfless and dedicated love for all persons, independent of race, income, gender, or status. I believe that it is just that Ben cares for the physical, but God also gave him a profound love for their souls."

"Sure! Those are good words, but what does one mean by *soul?*" Zack's words came forth more harshly than he really felt. Immediately he regretted it.

"My dear Zack, please don't think I am preaching at you. I am just trying to share some thoughts and feelings."

"You're not. I might feel that I was being preached to if it came from anyone but you." Zack's voice was softer now and carried intense honesty.

Angela smiled appreciatively. "The Bible teaches us that we are here on this earth for a short span of life. It also tells us that those who believe Jesus Christ is the Son of God will have eternal life. We are just passing through this life on the way to the perfect place. To heaven."

Zack really wanted to hear more, but Tshilaka, the cook, brusquely interrupted them.

"Monsieur Docteur Pascal has sent a messenger to ask if the young mondele can come and join them. He says he *must* come as soon as he is well enough."

Angela translated for Zack and then added, "Before you go off recklessly, take the remainder of the day, drink a lot of fluids, walk some, and take some food. After a good night's sleep, you can leave early in the morning."

"You're the boss." He took her in his arms and kissed her, at first with gratefulness, but then the kiss transformed to passion. Tshilaka stared at the floor and coughed.

CHAPTER 21

Ben had closed his eyes in prayer, expecting to feel the searing pain of a sword or bullet. No pain came, and then, without warning, he heard excited voices outside the hut. There was a thunderous commotion and apparent chaos. Without opening his eyes, he sensed the colonel had left the hut. Then he heard a hideous sound pierce through the pandemonium. Ben opened his eyes and found he was alone. His weak legs carried him to the window. Most of the soldiers had gathered in the area around the colonel's compound. Unadulterated fear permeated the air and some agitated soldiers were yelling and pointing at the forest edge, while others lay writhing on the ground. All were overpowered by fear. The rain had ceased but and a heavy mist had settled in. Ben saw nothing but shadows created by a partial moon casting its faint light over the field and trees. A shriek again burst into the darkness, and a shimmering image appeared from just within the tree line. It gave off a reddish-golden glow, and it seemed that it was from *this* the terrifying sounds came. The confusion and panic it was creating was incredible! The terrified soldiers crowded together for protection from this horrifying apparition.

"Ndoki! Ndoki," was being screamed by many of the terrified men. Colonel Ching was also experiencing anxiety and was briefly frozen into inaction. For a time he had completely forgotten his prisoner. However, indecision lasted only a few moments, for he was a leader of men who possessed great powers.

"Sergeants Bema and Belata, kwisa no mono!" He was shouting and his voice conveyed authority. One did not disobey his orders and the soldiers responded rapidly.

"Arrange the men into unit's of twenty-five and . . ."

Another piercing shriek penetrated the night air. The glowing apparition again appeared but now had moved more to their left and was closer and more intense. The men were again frozen into immobility, but only momentarily, because some feared the colonel more than they feared the Ndoki. Their total numbers had decreased greatly during the past few weeks because several men had deserted. Now, many were fleeing into the forest, escaping from this terrifying apparition. Fewer than a hundred men remained in this group of the Devil's detachment.

"Get you rifles and swords!" he ordered. "Go and kill the Ndoki. You know that my forces are far greater than his!" Some of frightened soldiers gained strength from the colonel's fierce words. Swiftly they organized into the units and rushed toward the forest edge. But once there, paralyzing fright stopped them again. The colonel watched his troops intensely. He was still dressed in just the loincloth and necklace, but he had lowered the repulsive mask. In the darkness, with the only light that from the lanterns, the monstrous leader stood with outstretched arms and fixed his glowing eyes on the trembling men. They could feel the effects of his savage temper. In the gross and murky air, his glistening body seemed to be caressed by flames. Before their fearful gaze, he had a serpent head but with outstretched arms on which were jagged claws. Fangs and blood had replaced the wooden mask. The apparition before them twisted and writhed as it moved toward the forest. A raspy voice—a voice from the very depths of hell—uttered the order. "Follow me!"

◇◇◇◇◇◇◇◇

Joel had planned well! He had sorted out and arranged the strategy repeatedly in his mind. Now, with the help of Maludi, he was able to implement it. First, he had found a large gourd and cleaned out the middle. Next, he carved eyes, nose, and a jagged mouth. Joel had never seen a Halloween pumpkin, but had created one. He then colored it white with some molds of which he was familiar. That had taken time because it was found only on the trunk of a certain type of tree that grew near streams. It was a soft, spongy material that at night gave off a fluorescent white glow. He then placed the kerosene lantern within the gourd and mounted it on a long pole. His handiwork was perfect for the nighttime, and he and Maludi spent quite a bit of time working on timing and positioning. His new friend would hold the luminous head up high into the air. Creating the blood-curdling scream would be easy, because most Africans were very good producing diverse sounds. The glowing gourd was to be held high, then brought down and covered by a cloth and quickly moved to another spot, and the scene was to be repeated. Now, this dramatic course of action was causing the desired effect. While the terrified soldiers were moving toward the forest in pursuit of the Ndoki, Joel circled around behind the hut that held Ben. He and Maludi had spent two full days spying on the military camp and its leader. They knew their schedule reasonably well. They had learned that by sundown some of the soldiers would be intoxicated with palm wine and beer. They reasoned correctly that their state of drunkenness would magnify the fear aspect of their plan.

Joel knew exactly where they kept Ben and how many guards were there, and he had carefully observed their behavior. He had become worried when he saw them take Dr. Ben to the colonel's hut but had no choice other than to turn his attention there rather than the prison building. He was overwhelmed with fear for Ben's life. The darkness and bedlam concealed his movements, and he was able to approach to within forty meters of where Ben was being held. The effect produced by their *Ndoki* far surpassed anything they had hoped for. The confusion, fear, and clamor were unbelievable, and when he saw the Colonel burst from the doorway, Joel's heart jumped with exhilaration. Circling to the back of the small building, he peered in through a window. At first, he saw only the flickering fire on the floor in the middle of the room. Then he saw the outline of someone, or something, looking out the front window.

"Dr. Ben," he whispered, "c'est vous? Is that you, Docteur Ben? I am Joel." He kept his voice low but hoped Ben could hear him over the pandemonium outside. Ben, for a few seconds, thought he was hearing things because of some hallucinogenic fumes emitted from the colonel's incense. He turned toward the voice.

"Please be very quiet, Docteur Ben. I have come to help you escape."

Suddenly, Ben recognized Joel's voice. But Joel was dead! He had seen the bullet enter his chest—his heart. Was this Joel's angel? In seconds, Joel had dug through the mud and bamboo lattice wall with his knife, making an opening large enough to crawl through. They could hear soldiers shouting in the distance. Most all the soldiers were now fervently involved in the chase—or at least they hoped that was true. Nevertheless, anxiety gripped them both because they had no idea where *le Diable Noire* was. He prayed silently that Ben would be forgotten a little longer. It took just a few moments for them escape the hut and reach the forest edge in the opposite direction of the frantic soldiers. Only then did they take time to embrace. Tears flowed freely from both, but they made no sound. Ben willingly followed Joel, allowing him to choose the path. He was amazed how well his legs were responding after so many months of captivity. They came to a small stream and paused to briefly rest.

"I think we can speak freely now. Docteur Ben, God has assisted me in wonderful ways to find you and I praise Him. Soon the soldiers will know you are gone and there will be teams sent to search for you. We must try to cover our tracks and pray they cannot follow us."

"Joel, I understand that we will be able to talk soon. Right now, all I know is that I thought you dead and you are alive!" Ben's voice faltered.

"Yes, I will explain. Now we must wade in the river. It is too small for crocodile, but we might be bitten by the bad fish and also there are many leaches." Ben knew the *bad fish* were piranha. The leaches were repulsive but rather harmless.

The water was cool and they drank vigorously. Then both entered the stream. It was shallow, not more than knee deep, but rocks and fallen limbs made walking difficult. After thirty minutes, they were chilled and exhausted, but they had not encountered any biting fish.

"We can leave the water now," Joel said, "I think we have gone about three kilometers (two miles)."

Upon leaving the small river, they found the vegetation to be dense and almost impenetrable. Twisting, turning, and crawling on hands and knees, they left the stream several meters behind them.

"Wait here, Docteur Ben, I will try to erase our footprints from where we left the water."

Joel began at the river, and using a tree branch, he methodically removed their tracks in the mud near the river, and then carefully brushed the ground and rearranged leaves and branches to their previously undisturbed condition.

"I think we will be safe now," Joel said when he rejoined Ben. "However, some of the soldiers are excellent trackers, so we must not stay here for very long. But now we can rest for a short time and talk."

"Joel, I cannot understand how you are alive. I saw with my own eyes the colonel shot you in the chest—at short range."

"It was the Word of God that saved my life," Joel smiled as he removed his punctured Bible from the ragged shirt pocket. "The Bible took much of the force of the bullet and diminished some of its killing force. But it was by God's grace that I was healed."

He hastily recounted the story of his injuries, the recovery, and the medical care by the young nurse. It took him only a few minutes to come to the present by leaving out many details.

"Then you created the Ndoki in the forest?"

"Yes, Dr. Ben, with the help of my friend." He told Ben about the young soldier. "If he escapes Ching's men, he will meet us at the village of King-walaka, about twelve kilometers (seven miles) from here. He plans to have two motorcycles there for us."

"Where are we going from there, Joel?"

"To Kikungu. The colonel's soldiers are marching back there. If we move fast, we can arrive there several days before they arrive."

Ben remembered the colonel's orders. "I heard them planning to attack and pillage some villages on their way to our Mission Station. To the best of my knowledge, the colonel does not send out scouting units before his assaults. If that holds true we could possibly have even more time. But why go back to Kikungu? His army mostly destroyed the Mission Station, didn't they? I doubt if any medical supplies, fuel, or anything else of value remains."

"That is true, Dr. Ben, but I have recent information that tells me there are some white people there. I do not know if they are Americans or European, but they have a Land Rover and some supplies. *Le Diable* may know this. Also, I do not know if they are aware of the advancing rebels. If not, they are in great danger"

Unexpectedly, there was a muffled sound in the forest to their right. It was impossible to tell how far away but it was the snapping of a branch. Once again, the arctic chill of fear penetrated deeply into their bodies—some of the Devil's soldiers had found them!

⬦⬦⬦⬦⬦⬦⬦⬦

Fear had frozen Ben and Joel into total silence. All their senses strained to detect any danger. Suddenly, a small antelope, a Reebok, burst onto the trail; it was trembling and sniffing the air. It stared at them for a few seconds and then disappeared into the bush. They were just starting to calm their racing hearts when a soldier appeared on the trail where the small animal had been. He was young, gaunt and looked exhausted. He had an army issued rifle in his hands and a revolver on his hip. He looked dangerous. Then suddenly Ben and Joel cried out almost simultaneously, "Dear God, it is Maludi!" The young man walked slowly to them and then from total exhaustion and the sudden release from his own fright, he collapsed into their arms.

CHAPTER 22

Zack's strength had returned remarkably well, and by the next morning he felt little physical restrictions as he prepared to leave. He met with the chief and two other men he did not know. They supplied him with an old Savage 30–06 caliber-hunting rifle that apparently had belonged to one of the missionaries who had liked to hunt. There were also two full boxes of shells. However, the object that Zack coveted the most was the oversized Beretta hunting knife. It was slightly curved and razor sharp. Sharing good-byes with Angela was incredibly difficult. Neither spoke many words, nor did they allude to the very real fact that they might never see each other again. Sometimes hearts can be so attuned that things felt and left unsaid are more meaningful than when expressed. They had attained that significant stage in their relationship. Nevertheless, their parting kiss had been salty with tears.

It was just before sunrise that Zack left bearing only the rifle, knife, and a water container made of hides. Only one man, David Mbote, accompanied him. David was a supple, muscular man who could have been good-looking except for a cruel scar across his forehead and nothing but twisted tissue where his right eye had been. He was shirtless, displaying linear scars deeply engraved in the flesh of his chest and back. He appeared incredibly brutal except for his totally disarming smile. He spoke a few words of English, for which Zack was grateful.

Zack was amazed at how strong he felt and how well his muscles responded to commands. It occurred to him to be grateful for having kept up exercising, even if not as resolutely as he should have. As they walked, Zack could not determine if the sandy trail had been made through the tall elephant grass by animals or man, but it made travel straightforward. Occasionally they passed through groups of large trees, giants among the dwarfs, which punctuated the vastness of the broad savanna. They journeyed for about an hour at a rapid pace, and Zack was sweating profusely but otherwise felt vigorous. David had instructed him to follow behind about ten paces and to stop abruptly if he did. Now, the agile African was a motionless statue. All his senses were straining to detect scents and sounds. He motioned Zack to leave the trail. They hid easily in the small group of tall trees.

"People come," he whispered, "good or bad, I not know." Several minutes later, a small group came down the trail. The assembly consisted of three men, five women, and a few active children. The women carried baskets on their heads and two had infants strapped to their backs. As they started to pass by, the women began singing a rhythmic song. Was this their way of informing Zack and David they knew they were there? David remained immobile and vigilant for several more minutes before he moved or spoke.

"There is village near." His still kept voice low, "We go around."

Progress off the trail was much more difficult, and they had to move in an irregular pattern passing through groups of trees, tall stands of grass, and almost impenetrable brush that contained long, cruel thorns. Zack incurred many rips in his clothes and cuts on arms and legs before learning to respect them. It was almost an hour before they returned to the path. It was wider now and more like a road. Zack studied David more closely as he stood immobile, listening for any inappropriate sound. He wore only slacks and tattered sandals. He had a rifle over his shoulder and a holstered handgun at his side. Zack had examined neither of his weapons, but he hoped they were functional. They continued the same intense pace until the sun was almost straight up—it was giving off very fierce rays. It was 11:20 a.m. by Zack's watch.

"Village near. Pascal kele wapi. Kwisa!"

He again left the road and entered the bush, caution woven into every fiber of his statuesque frame. Zack followed. Although he did not understand David's words, his body language had told him what he meant. Pascal was in the village. When they were close enough to begin to hear human voices and the sound of dogs, he motioned Zack to his knees and directed him to be still. He silently moved into the bush and disappeared. After several minutes, Zack's leg muscles were cramping and demanding to be repositioned. He was about to do so when he suddenly heard a twig snap behind him. Swiftly, he turned with the knife already out of its sheath. David stood there. He had come soundlessly to within five feet of him. He stared at Zack with steely brown eyes but said nothing for several seconds. Self-consciously, Zack replaced the knife into its scabbard.

"Come. It is safe."

They entered the smallest village that Zack had seen so far. Eight square huts were built into a semi-circle that surrounded a larger central hut. There were no people there.

"Where is everyone?" Zack inquired.

"They hide. They not know us. Have fear." David shouted something loudly and soon some older men, then women, and then a few children appeared on both sides of them. Soon there were thirty-five or so people around them. The children hid behind their mother's skirts with wide eyes fixed on the giant creature that appeared human except for its awful white skin. Carved wooden chairs were brought for them and they sat. Zack was offered water and tea, while David spoke with a man whom Zack presumed was the village leader. The women and most of the men returned to their houses or to their work, but the children stayed, staring from a secure distance. Approximately thirty more minutes passed and the early afternoon sun had become severe by the time David returned.

"The chief says that Pascal is there." He pointed to the south. "It is only a walk of one hour."

After traveling for about forty-five minutes, they came to a narrow gorge. It was several meters deep and thick with tree and vines. Zack could hear a river or a waterfall far below. They started to descend into this jungle below when, without warning, Pascal appeared not ten feet from Zack.

"Hello, my friend." He spoke quietly. Zack was beyond trying to comprehend these people's stealth. "It is good to see you, Zack. You look well. You appear to have recuperated from the bout of malaria."

"Yes, I am doing great, and seeing you makes me feel a whole lot better."

Pascal was dressed in dark jeans and a light blue shirt that had *Yankees* imprinted across the front. He had on tough appearing sandals with no socks. Zack noted that he had no weapon. They shook hands warmly, but their reserve prevented a more fervent embrace. Neither knew that the other wanted to share a warmer welcome. Pascal turned and he and his men started down a path that dropped downward at a steep angle. Zack and David Mbote followed. They were soon surrounded with heavy foliage, enormous trees, and impassable underbrush.

"I believe that we are safe to talk here," Pascal spoke softly, and the cascade far below them muffled his voice. He sat on the ground and motioned Zack to sit opposite him. Nothing was spoken for several minutes. Pascal seemed lost in thought. The stillness carried with it the damp odor of mold-covered trees and decaying leaves. Within seconds of their silence, the forest became alive with relentless shrieks, throaty gurgles, and high-pitched chirps interspersed with an occasional melodic harmony—the bird life around them was energetic. When Pascal finally spoke, it was with excitement sheltered by reserve.

"If the messages we are receiving are accurate, and I believe they are, Ben has gotten away from the rebels. Just a couple of hours ago a runner came from a village where the colonel's army is camped. He was almost too agitated to understand, but he told us that a horrible spirit attacked the soldiers, and during the confusion, someone helped Ben to escape. Do you remember the name *Joel?*" Zack nodded affirmatively and Pascal continued.

"Somehow he was involved in the getaway, and they tell us now that they have been gone for two days. But the soldiers are searching frantically for them. It sounds as if this colonel Ching is furious—almost out of control. No doubt he will order the death of some of his men if they do not find Ben, and with his history, their deaths will be terrible. Somehow, you and I and this small group of men must find Ben and Joel before the soldiers do. This will be not easy, and it will be very dangerous!" Pascal searched Zack's face for any clues as to how he was responding. He could read nothing in his steady eyes. "We had started making plans, but now that you are here, we need your expertise in the preparation."

During the weeks they had been together, Zack had begun to understand Pascal somewhat better. "Even if we find Ben and Joel it will not be over, will it, sir?" A brief sadness passed quickly through Pascal's eyes, and he was quiet for a few moments. "It will not be," he said with deep grief in his voice, "not until *le Diable Noire* is either captured or dead and his band of killers are scattered."

CHAPTER 23

D uring the ensuing three days, they traveled by night and rested by day. Pascal hated to lose the time by not moving during the day—it was precious time—but at all cost they had to avoid encounters with any of Colonel Ching's soldiers. They followed the deep valley cut by the river and this made travel very difficult. The trees, vines, and deep underbrush made an almost impenetrable terrain. Nevertheless, staying in the valley was necessary. Many times the men had to use their machetes to slice their way through this jungle terrain. However, Pascal and the others knew that the soldiers would traverse the savanna country, avoiding the heat, humidity, and dangers of the thick forest along the rivers. They also assumed the soldiers would not consider that others would struggle with the grueling obstacles in the tropical forest below. However, the landscape was very familiar to Zack. With the African night encompassing them and little communication between the small groups of men, his mind was released to allow memories from the past to flourish.

◇◇◇◇◇◇◇◇

During the winter of 1950, Kim Il Sing, leader of North Korea, ordered his troops to advance into South Korea. This movement was made despite the reluctant support of Russia and no clear mandate from the Communist Chinese. On Sunday, June 25, 1950, the United Nations Security Council met and approved a U.S. resolution demanding an end of aggression and the withdrawal of the North Korean army. The resolution was disregarded, and in the following days and months, President Truman felt he had to escalate the U.S. participation. The reasons were diverse and complex. Over the next three years, more than a million American soldiers fought in South Korea against the Chinese and North Korean armies.

Among a group of marines that were deployed to North Korea during the fall of 1952, as part of the United Nations Command, was a young lieutenant named Zack Kylie. He had graduated from the University in 1951 with a degree in Engineering, but being uncertain of the direction for his future, he joined the Marine Corps. He excelled in boot camp because of his athletic ability and was commissioned as a Lieutenant because of his college degree.

Zack was a born leader of men and embraced the challenges of the armed service with enthusiasm, albeit, with some misgivings. He and his group of marines were part of the second expeditionary force sent from a northern California Marine base to South Korea. During the first nine months in Korea, he and his men saw limited action. Their time consisted of a few excursions along the DMZ but without exchanges with the enemy. Zack was in the middle of his daily exercises when orders from the commanding officer arrived. He was expected at headquarters immediately!

Zack was standing at attention in the CO's office within ten minutes of receiving the order. By the following day, he and the twenty men assigned to him were on board a DC-3 bound for Southeast Asia. Their instructions were to destroy a major supplier of heroin that was being funneled through southern China to South Korea. The heroin was eventually finding its way to some soldiers of the U.S. Armed Services. Although not a major problem yet, the military leadership realized how devastating the situation could become. Wartime creates terrible pressures on the young men and women suffering loneliness, separation from family, and the sporadic episodes of gut wrenching fear. The more prolonged the war, the greater the menace from illicit drugs.

During the long flight to their destination, Zack and the men learned that this was a covert operation. They were to perform their duty leaving no evidence of United States involvement. If discovered, he and his men would not be acknowledged—they never existed! They were parachuted in about twenty kilometers (twelve miles) from their objective. The terrain they encountered was much like the landscape through which he and Pascal were now fighting their way. Their first five days were used for scouting of a military base. It appeared to be made up of a mixture of Chinese and North Korean soldiers. They soon discovered that each day six guards were dispersed to selected areas to the perimeter of their tiny base. Zack and his marines, using stealth and hand-to-hand combat, killed these guards one by one.

Another five North Korean soldiers were *equalized* while they were returning from the poppy fields where they had been brutalizing some native workers. One shot was fired during that attack but went unchallenged because the soldiers were used to having one of their own fire at some animal or bird. This reduced the enemy to an estimated thirty men. During each noon-hour, the communist soldiers congregated in small mess halls. The officers took their meals in a more elaborate building. Lieutenant Kylie took fifteen of his men and assaulted the main eating facility while his Sergeant simultaneously stormed into the officer's mess and opened fire. The battle was over in minutes. The buildings were then closed and stored fuel oil was thrown on them. The structures were torched.

After that, Zack radioed the pilot of the unmarked plane that had dropped them in. Within the hour, the DC-3 landed at the small jungle airstrip. It was then that the unforeseen occurred. A small group of military replacements for the stationed troops made a sudden appearance. Zack and his men had to fight their way through them to reach their plane. During the ensuing firestorm, he lost three of his men and five were wounded, including Zack himself. However, they made it to the waiting aircraft carrying their dead and wounded. Take off proved to be extremely precarious and their plane took several rifle shells, wounding the co-pilot and killing the navigator. They eventually arrived back at their original base in South Korea devastated and exhausted. There were no welcoming, no medals, and no formal recognition. Their mission never happened! Nevertheless, their superior officers knew that a tremendous amount of devastation, destruction, and death had been averted among their troops stationed in South Korea. Zack's wounds were initially treated at a field hospital in South Korea, and he was then airlifted to Okinawa and eventually found his way to the Oakland Naval Hospital. The horror he had seen, the bleeding bodies, the screams of pain, the burning flesh, and the cries of his dying colleagues, found a hideaway in Zack's brain. He convinced himself that he had camouflaged it well. The physical disabilities he overcame favorably, but unrecognized by his conscious mind, the terror and guilt were never completely conquered.

◇◇◇◇◇◇◇◇

Now as Zack struggled through the thick and almost impenetrable jungle, he continued to experience the strong sense of having been here before. They were organizing and planning to go to battle. They would be facing an unfamiliar but dangerous enemy. Some men would have to die, and Zack knew how to kill. During the last few hours of travel, his senses of hearing and smell had become intensified. His muscles were responding effortlessly and his thinking had become incredibly focused. Zack was once again back in the jungle of Southeast Asia—once more a Marine—a finely honed killing machine. But was it the same? Were these circumstances so different? Had he changed? Zack had always doubted the reality of such things as *flashbacks*. He had decided it was just psychological mumble-jumble. But suddenly they were there—the flames, the shrieks, the blood, and the mangled bodies—concealed images of horror long consigned to a hidden place in his brain. Suddenly, memories from his mental foxhole poured out the feelings of quilt and pain—terrible hidden torment that had been skillfully recognized by Pascal's insight and softly embraced by Angela's love.

CHAPTER 24

Their plan was simple but dangerous. They had to infiltrate the army in order to learn more about the relationship between the colonel and his most trusted officers. From some of the Congolese people, they had learned a little about Colonel Ching's methods of deployment, his arms, and his supplies. Pascal's small band of *militia* was made up of seven men. Somehow, they had to infiltrate the Devil's army. David Mbote was chosen because he was from the Kasai region and spoke Swahili and Kipende, the languages of the colonel. The second phase of their strategy, and the most critical, was to find Ben and him get him back to the Mission Station and to safety. The first stage depended entirely upon David being able to be accepted into the rebel army and quickly obtain information. David needed little instruction and no encouragement. He was ready to give his life for Dr. Ben. In contrast to the illusion created by his scarred and cruel face, David was not a brutal man, nor did he have hate toward the soldiers. David's only desire was for Ben's safety.

"We will meet at Mwadi at sundown six days from now," Pascal said, indicating the small village on the crude map. David nodded at Pascal and briefly looked at Zack. His dark eyes reflected no fear, only certainty. Failure was not an option!

After David had disappeared down the trail border by tall elephant grass, Pascal turned to Zack. "Ben should be about here," he said, pointing at a small town some twenty kilometers (twelve miles) north of them. "Some villagers who came from there this morning tell us that their people have Ben and two other men well hidden. They say Ben is weak but otherwise seems well."

"When can we go to meet him?" Zack asked.

"There is a problem. A group of seven or eight of the colonel's soldiers is headed to investigate the village where Ben is hiding. An informant may have told then about Ben, or they may be just randomly searching. However, they must be stopped and not allowed to get information back to their main group."

"Do we have time to intercept them before they find Ben?"

"I believe we can," Pascal replied, "but we must leave the forest and travel the savanna tonight. The soldiers will probably not march right now because of the moonless night. They will stay by their fires for fear of the demons in the darkness."

Zack noticed again that Pascal had no weapon and again speculated about this, but had too much respect to question him. Four of the other men had rifles, the model of which Zack could not identify. All had great knifes in sheathes on their belts. Two of the men were holding large, vicious-looking machetes.

There was a sliver of moonlight delineating the path for the first hour. But then clouds hid even that splinter of light, and the trail had to be felt under foot, more than seen. A native by the name of Nganda was in the lead. He was tall, especially by Congolese standards, and painfully thin. He appeared even frail. Yet, well-defined muscles stood out on his arms and chest, and his movements were strong and focused. He did not appear to be a man who should be taken lightly. Zack was in total awe of how well he could see in the darkness. By each of them trailing closely the person in front, they kept a steady pace; sometimes a rapid walk and at times a slow jog. They had traveled about two hours before stopping. Zack estimated they had covered seven to eight miles. The night was cool, but humid, and they were all saturated with sweat. Each drank sparingly from their water containers and rested.

Pascal spoke in a hushed voice, "If our information is correct, the small band of soldiers should be about a mile from us. Zack, you and Nganda are on your own now. You have to reach those men and make sure they do not get to Ben—or be allowed to return to the main unit!"

◇◇◇◇◇◇◇◇◇

At about the same time that David Mbote was moving to the southeast and getting close to Ching's main army, Zack and his friend were moving rapidly to the east. They had to intercept that small gang of killers!

Simultaneously with the others, Pascal and his natives started northward. By moving rapidly, they hoped and prayed to catch up with Ben and Joel by two difficult days of walking.

Pascal and his men moved rapidly and unimpeded. The trail was narrow but well used. They passed through a few small villages where the people were friendly and cooperative. From them they learned quite a bit of the status of Dr. Ben. It was through them that they learned that Ben, Joel, and another man had traveled by motorcycles. However, it was only a few miles before one of the cycles broke down. Before long, the other ran out of fuel—they were now traveling on foot. The loss of the motorcycles had made the travel ahead of them more prolonged than they had projected. It was on the third day that they caught up with the three men. When Pascal's group finally found Ben and Joel, they were sitting a few paces off the trail—thirsty, hungry, and totally exhausted. Fear had gripped them at first because Pascal and his men had appeared in such complete silence. Ben's first thoughts were that he had come so close to freedom only to be recaptured by the Devil's militia.

Reunion of friends is almost always emotional. A reunion of hearts and souls is one of fervor and enchantment. Tears ran freely on the cheeks of Ben and Pascal who were unified in ways far beyond camaraderie. The two men were more than professional and cultural brothers. They were united mentally, spiritually, and emotionally. Indisputable friendships are rare on earth. Such friendship means identity in thought, heart, and spirit. These two men had long ago entered into that relationship. Great distances and time had not diminished it. Their friendship, based on years of toiling, learning, and struggling together, had developed an intense and resilient relationship sustained by their mutual love for the God. As their friendship had grown, they had learned to share their deepest sorrows. All the more, as their relationship solidified, they discovered something even more exceptional—they had learned to share their secret joys. Now, as they greeted one another, even after all the years of separation, it seemed they had never been apart. They were completely unashamed of their tears. After several moments, Joel and then Mutadi joined them. The other men sat a small ways apart, but they, too, felt a wonderful camaraderie with these men.

Zack and his new friend, Nganda, had found their objective on the second evening of travel. By midnight of that day, the small band of soldiers following Ben had been *neutralized.* He and Nganda had then traveled until the light of daybreak was starting to erase the night. It was only then that they found a small thicket of gnarled underbrush and slept.

As Zack and Nganda were sleeping the sleep of exhausted warriors, David had penetrated the ranks of the colonel's military. It had been easier than anticipated. At a small market he had used his meager funds to purchase several bottles of whiskey. Good stuff by Congolese standards. In addition, he purchased some rice, canned meats, and two large sacks of flour. The pack on his back was burdensome but made him appear to be a poor, itinerate trader. The whiskey made it especially easy to move into their camp. Within a very short time, he had several of les soldats around him and the bartering had begun. The men were tired and bored and enjoyed the interlude of arguing over the price of the food and drink.

With his supplies sold, it was simple for David to strike up a relationship with a few of the soldiers and even easier to convince them he had no place to go. It created no suspicion when he asked them if he could join them. He shrewdly let them know how much he hated the whites, especially the Belgians and the Americans. This quickly endured him to some of the Colonel Ching's troops. In the lower ranks of the colonel's army, men came and went frequently, so none thought much about his sudden appearance. If any suspicions did occur, David easily dispelled them because of his knowledge of the region and languages.

By the end of the fourth day in their camp, David had gained some useful information. During that time, he had seen the colonel only once and that brief encounter had shaken him. There had been forty meters between them when *le Diable* stepped out of his hut. Their eyes had met only briefly, but long enough to make David's blood run cold. He experienced an irrational fear that through that brief exchange, the *le Diable* knew who he was and why he was there. David suddenly had the vision of a dead man lying on a funeral pyre. The man was he! David was a fearless man, but for a few seconds he experienced an absolute terror such as he had never experienced before. Then, the colonel had abruptly turned away and walked toward the forest edge. David never saw him again and for that he was grateful.

In a short time, he learned that there were approximately one hundred men in the camp. Other than the small group that had been dispersed to search southward, there were no other groups separated from this main section. Many of the recruits in this motley army were discussing attacking the larger village of Katambo that lay about fifty kilometers (thirty miles) to the east of them. The market there was rather large and well stocked. In addition, they were told of many young women in the town. Sometime during the next few days, they believed their leaders would give them the orders to attack Katambo. Then, when they had finished pillaging the homes and marketplace and having their way with the women, they would march north to the Kikwit road. They planned to travel that road for several kilometers and then march west to the Mission Station. They hoped some of the missionaries had returned and they could renew their supplies of medicines. A few of the more cruel soldiers relished the idea of raping some more white women. However, it would be many days before they could arrive there. Another important piece of information David was able to gather was that the colonel rarely sent a reconnaissance party before an assault. On the fourth night of David's stay in the military camp, he noiselessly disappeared into the darkness. He did not believe any of the soldiers would be of danger to him, not in their usual disordered state—they would not miss him. He knew that men came and went frequently among the enlisted soldiers. Yet, David remembered his brief encounter with *le Diable Noire* and recalled the words of his grandfather. "A lion always sleeps with his teeth." He trembled imperceptibly.

David felt that without unexpected delays, he should arrive at the Mission before Pascal and the others. After moving far enough from the encamped soldats, this powerfully built, impoverished African with the disfigured face knelt alone in the obscurity of the Congo night and prayed. He asked for safety of the other rescuers and to guide and protect Zack and Nganda.

◇◇◇◇◇◇◇◇◇

Totally unknown to either Pascal or Colonel Ching, a regiment of government soldiers was just now being dispatched from Bukavu, a major city in the far east-central area of the Congo. These Congolese troops were poorly trained but accompanied by some fighting men from South Africa, Belgium, and the U.S.A. These were soldiers with great amount of experience. These *dogs of war* were an efficient, skilled, and well-trained private army—and deadly assassins. David's prayers might be answered by courses of action of which he had no knowledge.

CHAPTER 25

Zack and Nganda arrived at their place of rendezvous several hours before Pascal, Ben and their team. Zack ate supper eagerly that evening and slept the sleep of the exhausted. He awakened refreshed the next morning, grateful there had been no dreams. A night thunderstorm had left the air cool and musty. Thick clouds still hung low over the village giving the surrounding huts a ghostly appearance.

His watch disclosed the time as 5:30 a.m., but there was already some activity in the settlement. A few of the natives moved about like shadowy phantoms in the fog. Zack felt the need to walk and think. It would take a lot of thinking to even begin to sort out the events of the last few hours. He had walked further than he had planned, but the trail seemed safe and was certainly easy to negotiate. An hour later, the fog had burned off and the equatorial sun had extinguished the gloomy clouds. Zack first saw them from a long distance and he instantly hid, thinking they might be enemy soldiers. As the distance between them shortened, he recognized the group to be Pascal and some others. The band moved in single file. In the group was a thin, slightly bent man whom Zack knew instinctively was Dr. Ben Wells. Zack stared intently at the man as the group approached. He had not yet moved back onto the trail from where he had hidden. He could not take his eyes from the man about whom he had heard so much. Despite his thin frame, the man conveyed substantial strength and vitality. His gait seemed to be one of determination, steadfastness, and perseverance. Soon, they were close enough for Zack to clearly see the man's set jaw and furrowed forehead. Despite his thinness, he displayed a robust exterior, as if daring the world to meet him head-on. However, there was cheerfulness in his eyes that defied the formidable exterior. He appeared to be someone who could walk all day long without tiring and also gave the impression that he would give of his heart with the same intensity. When

Zack stepped forward on to the trail, the startled Ben turned to gaze at him. Finally, here was the man about whom so many had spoken with such esteem and reverence. For a brief moment Zack felt a mixture of irritation and disillusionment. Standing before him was just a man, more fragile and bowed than he had first appeared on the trail. His thin shoulders sagged, as if weighed down by a heavy load. Yet, Zack was instantly drawn to the man's eyes; dark green eyes that gazed keenly into his own. In brief seconds it seemed that Ben had explored Zack's mind and soul, leaving nothing unexposed. Astonishingly, Zack saw in Ben's face serenity mixed with strength and genuineness. A few moments of stillness passed and then the frail appearing man spoke. His voice was deep and vibrant. "Zack, how good it is to met you." He extended a slender hand, but his grip was dry and firm. "My dear friend, Pascal, has told me so much about you!"

Standing here on a sandy path in the heart of Africa, Zack was impacted powerfully by the bearded and disheveled missionary physician. He curiously felt himself to be in the presence of greatness.

It was only a ninety-minute walk from this gathering place to the Mission Station. Angela had already received the news that they were approaching and had come down the trail to meet them. When she sighted the bedraggled group, she broke into a run. The first face she sought was Zack's. Their eyes met in a reunion that only those deeply in love can exchange. Relief, joy, and passion radiated from her eyes as she threw her arms around his neck and kissed his bearded face. She then hugged Pascal joyfully and afterward turned to Ben. "You must be the person I have heard so much about!"

"And you are Angela. My, you are even lovelier than they described." He took her hands in his. "What a pleasure to meet you. Actually, I met you and your parents many years ago. You were passing through Leopoldville on your route back to Brazzaville, across the Congo River. You were just a little girl at the time." He smiled. "I am anxious to get to know you much better, but now you go to your young friend there," nodding at Zack.

The short walk back to the Mission Station passed in silence. Zack and Angela held hands, and she was inwardly thanking God for Zack's safe return. Zack was taking great pleasure in the amazing woman at his side.

After all the months of absence, the grounds and buildings did not appear much different to Ben than before being taken prisoner. Some of the furniture and office supplies were missing and many windows had been broken, but the workers had repaired Ben's home well. Angela had prepared a snack of bread and fruit, and they ate eagerly and took enormous pleasure in drinking cold water from the kerosene refrigerator. After eating, Angela assisted the cook in heating water on the wood-burning stove and the filthy travelers followed one another in baths, shaves, and clean clothes. The resulting metamorphosis was remarkable. Darkness was trespassing on them when Ben, Pascal, Zack, Joel, and Angela gathered in the old-fashioned living room. Some of the Congolese men sat on the floor in middle of the room. Pascal seemed to be in deep thought and Zack was withdrawn. Pascal was the first to break the silence.

"Zack, we have related to you much of what happened to us after we separated six days ago, but you have not shared with us what happened to you and Nganda." They all turned to look at Zack. Angela sensed immediately that Zack was struggling with something, and when he spoke, it was with measured words.

"When we left you, Nganda," nodding at his friend, "and I circled north toward the village where we heard the soldiers were. However, before we got there, we encountered an isolated house. There was a man sitting by a fire outside—he had a rifle on his lap. We could hear the sound of voices coming from within the hut. As we hid and watched, a couple of men came out, relieved themselves, and went back in. We realized that we had found the band of soldiers we were looking for." Zack's voice had become unemotional and detached, as if he were not the one speaking.

"Nganda and I waited until the activity from within the huts ceased and the sentry began to nod. We were about to make our move when the guard suddenly got up and peered around into the darkness. We thought he had heard us, but then he added some wood to the fire and sat down again. After he started nodding off again, I signaled to Nganda to slip to the side of the hut and stay there until I motioned to him. It took me almost thirty minutes of a slow crawl to get myself close enough to the sentry. Then . . . well . . . I got the job done. The soldier died instantly and soundlessly." Zack paused. His eyes seemed to be witnessing a horrible scene. "I carefully lowered his body to the ground. I, ah . . . I rem—I remember that his head was twisted at a grotesque angle. His neck broke as easily as a limb of a tree. Then, as quietly as I could, I joined Nganda at the side of the hut. The sound of snoring from within the hut was strong. A quick glance inside revealed a pot of glowing embers in the center of a single room. Five sleeping forms lay on the floor in an array of positions. Their rifles were stacked together against the wall near the doorway. Nganda and I tried to enter the hut as silently as we could. I remember the rotting door made a grating sound as we pushed it open. And I was scared. One of the soldiers awakened and screamed as we entered. Right away the others were awake! They were slowed by sleep and probably large amounts of alcohol. It was over in seconds. My knife found the throats of two of the men as they charged me. A third one I killed as he was reaching the guns." Zack's face darkened and his voice became more emotionless. It was as if he were giving an account to his commanding officer. "The knife entered just below the ribs, angled upwards through the stomach. I am sure it perforated the left side of his heart. I remember turning to defend myself, but there were none left. Nganda's machete had essentially beheaded one and disemboweled the other. I don't believe I have ever seen a more gruesome sight. We went about hiding the bodies in some nearby brush and swept the dirt floor in an imperfect attempt to hide the blood."

Zack stopped speaking for what seemed an eternity to his companions—all of them respected his silence. When he spoke again, his voice was composed and the harsh edge was gone.

"After we attempted to conceal the evidence, we circled west to meet you. That small band of soldiers was no longer of any danger to Ben." Angela heard something more in Zack's voice and it frightened her. He sounded sad, almost defeated. Ben and Pascal also recognized that Zack was wrestling with intense emotions. Pascal spoke first.

"Killing another human being has to be a living nightmare!"

"But I have fought in war before, and. . . . and killed before. It was just something that had to be done; something I was trained to do. But now it seems so strange to me. Somehow so different! Why?"

Angela was certain she knew. She had seen God working in Zack for quite some time. However, she said nothing. She did not feel the time was appropriate.

Zack continued, "We have just slaughtered five men, and how do I justify that killing? How do Christians as yourselves defend killing anyone?" He paused and then continued, "I have heard people speak about *just* wars. But what does that mean? Does it imply that God uses men like me to fight a certain type of battle, and when through with us, He sends us to hell?"

The three Congolese men had been requested elsewhere, leaving only Ben, Zack, Pascal, Joel, and Angela. Zack's question, actually more of statement, weighed heavily on them. Ben studied Zack's expressions intently and Angela prayed silently. Pascal spoke first.

"The concept of peace at any price developed genuinely from Christ's teachings of love and peace. While studying in Europe, I became friends with many Christians of the Anabaptist denomination. They passionately believe that all war and killing is evil and teach the concept of peace at all cost. I have enormous respect for them. I have often prayed that their cause and beliefs will triumph. They are right, you know. If everyone followed Jesus' teaching—peace, not war; forgiveness, not revenge; turn the other cheek, not retaliation—there would be no more battles, no more devastation, and no further killing. This could happen in a perfect world. But we do not live in a perfect world. So then, the question arises. Are there conditions in which Christians should intervene, even with force, if necessary?" Pascal paused and looked at Ben, sensing he wanted to speak.

"Zack," Ben spoke his name with affection, "I believe that most Christians are committed to the sanctity of life and to peace."

As Ben started to speak, Angela arose and moved over next to Zack. She squeezed his hand and she heard him sigh, almost imperceptibly.

Ben continued speaking in his resonant voice, "You can appreciate by what is being said here that many Christians have labored tremendously with these same questions. Throughout the history of the Christian church, people of faith have searched to find the correct answer. Much of my life has been spent here in Africa. This is a country where evil forces, vicious leaders, and widespread prejudices dominate. There has always been starvation, murder, and devastation. Must we accept and adapt to evil and turn our faces on suffering for the fear of doing something wrong? Can we Christians turn our backs on every terrible and vile act, telling ourselves we are doing so for the sake of God? At what point does passively accepting evil become in itself anti-God?" Ben thought deeply for a few moments. "I think I can speak for all of us here when I say that we believe that Jesus teaches we must resist cruelty, oppression, and killing by every means available to us—first of all, through love. However, we must recognize that in this imperfect world there will be times when Christians will be called to resist evil with revolt—even war."

Joel had sat quietly, listening intently. He now opened his Bible and quickly found the verses for which he searched.

"Sirs, may I read something very briefly." His voice was humble.

They all spoke in near union, "Of course."

Joel read with heavily accented but accurate English. "In Ephesians 6:10–12, the Apostle Paul tells us 'Be strong with the Lord's mighty power. Put on all of God's armor so that you will be able to stand firm against all strategies and tricks of the *Devil*. For we are not fighting against people made of flesh and blood, but against the evil rulers and authorities of the unseen world, against those mighty powers of darkness who rule this world, and against wicked spirits in the heavenly realms.'"

He closed his damaged Bible and in the common African manner, he stared at the floor, but spoke with a perceptive voice, "Right now are we fighting flesh and blood, or are we fighting the instruments of our authentic enemy, Satan?"

The group sat humbly and in total silence. Finally, Ben broke the quiet. "Please, let's all think hard and pray on these enormous problems. We cannot resolve all these difficulties, but we can pray that God will guide each of our hearts to deal with them in a way in which He would have us."

This small, diverse group remained in stillness and in unrestrained communication with God for a long time.

CHAPTER 26

They all retired for sleep shortly after their meeting and prayer. It was approaching 10:00 p.m. and a half-moon was lashing out against the darkness. It was a huge yellow semi-circle that sculptured the horizon and silhouetted the large palm trees. Pascal's mind was racing with strategies. The night air was cool inside the mosquito netting, but he was perspiring lightly as sleep escaped him. Finally, he decided to go for a walk—maybe even a short run. The mission grounds would be well-lit by moonlight. Beyond the hospital lay an area that the workers kept cleared of trees and brush. They kept the elephant grass cut with the regular use of machetes. This was the mission's landing strip, and although no planes had landed there for several months, the men kept it cleaned in anticipation of a time to come. During the years he had spent here, Pascal had jogged the strip many nights. It was a peaceful and secluded, conducive to thought and prayer. It was also comforting that he had little chance of stepping on a night adder or encountering a cobra. Even as a young man, most of the antelope, elephant, and zebra had been killed or driven away. Without these, one rarely came across a lion or leopard. Nights hawks would occasionally dive at him and a hyena would infrequently make a cautious appearance. The night air was serene and the temperature pleasant. He walked rapidly.

During the past several days he had formulated one plan after another by which he could isolate and capture this maniac and his most trusted officers. However, each time he devised what seemed to be a formidable strategy, he would realize certain dangerous flaws. He could not—would not—unnecessarily endanger the lives of any of his people. The more he learned about this colonel, the more he seemed an enigma. There was no doubt the man was exceptional, and he obviously possessed some military experience. He also had the ability to lead men. Yet, his behavior was erratic and even bizarre at times.

This man was either very insane or so obsessed with evil that he had become totally conquered by it. Could he be both insane and possessed? It was possible, especially here in the heart of Africa where vile spirits wandered unrestrained. Recent information he had obtained from Ben and Joel had begun to convince him that *le Diable Noire* was more than just crazy. He both controlled and was controlled by demonic powers. To prepare tactics against a good military leader was one thing—to fight against the powers of Satan was quite another!

Other thoughts that had given Pascal some sleepless nights recently were the recurring memories of his older brother. He had not considered him for many years. He assumed that his memories were being brought back now by his return to the Congo, to his people, and to the land that contained so many memories. It had been years since he had felt the fear and resentment he held for him. Now, he was remembering the pain, terror, and torture his brother had inflicted on him. Feelings he had delegated to the recesses of his mind were returning. Pascal believed he knew why the memories were coming again, but everything in him wanted to obliterate them. He did not want the feelings about his long dead brother to resurface. He believed for years that he had completely forgiven him through his faith, as he had the murderers of his mother and sister. Now he began to doubt that he had. Hate permeated him as he recalled the horror, the torment, and the anguish Antonio had caused him. He remembered the relief he felt when his brother had disappeared. He could still vividly recall the liberation he felt when he received the news that he was dead. Pascal was certain that after he had been back in the Congo for a while, he would be able handle the feelings better. But, with his return to Africa came many memories. Some were beautiful, but many were repulsive and frightening!

Now as he walked, appreciating the solitude and the feeling of his muscles and heart being exercised, Zack's words came back. The words had affected him intensely. Zack had asked, "Does God use unbelievers like him to fight His *just* wars, and then when finished with them, send them to hell?" Pascal realized fully that the battle against the colonel and his army would have to include some nonbelievers—and some might be killed. There was no strategy he could mentally design that did not hold this great peril. Where was the rationale? Where was the fairness? The certainty that the colonel had to be stopped was not in question. If he was not, many more of his people would be made to suffer horribly, and many more would die terrible deaths. Missionaries would continue to be raped and murdered. Poverty, disease, and starvation would become still more widespread. Even during the terror-filled years as a boy hiding in the forest, he had never encountered anyone as monstrous and hideous as this crazed madman. All the plans he had mentally devised had to include Zack, Joel, Maludi, David Mbote, and Nganda. All had shown great loyalty and bravery. He did not feel that Ben would be strong enough for any physical assistance, but they needed his experience and wisdom. To be successful, Angela would also have to be involved. Additionally, he would have to include some of the young men from the village of Kikungu. Some of these indigents knew Jesus Christ as their Savior, but many were nonbelievers, atheists, and animist who would fight to protect their homes and families. So where was the fairness? How does one respond to Zack's question? Pascal prayed that he would have time to talk further with Zack.

In every plan that Pascal developed in his mind, a key element ran through them all. To be successful, he would have to make first contact with the colonel! Somehow he had to meet him and dialogue with him. Then, in some way, he had to isolate him from his loyal officers. The undertaking seemed unachievable! Yet, he had formalized plans well enough in his mind that he was now ready to discuss them with the others. He would especially value Zack's counsel because of his military experience. Pascal suddenly felt more relaxed. As he turned on the path to return to the house, dark clouds were gathering. The brilliant stars and bright moonlight were now hidden. Lightning began to burst within the huge clouds. It would rain soon—in rebellion against the advancing dry season.

CHAPTER 27

It was late afternoon of the following day before the various duties of the group finally allowed them to meet. Pascal, Zack, and Joel had already assembled in the small dining room and were sipping freshly brewed tea when Ben entered. Sounds radiated from the kitchen where Angela and the cook were preparing the evening meal. The four men spoke little and all seemed especially tense and lost in thought. Each knew that events were rapidly progressing to a conclusion and many vital decisions had to be made very soon. Ben appeared weary and stressed, but his eyes continued to show thoughtfulness and kindness. In contrast, Zack and Joel gave the impression of being rested and enthusiastic. Zack especially seemed to have resolved some of his internal struggles. As usual, it was difficult to read Pascal—rested or exhausted, relaxed or anxious—his demeanor never changed. He was the first to break the hush at the table. "We are too small a group and have far too few weapons to directly attack the colonel's army. Somehow we have to divide them. I am thinking in particular that we have to separate the colonel and his officers from the regular soldiers. But how? I have been struggling for a long time and have come up with some tentative tactics. Now I want to hear your thoughts. I need your advice. Ben, please, because you probably know more about this man than any of us. Can we begin with you?"

Obviously Ben had also been thinking about their situation and had devised some plans of his own. He spoke quietly but with conviction, "The colonel, in my opinion, is insane and totally evil. But he is also extraordinarily intelligent and has finely honed instincts. However, there is much more involved. I have no doubt that some will think me a little crazy when I share this—I believe that he is more than just a mere man. I am sure that he is possessed with demonic powers that are so violent and deadly that we cannot wage war against him as if he were just a powerful man—or competent military leader. I have seen him exhibit horrible supernatural control over his men and have been very near to some of the soldiers when strange forces have attacked them. I really think that he is a true monster who, sometime and somewhere, gave his soul to Satan and now is dominated by supernatural capabilities that are far beyond human."

"Are you telling us that you believe him to be too strong for us to consider fighting against him?" Zack asked kindly.

"Not at all!" I believe with all my heart that the dark forces of evil, demonic forces, if you will, do exist and especially here in the depths of Africa. Demons, evil spirits, and the powers of darkness have been released and worshiped here for centuries. Nevertheless, none of the forces are stronger than the power of God. No, I am not saying that he cannot be defeated, not in the least. In fact, I think that we can use some of those evil powers against him. During the last several weeks of my captivity, I saw the colonel becoming progressively more erratic, more irritable, and indecisive. In our last encounter, just before Joel rescued me, I sensed fright and vulnerability in his actions. I actually think that he is no longer certain he is in total control over the demonic spirits. I believe he is wondering if they are starting to turn on him. However, I do not question that he still has strong dominance over the men who remain with him. But it may not be with the totality that was there previously. The deception that Joel and Maludi perpetrated on him may reveal just how exposed he is becoming. Also, I think his men are noticing his increasing indecision and vulnerability. We know that many of the soldiers have deserted him and others are continuing to do so. The dreadful control he has exerted over these men has been undermined. Oh, they still fear him, and I have no doubt that he is still manipulating them and even killing them with his satanic powers. Nevertheless, some weakening and uncertainty has crept in. This, then, might be one small opening through which we can defeat him."

Their cook appeared with tea and biscuits, and for the next several minutes they spoke of small things. However, the tension was too intense and the conversation quickly returned to the task before them. Ben spoke again. "What lies ahead is a tremendous task. I remember reading several years ago the words of Abraham Lincoln spoken during the terrible days of the Civil War. President Lincoln said, 'I have been driven many times to my knees with the overwhelming conviction that I have no other place to go.'"

No one spoke, but, simultaneously, Ben and Pascal got to their knees. Zack and the others bowed their heads reverently. The small, frightened group prayed quietly. After a few moments the silence was broken by Zack's voice. He had no memory of ever praying before and certainly not aloud. His voice carried with it a composed strength. Zack had not intended to pray but suddenly found he was talking to God—a being whose existence he had totally rejected a few months before. The words formed slowly but flowed easily. The assembled friends around him were mesmerized as he prayed. "God, I don't exactly know what I want to say. I don't even know if you are hearing me. God, please help us to develop a plan by which we can stop this madman. There has been so much suffering, pain, and death, and it isn't fair . . . or right. So God, help us put an end to all this and please God, don't allow any of these wonderful friends to die. God, if you will help these people I will . . . I mean, I don't know if I can bargain with you, but if you will save these people, I will give you my life to You . . . and . . . ah . . . to be used as You will." He paused and his voice was strong as he finished. "Amen."

Angela was standing at the kitchen doorway with tears flowing down her cheeks. She fought back the overwhelming urge to go to Zack and hold him close, but she was sure it would have only embarrassed him. Her tears continued to flow freely as she watched him raise his head and open his eyes. As he did, he found the others looking at him intently. Their eyes held unmistakable joy and appreciation. Zack felt embarrassed, inadequate, and even foolish. He did not realize that he had shared a remarkable prayer, not because of any theological eloquence, but because of its heartfelt honesty. The others all knew that the genuine, childlike prayer he had spoken was the type of prayer that God asks from His people.

"Thank you, Zack, for sharing with us." There was profound respect in Pascal's voice. "Zack, we all need your opinions very much. Of all of us, you are the most experienced."

Yeah, experienced in killing people, Zack thought miserably. He did not say this aloud.

"How do you think we can best defeat them?" Pascal continued his question.

"I have not settled on a definite plan, but I have certainly been thinking of several tactics that I believe could succeed. My thoughts pretty much follow what was just described. Colonel Ching and his officers must be isolated from the main group. If we can do that, I think we can destroy his rag-tag army with just a few troops of our own—hopefully with a minimal amount of danger."

Pascal said nothing but was rather amazed that Zack and Ben both were describing things he had been planning. It was as if they had been reading his mind.

Zack continued, "I think that with four or five good men, we can quickly destroy a lot of their weapons. From what I saw during that last encounter with them, they seem to have a habit of placing all their guns in a neat stack near the doorway of their huts. Apparently they feel that if a surprise attack occurs, they have quick access to their guns. David can help us here since he spent a few days in their camp."

Ben spoke loudly enough to be heard by the cook in the other room. "Nzala, when you have finished with your duties in the kitchen, would please find David Mbote for us. Tell him that we would like to speak with him . . . No, tell him we need his help."

Zack continued speaking, "I will gladly share some other thoughts about attacking these murderers. First, though, would one of you tell me how we could best isolate the colonel from his soldiers?"

Pascal started to speak, but then decided not to express aloud his feelings of complete agreement with Zack. He was hoping to hear some unprompted thoughts from the others. They needed Angela to join them. She was in the kitchen and he was sure she could overhear most of their conversation. Her experience in Africa would be invaluable.

"It seems to me," Ben said, "that we need someone the colonel knows, even someone like myself with whom he is familiar."

"You would be committing suicide!" Angela had just entered the room. Her words were blurted out impulsively. Ben smiled. "Angela, I have no desire to be a martyr. I still have too many things I want to accomplish."

Pascal now entered the conversation. "He and his men do not know me, so it is very possible that I may have the best qualifications. He apparently hates the Belgium, but as far as I know he has no great difficulties with the Americans. I still speak French, so we can communicate. He does not need to know that I understand his mother tongue. My thinking is that we can form a small group and approach him as if we are an official party. I can try to convince him that I am an American who has heard of him, admire his cause, and might be interested in giving him some support. Possibly we could pull this off if we play to his ego."

The others could say nothing. Each realized the potential dangers imbedded in such a plan but also recognized its straightforward cleverness.

Ben had actually developed similar tactics but decided against them because it would mean exposing Pascal to great danger. Now he felt he needed to express that.

"Pascal, I believe that you may have worked out a very good plan. But I think I can speak for all of us when I tell you that we do not want you open to such enormous risks."

"I appreciate your concern, but we must act soon, or all of us will be in even greater danger."

"Very true," Ben replied. "There is no doubt time is critical and we must proceed very soon. But right now we are running out of daylight. Let's eat something and then think things out tonight; by morning we can present some specific ideas on how to defeat the colonel—with a minimum of casualties on either side."

After their evening meal, they started to leave when Ben said, "Oh, Zack! Would you please read something for me? It is in the Bible—the book of Judges, chapters six through eight? There is a Bible on my desk in the study. I think you might find some helpful information for us in those chapters."

The equatorial night had descended with its normal gruffness. Angela found Zack sitting alone on the steps of the veranda. The sky was moonless and the night complete. Only the flickering light from Zack's lantern broke the darkness by casting shadows on his face. For the thousandth time Angela thought just how attractive he was. There was something else of which she was becoming increasingly aware. Despite all the physical adversity they had faced during the past few weeks, Zack actually was looking more youthful—and more at peace. "Do you mind a little company, or would you like to be alone for awhile?"

"Please join me, Angela. I was hoping you would." When Angela sat beside him, Zack put his arm around her waist and drew her close to his side. Angela placed her head on his shoulder, experiencing the ever-growing sense of completeness. Neither spoke, but both were enjoying the moment and as they looked out over the vast obscurity of the valley below. In the distance, lightning flashes bolted across the sky like fiery arrows aimed at the rugged peaks. The clouds were deceiving the parched land below. No rain would be coming that night. The dry season was beginning. The oppressive heat of the day had been driven away, and it was now time to benefit from the coolness of the night. An evening breeze teased the limbs of the palm above them. Somewhere in the distance a nighthawk screeched in flight and the familiar sound of drums drifted to them. Angela felt so fulfilled next to Zack here in her beloved Africa. She prayed silently that he might also feel, even slightly, the way she did.

"I am afraid that I made a fool of myself this evening." Zack dissolved the silence.

"How? When?"

"With the prayer. I can't understand why I did it . . . eh, pray like that. I honestly had not expected to pray, let alone aloud."

Angela took his face in her hands and turned so she could gaze into his eyes before she spoke. When she did, she was not prepared for what she saw. His hazel eyes were so soft and contained such consuming love. For a few moments, she found she could say nothing. She kissed his forehead, his eyelids, and then their lips meet, tender but passionate. They trembled in each other's arms, and when they reluctantly separated, they both felt overpowering passion. Angela swallowed hard and fought to keep her voice calm. "Zack, you didn't make a fool of yourself. In fact, all of us thought we had heard one of the most magnificent prayers ever spoken."

"But why?"

"For the reason that you had not planned to pray. You were talking to God the way He wants us to. Authentic prayer is just simply visiting with God. The words are ours, but genuine prayer is spoken with the guidance of the Holy Spirit within us. The Bible says that we are all to come to God openly and trusting as little children. You did! I just thank you for allowing me—for us, to listen in." They sat quietly for several minutes, arms locked around the others waist, their physical natures wanting so much more but their spiritual awareness in harmony. Finally, Zack spoke as he arose. "We have a big day tomorrow, and I have some reading to do tonight." They stood and embraced. Their lips again united in the complete ecstasy of new love.

The only light in the house came from Ben's bureau. Zack glanced in to find Ben sitting at his desk, his lamp's flame turned up high. He had obviously been studying and writing. "I don't want to disturb you, Ben. I just came to get the Bible you mentioned."

Ben lifted it from the corner of his desk and handed it to Zack. "Thanks for your prayer tonight, Zack; you will never know how much it meant to me." Zack stared at this dynamic and imposing man and saw sensitive warmth in his eyes. "Thanks," he managed to stammer.

Zack closed the bedroom door behind him, quickly undressed, and slipped into bed, anchoring the mosquito netting around the mattress. Tonight he would use his flashlight and the precious batteries because he wanted to carefully read the chapters that Ben had recommended. Thankfully, Ben had marked Judges and the specific pages for him. He had no idea where to find them. He opened the Bible at the marker and began to read.

◇◇◇◇◇◇◇◇

After Zack left, Angela spent several minutes on the veranda alone, enjoying the glow of love and trying to calm her rapid heartbeat. Could any woman be given more? She was with the man she loved, at home in the place she was certain that God wanted her, and surrounded by wonderful Christians. This evening she had experienced the greatest of all joys. She was witnessing a man, her man, come into God's family. *Can one have an acute heart attack from too much happiness,* she thought foolishly. Silently, she spoke a brief prayer and bent down and extinguished the lantern flame.

As she entered the bungalow and started down the hall, she saw the flickering light coming from Dr. Ben's office. She paused at the doorway and found him still at his desk, an open book on his left and writing paper before him.

"Please, come in," he said. He somehow knew it was she, but she was sure he had never looked up. Angela marveled at this but said nothing. The lantern's light made it difficult to see his face clearly, but his manner was alert and vigorous.

"I was just heading for my room and saw your lamp on. I don't want to bother you."

"No, no. I appreciate you stopping. I am just jotting down a few thoughts before retiring. We have never a quiet moment to talk, so I appreciate this time."

"Thanks." Angela paused. "May I ask you ask you something personal, Dr. Ben?"

"Of course."

"When we first arrived here, we found your bureau ransacked. While cleaning up, I couldn't help but see a lot of your papers. I found many journals, articles for publication, and research manuscripts. I am totally amazed at how you found the time, especially after long hours in surgery, hospital rounds, and seeing hundreds of outpatients a week. You must have spent a lot of late nights, like now."

"That is true, Angela."

"But why do you do all this. The research I can understand because it can benefit the medical community and patients. But why the reflections and writings on so many subjects and all the wonderful personal thoughts?" A few moments of silence ensued. Angela could see the shadowy outline of Ben's head as he leaned back in his chair. His eyes were closed.

"That is a fair question and also one difficult to answer. I will try to make my reply brief." Ben began to speak as if he had answered this question many times. "My father never had an opportunity for an education. He was born to poor farmers in central Kansas. His parents died when he was very young, and my father was working full time by the age of ten. By the time he married and I was born, he was a tenant farmer west of Wichita. Though my father had no formal education, he had a burning desire to learn. He read everything he could get his hands on. When we kids asked him questions, he always became excited and sometimes shared a lot more information than we wanted. My brothers and I and our friends thought he was sometimes showing off all of his knowledge. It was several years later that I realized the truth. My father loved to learn. It was exciting to him, and he never realized that others were not as thrilled about learning as he. He was not more intelligent than others; he was just *wired* to love learning. By the time I got to high school and then to the university, I discovered that I also found learning exciting, whether it was biology, Shakespeare, or chemistry, I could not find enough time in the day. I discovered that I, too, was *wired* the way he was. But I did not want to turn people off, as my father had. So now, I research and write to put my excitement on paper, hoping that it might come into the hands of someone who will be interested. Maybe that is part of the reason God put me here in Africa, instead of at a large medical center—I don't know. However, of this I am certain: education does not impart intelligence—only facts. Intelligence is born only when man recognizes that his mind is a gift of God from whom all true knowledge comes." Ben paused. "Sorry, Angela, for such a long-winded response to your question."

"Don't be! I am grateful that you shared," she said with deep feeling. She arose and kissed him on the cheek. "Good night and thank you." As she left the bureau she sensed, more than saw him return to his writing.

CHAPTER 28

A brisk breeze agitated the palm trees the following morning, another signal the dry season was beginning. During the next four months there would be no rain. The lofty elephant grass would turn brown, then shrivel and die. Their land would become parched and lifeless. The few elephant, zebra, antelope, and other large animals would move away in search of green grass and leaves. The large cats and other carnivores would follow their prey. Now the cobras would move nearer to human domiciles, seeking the relative coolness and dampness of buildings.

The molten sun was just extracting itself from the night's darkness as Dr. Ben and the others met in the freshness of the morning. Later, they would take the time for attention to their bodily needs such as the shaving, showering, and brushing teeth. Once again, unimportant conversation was minimized by the necessity of time. Present along with Dr. Ben were, Pascal, Zack, Angela, David Mbote, Nganda, and there was a new face—Pastor Ndela—whom Ben had requested to join them. He represented the people of the village of Walapi that lay about twenty kilometers (twelve miles) north. Maludi and Joel were absent. They had left earlier to visit his family.

Ben began the discussion. Those present had placed him in de facto leadership for reasons that were obviously known to all. No one else had even been considered.

"David, may we start with you. Please share any ideas you might have. I will translate."

For the next several minutes, David spoke precisely and thoughtfully. Zack particularly was astounded at how fluently his quiet friend presented his views. Having recently infiltrated the rebels, he was able to give important information relating to the soldier's habits, organization, and very importantly, some details concerning their weapons. The group was extremely pleased to learn that the number of their weapons was quite limited. David told them that some of the officers had handguns, mostly Chinese made. Also, he had seen some Russian automatic rifles and a few grenades. There was one worrisome detail. He had seen a large, Russian made truck in which they kept a powerful arsenal. It held mortars, land mines, and some types of field guns. What else he did not know. David's *friends* told him that a lot of their ammunition had been used up a long time ago. As to the enlisted soldiers, most had very old equipment, such as single shot rifles or ancient shotguns. Others had to be dependent on their knives or machetes. Mostly their uniforms were in shreds and their boots worn out. Many had discarded the boots in favor of cheap sandals. David had discovered that a lot of the colonel's army was very young, many in their teens. Their allegiance to one another was very fragile and David sensed that their loyalty to Colonel Ching was extremely precarious.

"Thank you, David. We will return to you again a little later," Ben said with enthusiasm. "Angela, you have so much understanding of Africa and its people; we would appreciate your thoughts very much."

Angela was prepared because she had spent time, organizing her thoughts the past several nights before falling asleep. "First, I want to say that we all hear so much about the horrible conduct of rebel armies like those of the colonel. I just want people to know that they do not represent the majority of the Africans. I have always found the Africans to be sociable, sensitive, and compassionate. It is sad that the few drunken, drugged soldiers led by a maniac must reflect on all the others. But also I know that there is a vast difference from tribe to tribe. In addition, superstition and fear of evil spirits are rampant here in Central Africa. This influences their actions a lot. But when you get to know them, you find they are great people to befriend and work with. I am certain that many of the Africans population right here resent the rebel soldiers as much or more than we do. Actually, probably more because the natives have suffered far more from their cruelty than we can even imagine." Angela realized she was saying these things for Zack's benefit. But also, she wanted the Africans there to know how she felt—and how she was sure the other felt. She turned to the minister. "Would you agree, Pastor Ndela?"

"Ai, yo kele une verite," he replied, vigorously. "That is true."

Angela continued, "I believe we will have to include the inhabitants here at the Station and the nearby villages into our plans. In addition, we need to send a few trusted men to begin talking with the leaders in the other villages. I believe they will cooperate because they want to stop the killing as much as we do. I think Joel, when he returns, should be invited to do this. If we unite in our effort, we have a good chance of defeating this revolutionary army."

"Splendid! I am glad you are on our side, Angela!" Ben said with pride and a smile.

"Who is next? Zack, did you have the time to look at those chapters in the book of Judges?"

"As a matter of fact, I got so involved I read the entire book."

Ben smiled perceptively. "Any insights you found that might help us?"

"I will try to be brief, but this man Gideon was absolutely amazing. What really came through was how God can use a poor, unskilled man and make him a great military leader. That was amazing! However, I will leave that for another day." Zack could not hide the eagerness in his voice. "I discovered at least four strategies from Gideon's military genius that I think we might use. First, he sent messengers out to surrounding cities to gather recruits, just as Angela has suggested. Second, he separated the enemy from any water supply. In his case, it was the Jordan River. Third, he discovered that great numbers do not necessarily make a strong army. Fourth, he used psychological warfare by making a few seem to be thousands."

"Comment? How?" asked Pastor Ndela after Ben had translated Zack's discourse. The excitement in his voice was shared by the entire group.

"As to the psychological warfare, Gideon had a relatively small group of men take pottery, trumpets, and torches with them. The smashing of pottery, the blare of trumpets, and the flare of torches produced the impression of an enormous fighting force on the move." Zack paused, wondering if he was saying too much.

"Please, share with us more about Gideon and his battle," Angela requested, although she knew the account very well.

Zack continued, "A great many of the enemy lost their courage and broke and fled. What had seemed to be great army facing Gideon was greatly decimated by fear."

"Excellent!" Pascal spoke earnestly. "So in order to carry out these tactics, we first need to send a few good people to nearby villages to recruit support. Angela has already made excellent contributions on that phase. Then we need to develop a plan to shut off the water supply to the rebel soldiers. After that, we need to develop a tactic of psychological warfare. That phase might be the most challenging."

"Well, as I said, I am amazed how much practical information I gained from the account of Gideon's war. I have just presented a rough draft with which to work. As you have indicated, Pascal, many details must be put together in order to win the war."

"But now we have some very specific ideas to build on." As Ben spoke he turned to pastor Ndela, who was quietly speaking to them.

"Si vous plait, je voudrais vous recontrer quelque chose." His pastor's voice was almost a whisper

"The pastor has something he would like to share with us." Ben continued to translate into English for Zack and into Kituba for the others. "The pastor is saying that he received information this morning on their short-wave radio from a staff member of the Baptist church at Bekoni. Bekoni is a village approximately two hundred kilometers (one hundred and twenty miles) to the east. He learned that the rebels are near them and moving in force toward us. They are in great fear, and most of the village people are hiding. Depending on how many villages they assault, they can easily be here in one or two weeks' time. He says that we must work swiftly!"

With a sudden shattering blast, a lightning strike hit very near the small group, deafening them and causing the hair to rise on their necks. They rushed to the door but could see only one small, innocent appearing, white cloud in an otherwise clear, indigo sky. It was only moments later that several men arrived, all shouting in unison.

"They are saying that the roof of the church is on fire," Ben told them. "I will go with them. Please remain here and thrash out the plans. I will return as soon as I can."

Zack's eyes converged with Angela's. Instantly, she sensed what he must have been thinking. Was this some type of omen, this intense lightning strike from a clear sky? Were the powers from *le Diable Noire* telling us that he knew we were here and that he did not fear our God or us? He and Angela shared their thoughts and discovered that it was exactly what they were both thinking. "It is absolutely irrational, I know! But yet . . ." Angela's voice trailed off, her thoughts drifting into Africa's eerie cosmos.

CHAPTER 29

During the next three days the small group spent almost every waking hour in planning. On the fourth day Joel returned and with him was a lovely young woman. He introduced her as Rachael and shared with them that she was the nurse who had saved his live after being shot by the colonel. With them they had some medical supplies including antibiotics, anti-malarial, and a few analgesics. Additionally, they had bandages, tape, and various ointments.

"There is something that I want to share with all of you." Joel had wanted to wait for Pastor Ndela to return, but his schedule was uncertain and Joel was excited. "Rachael is my wife. Her pastor married us before we returned!"

"Joel, you ornery, young scoundrel!" Ben's voice was crisp and sounded unkind. Joel's face fell and everyone turned to stare at Ben, but by then Ben's face had broken into an incredibly broad, heartwarming smile. "Joel, this is fantastic!" Dr. Ben embraced his *son* tightly and beamed like a proud father. He then took Rachel's hands in his and looked deeply into her eyes. "I don't know you yet, but I see you are a very beautiful. Also, I see kindness in your eyes. If Joel loves you, then you must be a very special young woman!"

After they all had shared congratulation, they grudgingly returned to their all-consuming issue—their encounter with imminent disaster was too near.

Their fifth day of preparation was a Sunday, and they decided to free the morning from their tough schedule. Those who desired church services could do so and the others could have some quiet time for reading or reflection. Zack and Angela decided to take time for companionship and attempt to completely forget all the pressures. So far, several very solid strategies had been formulated. One of the plans was for Joel and Rachael to travel by motorcycle to nearby villages. They all felt certain there were many families in these villages who had relatives or friends whom had been beaten, tortured, or killed by these pillaging rebels.

If organized, they would fight to prevent the chaos and destruction to their own villages. Their recruits were to include only those men who were physically able and seemed committed. Each man would be requested to collect pottery, tom-toms, ivory horns, and also whatever weapons they had. Joel and Rachael were given seven to ten days to perform their recruitment and return. Their *war plans* also demanded that they evacuate the Mission Station and allow the insurgents to take it over. One fact they were counting on was that Colonel Ching did not know that the only available water during the dry season had to be carried from springs far down in the valley. It required a strong man at least three hours to descend to the floor of the gorge, fill his containers, and struggle back up the steep slope. When the colonel had attacked before, it had been during the rains and the barrels had always been full.

On the following Saturday, Zack took David and Nganda and six other men and made the demanding climb down into the valley to survey the area. The two springs lay about one-quarter mile apart. The cool, fresh water flowed directly from the rocky hillside, forming a small pond that flowed into a small stream. Nobody seemed to know where the water came from; it had just always come out of the rocks. There were some snow-capped mountains in eastern Congo, but they were three thousand miles away. The fresh, clean water had always been available and during the four months of the dry season served the people well.

The first three days of the week were filled with a flurry of activity for Zack and his men. They made numerous trips to the springs, carrying buckets of water with which they filled multiple barrels. These were then loaded into their Land Rover. They hauled these large containers to a thick grove of trees a few miles to the south. After ten such trips, they felt they had cached enough water to last several days. This finished, they returned to the springs in the valley. It took a full afternoon of grueling labor to shovel enough rocks and dirt to block the springs. The pools that were formed would become rancid very quickly. But to facilitate the spoiling of the water, some of the men cut branches containing green berries and threw them into the water. Almost immediately these produced one of the foulest odors Zack had ever smelled.

So far, they had implemented two phases of Gideon's conspiracy. First, they had sent a team to enlist some of the villager. Second, they had interrupted the enemy's water supply. Now they had to devise the most intricate and important part of the plan. In the Bible account, Gideon had destroyed the altar of Baal, the enemy's god. Their enemy's god was Ching. This fanatical leader still had great supernatural control over his army. There was one aspect of their plan that had to be done but they all loathed—Pascal would have to be the one to make the first encounter with Colonel Ching. Pascal was African and an American. Also, he was educated, articulate, and enigmatic; everything the colonel wanted to be. Already, they had begun to paint the Land Rover to appear like an official vehicle. One talented man had even decorated the door with a close reproduction of the emblem of the American Embassy. The plot now was for Pascal and a select few to leave the Station and meet the rebels before their arrival at Kikungu. Time was moving rapidly and a catastrophic moment in an anonymous chronicle was about to occur. It was known only to God and cared about by almost no one except the tiny group of people whose lives had become strangely entangled.

CHAPTER 30

Colonel Ching spent several days in seclusion. Only his idols, fétiches, and hideous spirits surrounded him. Two prominent situations had tormented him for several days. Primary was the growing unrest and disloyalty among the men. Second, he was beginning to recognize he had strayed far from his original crusade to complete his Marxist-Lenin program. When he formed his army, he had desired to defeat the leadership of Patrice Lumumba, who, contrary to common thought, still had close relations with Belgium. When Ching had first begun recruiting and training the soldiers, he had the burning need to bring the teachings of Karl Marx to Central Africa. He had learned while studying in China that one of the great teachings of Marx was that all history of mankind reflected the struggle of the social classes.

Marx advocated that the conflict between the two classes, owner and worker, must lead to a revolution where the working class would triumph and the bourgeoisie (owners, rich) would no longer exist. Karl Marx dreamed of a world revolution, and Colonel Ching wanted to be a part of it. Ching was now wondering when and how had he strayed from his great yearning to lead a widespread revolt against the current popular, but unstable government of President Kasa-Vubu and Prime Minister Lumumba. However, he still believed that his foundation remained, and if he had become a little sidetracked, it was only because the multiple raids and plundering of the villages were necessary to finance his great movement.

Soon, he would move against larger cities, such as Stanleyville and the surrounding area, accumulating wealth and new human resources. Then, he would be able to march eastward, following the Congo River to the seat of government at Leopoldville. There was no doubt in his mind that he would lead a liberation army to the very steps of the capital of the Congo. However, that was the future. Now the primary action was to gain back the control of his men. For several days he had worked out a plot that he had already begun implementing. The day before, he had dispatched one of his most trusted officers eastward with information so secret they were the only ones to whom it was known. That evening he had arranged for a *state dinner* with his officers and a few *trusted* enlisted men. Actually, the colonel could trust no one absolutely. *What is trust?* He thought. *Trust is a logical decision based on current information that the one you have trust in has shown the least suspicion to be a traitor.*

This banquet would be exceptional with freshly killed antelope, rice, and fresh luku. They would consume fine bourbon whiskey that he had long ago confiscated and hidden. They would feast and drink like royalty, and then afterward he would include them in shaping strategy. He would make them feel like officers with authority. Like most followers of the Marxist Doctrine, Ching felt no contradiction in dining like an emperor, in the midst of poverty, and at the same time proclaiming that all men should live equally.

Lieutenant Lobongo had known the colonel for many years. He had always admired him and trusted his ability to lead. He also totally feared him. Recently, he had noticed worrisome changes in his leader, and during the last couple of weeks, his qualms had begun to increase greatly. When Colonel Ching called the secret meeting, Lobongo was instantly filled with dread. However, their discussion was cordial, professional, and he was impressed with the colonel's comprehensive and extraordinary plan. The lieutenant knew that the turmoil and suspicion within the soldiers was obvious to many, but something he had not considered was the fact that Colonel Ching was so perceptive—but his eerie proposal showed it. Lobongo was in total agreement with the reasons for the colonel's strategy, but his part in it terrified him. He left late that night while most of the soldiers were sleeping. As he departed camp, he purposely passed the colonel's hut. A ghostly glow came from within, and he was certain that he heard deep, rumbling sounds that resembled that of a leopard. A lesser man would have been frozen into inaction. It took all the courage Lobongo possessed, along with his morbid fear of disobeying the colonel, to drive him into the forest and the darkness.

The leopard men were a myth, or so believed the mondeles—those of the white skin. For centuries in central Africa, tales of this half man, half leopard had terrorized children and adults alike. Some believed them to have their origin from a powerful Nganga (witch doctor), who copulated with a leopard. Others believed that certain individuals, those who possessed the Ndoki, had the capability of transforming themselves into wild beasts in order to punish a person guilty of murder, incest, or who were causing sickness. Of course, the early missionaries presupposed that they were merely villagers in disguise—they were just mere men clothed with the yellow-lined bark of a tree painted with black spots and spirals, emulating the pattern of leopard skin. The headdress, made of the same materials, was constructed to cover their heads and fasten around the neck. It had small openings for the eyes and nose. The garment reached to the waist and was then anchored by a rope to which was attached the tail of a leopard. These leopard men devised a small earthenware bell that could produce a startlingly real imitation of the leopard's low growl. In addition, metal *hands* were fastened to the wrist upon which were attached sets of claws. These claws were used to scratch and tear flesh from the victims. Whether fact or fiction, the leopard men struck terror into the hearts of the natives.

Typically, human devices used to produce superstitious fear, if effective, became widespread throughout a country. But strangely, these leopard men were never seen beyond the Bandundu region along the Kwilu River.

Ching had assigned to Lobongo the job of finding these mystical creatures.

CHAPTER 31

Colonel Ching was actively driving his officers into a more cohesive unit, and they, in turn, were organizing the enlisted men. He had forbidden the use of any form of alcohol and drugs. His order had gone out for them to wash and repair their uniforms and to straighten up their encampment. Soon they would start being a military unit again. During the next few days, his officers arranged the men into divisions. Early morning exercises and marches were organized and discipline became firm. Ironically, the men responded to the rigid demands with renewed self-esteem and enthusiasm. By the end of only five days, their guns had been cleaned, tattered boots shined, and uniforms washed and stitched. At the end of the second week they were ready to move on to the Kikungu and more of the white man's wealth.

At the present, Colonel Ching had received no news from Lobongo. But it did not matter as much. He no longer needed the leopard men to create fear in his soldiers. If they started to march now, they could reach the Station in about two weeks. The moon would be full then. There would be no better time to turn the leopard men loose on the inhabitants there rather than on his men. These creatures could enter the village of Kikungu and the Mission Station first, making things much easier for his army.

At approximately the same time the colonel was completely reorganizing his troops, Pascal, Pastor Ndela, Nganda, and their fresh driver, Sobito, were loading the newly designed Land Rover. They now knew, with relative certainty, the location of the rebel army. They were sure they could find the road they were on. The plan was to encounter them about a ten-day march from the Mission, which would mean approximately a two-day drive. Their campaign was well planned, and they were feeling reasonably confident. If they could pull it off, they anticipated making contact with the rebels, introducing themselves to the colonel and his officers and then deceive them into thinking they were representatives of the United States. They had to appear to be genuinely interested in the rebel's efforts and make Ching believe they would support him. If this could be accomplished, they might convince him, along with three or four of his most trusted leaders, to travel in the Land Rover back to Station with them. If the deception worked, they would isolate them from the main army—the most crucial ingredient of the entire plan.

Conviction is a fragile thing and so easily manipulated by unexpected events. At the time of preparing for this vital encounter with the rebel leaders, they knew nothing of the leopard men. However, the leopard men knew nothing of Joel Lusombo. Even more intriguing was that neither group knew of the *dogs of war* who had been engaged and assigned by the Belgium government to search and destroy a one Colonel Ching and to disperse his rebel army. These mercenaries cared nothing of the politics of the country or the inhuman actions of this revolutionary leader. This group of men was a highly trained and disciplined unit that had established a worldwide reputation for getting the job done.

Pascal and his team moved slowly, but steadily. Their route, built by the Belgium some twenty years ago, had deteriorated to being multiple ruts that hardly resembled a road. Deep potholes, soft sand, and fallen trees made travel tedious. Four days before their departure, they had sent out two scouts. They were trying hard to leave nothing to chance. Now they received word that they should rendezvous with the insurgent army in about thirty-six hours. Pascal was becoming increasingly aware of the tension building in his group. It was something he felt more than saw. He had anticipated this because of all the terrifying accounts that had circulated about this curse of central Africa. But what he had not expected were the terrific struggles intensifying within him. For years, he had prided himself for being able to remain composed during any situation, no matter how critical. However, during the past several hours he had found himself frequently gritting his teeth, the muscles of his neck were tight, and he was aware of a mild increase in his heart rate. These were all symptoms of anxiety, he knew, but there was something more—he was also experiencing pure, unadulterated fear! But he was certain that these feelings were to be expected. However, the fear was strange, more of a *free floating* anxiety that seemed to have its origin above and beyond their circumstances.

He had not felt fear such as this since he was boy. It was reminiscent of the times of hiding in the forest with his family or when he would try to get way from the cruel, inhuman actions of his brother. Pascal shivered despite the heat. Cold sweat tracked its way between his shoulder blades. He was experiencing an overpowering need to escape. A foul aura surrounded him, and he had the irrational thought that ravenous, demonic forces were poised to devour him. It seemed that all his intellect, strength, and abilities were being crushed, leaving him vacant and defeated. Silently, Pascal began to pray more earnestly than he had ever before in his life. Verses from Psalm 34 came to him. "I sought the Lord and he answered me: he delivered me from my fears."[2] Within moments, his strength began to return, and the mysterious fear started to abate. The experience of total devastation was fading, but the muscle tightness and palpitations remained. He was nearly in control again except for a persistent feeling—the unbearable premonition of impending doom!

---

2   Psalm 34:4

CHAPTER 32

On the evening prior to Pascal and his team's departure, Angela, Joel, and Rachael spent the evening together. As Angela became more comfortable with them, she realized how deeply founded they both were in Christianity. Joel had suffered incredibly during the past several months but seemed to have no bitterness. On the contrary, he revealed peacefulness and a forgiving spirit. She was also impressed with Joel's intensity and resolve. In addition, she found Rachael to be very special; affection and gentleness radiated from her. Angela grew quickly to love them both. She was so thankful for these brief moments she had with the young couple. Interludes like these borrowed a little serenity away from the fright of their rapidly encroaching destiny.

Suddenly, a young Congolese man pounded excitedly on their door, disrupting their short-lived calm. He was unknown to any of them but spoke Kilunda rapidly. Joel kindly invited him in, offered him cool water, and gave him a few moments to gather himself. They talked for several minutes, and then Joel excused himself as he led the visitor out. When he returned, his face was grim. "He is telling me that a group of the leopard men are coming toward us. They are fully dressed for violence and murder! These *animals* have not been seen in the region for a long time!" The stories about the leopard men were well known to both Angela and Rachael. Both young women shivered instinctively.

"Why are these horrible creatures suddenly appearing now?" Angela's voice held a terrible uneasiness. She and Joel looked at each other, their thoughts obviously on the same track. "Do you think Colonel Ching could have something to do with their sudden reappearance?"

"I was thinking exactly that," Joel replied. "This has to be more than a coincidence. But why? Why should he want to send them against us unless he thinks that there is danger here for him? Do you think he has heard that there are white people here?"

"Yes! Why else would these awful beasts come forth at this time? I don't think that they have been seen for several years. However, if this is true, Pascal and the others should be warned. But there isn't much time! We must find Dr. Ben and tell him!"

They found Ben at the hospital in the middle of rounds on the tuberculosis ward. They watched him for a few moments, captivated how calmly he moved from one gaunt and gruesome patient to another. *How does one ever get use to the dreadful odor and the impact of seeing those emaciated bodies?* Angela reflected silently.

"We are sorry to interrupt you, Dr. Ben, but this is important!"

"No problem. Please, let's step outside where the air is fresher."

After they recounted the news to him, Ben was silent for quite some time before speaking. "Knowing this colonel Ching as I do, I doubt if he would actually recruit the leopard men to attack us. I am certain that he knows he has the forces enough to destroy us even with a few expatriates here. And if he believed there were government forces here, he would bypass us and strike elsewhere. My thought would be that he has engaged the leopard men for other reasons. I am certain it would take someone like him to activate these creatures. The way he has been losing control of his soldiers, I wonder if he is going to use these creatures to manipulate them. However, I cannot be sure of that."

Can you think of any way we can hold back or prevent these *animals* from coming?" Ben asked, but before they could answer, he continued, "We have about three or four days before we must evacuate. Some of the male nurses have volunteered to remain and continue caring for our patients. They will cooperate with the rebels as best they can. Hopefully, this will diminish the danger to them. None of the staff or patients know where we will be and so even if interrogated they cannot tell. We are taking all the women and children with us. If the colonel's plan is to use the leopard men to create fear in his men, or attach us, they must do so within the next few hours. Joel, what are your thoughts?"

"I know a powerful sorcerer that might be able to help us. I know him all too well, I am afraid." Joel briefly related his experience with the *witch doctor* when he lay so critically wounded. "He might have the power to turn the leopard men away. But I must share one thing; it is the power of Jesus Christ we must trust in. My grandfather had an old saying," Joel lapsed into French:

"L'éléphant ne peut pas pourchasser par une scorpion? Ou bien, Jésus, fils de Dieu, peut-il être chasser par n'importe quel moyen de sorcellerie? Certainement pas l'éléphant! Encore moins Jésus!" (The elephant cannot be chased away by the scorpion. In the same way, Jesus, the Son of God, cannot be driven away by means of sorcery. It is certain for the elephant; still more about Jesus).

"Thank you for sharing that, Joel. The sorcerer might be an answer to the situation, but I am not going to let you put yourself in any unnecessary danger! Can you trust this shaman?" Ben asked with concern.

"No, I don't think I can trust him, but I feel that he will respond to my appeal." Joel then spent a few minutes trying to explain why he thought the *witch doctor* might feel compelled to help him.

Ben stayed in deep thought for several moments, and then said, "I pray that you are correct. It is not like we have a lot of choices." Ben stared in to space for what seemed an eternity before speaking. "At the first sign of danger you get the blazes out of there! Promise?"

"I promise."

"Okay, Joel. Well, I don't have much money, but hopefully I can find enough to entice the Ngangu to come back with you or in some way get him to use his powers."

"With the hospital's motorcycle, I can reach his village within a day. It will take time for the necessary negotiation, but I can probably be back by late tomorrow." Joel was excited but guarded. "I will leave within the hour."

Joel turned to look at his new wife. The heartrending glance exchanged between them tore at Angela's heart.

The sun seemed to have reached its pinnacle more hastily than usual. Pascal and the others were sweating profusely as they struggled to remove a fallen tree from their path. They were extremely cautious because it seemed the trunk of the tree had been recently cut. Without forewarning, an armed man appeared on the road a few yards from them. He wore a ragged military shirt, torn jeans, but sturdy boots. Several days' beard partially concealed his face. He had a cartridge belt over his shoulder, a revolver on his right hip, and a large knife sheathed on the other. The automatic rifle balanced in his left hand was indifferently pointed in their direction. He was a small, agile appearing man of indeterminate age. He had the complexion of Eastern Europe. His forehead was deeply carved with furrows that were intersected in the middle by a single vertical groove. His eyes were dark, cruel almonds that also displayed intelligence. A circular scar over his right temple reminded Zack of a skin graft, but he doubted that it was. He was obviously powerful despite his slight stature. Within seconds, three more men appeared from the brush to their left and then four more on their right. They were all similarly dressed and armed.

"Do you speak English?" The dark man's voice was sharp and accented.

"Je parle un peu le Francé and a little English." Pascal said, deliberately trying to keep the stranger off balance. "The other men here speak French and Kituba." Pascal nodded toward the others, deliberately failing to mention Zack as English speaking. He did not exactly know why he did so. He then walked toward the man in the road, his hands raised.

"May I ask who you are?"

The swarthy man in the trail glared at him and then said, "You can, but first, *you* are going to answer some questions." Pascal continued to close the distance between them arousing no apparent apprehension in the man.

"We are from the missionary village of Kikungu. It is about thirty kilometers (eighteen miles) to the west. We have come here to contact a rebel soldier and his troops." At this, Pascal noted a slight movement of the man's eyebrow, nothing more. About five feet separated them when Pascal suddenly stumbled slightly. This caused the man's eyes to shift slightly, but it was enough. Within the next second the man found himself in a steel trap, his arm jammed up his back in a powerful grip. His own knife pressed deeply against his throat, Pascal was almost lifting the man from the ground with his twisted arm. His pain was intense.

"Tell your men to drop their weapons or I *will* cut your throat!" The severity in Pascal's voice carried no doubt of his resolve. "Unless you are part of Colonel Ching's army or bandits bent on attacking the Mission Station, I mean you no harm."

"We are neither!" the man growled through gritted teeth. "Then tell your men to drop their guns and stand together in the road!"

"Do as he says! Lower your guns and come over here!" The captured man's voice broke as he fought the pain while giving orders to his men. He spoke in two languages, first French, and the second Pascal thought might be Polish. Noticeably, the men were hesitant but then obeyed their apparent leader. Pascal released some pressure on his prisoner's arm but kept the vicious knife pressed firmly against his throat. Sullenly, the others dropped their guns and came as a group to stand in front of Pascal and Zack, who now had moved to his side. Zack had his revolver aimed lethally at them.

"I will ask you again; who are you and what are you doing here? And please, no lies, we do not have the time." The severity of Pascal's voice was unmistakable.

"We have been hired by the Belgium government to stop a certain Colonel Ching. Belgium wants them defeated and this colonel neutralized!" Pascal believed him. He had seen mercenaries in the past and had little doubt these men were who he said they were. However, caution did not permit him to drop his guard. "You, apparently, are in charge." Pascal's voice was a stern whisper.

"Yes."

"How many of you are there?"

"We started with fifteen, but a couple of them got hurt. We left them behind to get care."

"I assume you are well armed."

"Yeah, well enough, I think, but then we are not certain just how many or what kind of weapons the colonel possesses."

"Are you American?"

"I fought with the Americans, if that is what you mean. It was during the Korean conflict."

"What rank?" Zack interjected.

"I was a captain when I retired. In the Green Beret, if that means anything. Then I bounced around Asia and Europe for a while trying to decide what to do. That's when I formed this group of former soldiers, mostly Marine and Army Special Forces, into a private militia. We hire out to countries that need our particular talents."

"Believe it or not," he snarled, "we try to connect with only causes we believe in."

"Where in America are you from?" Zack asked firmly.

"Originally from New York City. My parents were Armenian immigrants. We moved to Boise, Idaho when I was in high school."

"Alright, monsieur, I am going to release you now. I will take the chance because I believe you. It seems that we might be able to help each other." Pascal slowly released the force on the knife at the man's throat and let go of his arm. The man turned carefully to face Pascal, messaging his shoulder. His eyes contained reluctant respect as he asked, "Where did you learn to pull that off?" He paused for an awkward moment. "It's been a long time since anyone beat me like that." A peculiar smile touched his lips. "That's why I have lived this long!"

Pascal grinned faintly, "I will tell you on another occasion, when we have more time."

Even though there were several hours of daylight left, Pascal and Zack decided on an extended stop. He asked their companions to arrange a meal. In a short time they were able to have food prepared for the small assembly of soldiers. Pascal and Zack discussed the situation in some detail with the group leader—Varstan. They learned he had been named after an ancient Armenian military hero. Varstan was joined by his second in command, a huge, muscular, blond Belgium who had a large, thick scar on his neck that pulled his chin toward his left collarbone. The scar tissue distorted otherwise flawless features. Varstan introduced him as Mercier Raynaud.

The Americans shared their food with these adventurers who were enormously hungry and very appreciative. While they ate, Zack found he quickly connected with Varstan and Mercier because of his own Special Forces background. When Vars, as his second in command called him, learned some of Zack's background, they also became a little more trusting. Soon they were sharing information and began to reveal their individual plans for fighting the rebel army.

As Pascal's people were cleaning up after the meal, Varstan's men relaxed. Some slept and others lounged in the shorter grass cleaning weapons. Shortly before sunset, these four men had formulated a reasonable strategy, or so it seemed to them. Pascal and his group would continue the proposed plan they had formulated. They decided they would still try to get the colonel and a few of his trusted officers to ride back to the Mission Station in their Land Rover. If they could rendezvous as planned, this would leave Ching's soldiers about a two or three day march behind them. If this worked, the time would be used to make the colonel feel comfortable and trusting. Then it was decided that Vars, Mercier, and the others would go north to join forces with the villagers. Zack describe his *Gideon plan* to the captain and the Belgium. Vars was captivated by it and wanted to know how he had come up with such a tactic. Zack told him, expecting ridicule. Vars, however, was quiet for several moments and then said, more to himself than to the others, "I knew that I had heard or read that somewhere before."

Both groups slept restlessly. Early the next morning, before dawn was absolute, they broke their makeshift camp. The two parties separated feeling relatively confident about their plans. By this time tomorrow, Pascal, Zack, and their brave Congolese colleagues should come face to face with the *curse* of central Congo. Very soon they would encounter the brutal soldiers and their leader, who was either a tortured man or a satanic fiend. They were deliberately moving toward events they had no way of predicting or even imagining. Were they preparing to fight against flesh and blood or a crazed devil?

CHAPTER 33

W hile the *dogs of war* were enjoying their first passable meal in weeks, Joel was in a terrifying encounter with the great Ngangu Ankisi. He had found him in the same village in which he had healed his wounds. The village was far more neglected than Joel remembered—decaying grass roofs and crumbling walls spoke of disregard and abandonment. The odor of sweat and smoke permeated the air. The villagers were dressed in tattered clothes; many appeared chronically ill. But they were kind and gracious to him and took him immediately to the celebrated medicine man. He sat in a hand carved wooden chair on the dirt floor in the middle of his hut. Dark shadows in the room added to the ominous aura of the specter before Joel. The Ngangu's lips did not seem to move as he spoke. The voice was deep and rasping; Joel had difficulty determining from where the voice came.

"You have come because of the leopard men," he stated. "But why do you think I can help you?"

"I have seen and experienced your mighty power, and I believe you can use your influence over the spirits for good and for evil." Joel managed to keep his voice calm. The medicine man was deadly quiet for a long time, and Joel had finally decided to leave when the Ngangu spoke.

"I cannot deny you help, Joel; the spirits will not allow me to. When I saved your life, part of my soul entered you, and now I must defend you to protect me."

Joel sighed deeply. He had guessed correctly. God had answered his prayers!

"Tell me, what danger do these *animals* cause you?" Joel felt the question was pointless. The Ngangu already knew the answer. But he went ahead and rapidly related their situation. When he finished, he sat in silence until the *witch doctor* spoke.

"You must leave now. I will help you!"

Joel wanted to ask questions. He needed to find out how and when the help would come. But instead he got up to leave. He stopped at the doorway and turned around to ask questions, but the Ngangu Ankisi was gone.

Night had advanced on Joel with a cavernous gloom. There was a chill in the air, and the old wounds in his chest began to ache. With the pain came menacing memories of his first encounter with this healer; this man whom he had prayed was a prophet and not Ndoki. Joel's lean, muscular body felt fragile and vulnerable as he lifted the motorcycle. The route was difficult during the day but would be nearly impossible at night, particularly in darkness like this. He knew that if were not for God's presence with him, he could easily become disoriented or would succumb to his childhood fears of evil spirits, and the Ndoki. He spoke aloud for anyone to hear—an intense prayer to God. Then he started the motorcycle's old engine.

◇◇◇◇◇◇◇◇

Angela and Rachael sat in the shade of a giant bamboo tree trying to stay comfortable in the midday sun. The village in which they had chosen to hide was at a much lower altitude than the mission. It lay in a valley near a rapidly moving river. The heat and humidity were oppressive. Rachael sat with her knees clasped in her arms. She was near tears as she retold the story of finding Joel near death and how she had nursed him back to health. While they talked, the mamas came and went with their daily activities. They frequently stopped by to offer care to these guests in their midst. The elders from the Mission Station had chosen this village in which to hide for several reasons. One was that they knew that the soldiers liked to avoid the river valleys. Many Africans had learned that people became ill and die much more in the lowlands along rivers. Also, they all *knew* that the bad spirits lurked in the forests surrounding the waterways.

This was the mondele's third day in the village of Kinsantu. Angela and Rachael were sturdy women with great faith, but they were becoming more and more anxious.

"I worry so much about Joel."

Angela put her arm over Rachael's shoulder as she shared. Rachael was instantly comforted and deeply appreciative of Angela's compassion.

Rachael continued. "Joel is strong and very capable, but there are so many dangers on his path! And I know the powers of the great Ngangu Ankisi. He can do terrible things to people and call forth the Nkuyu, the evil ones who have died but return to do dreadful things to the living."

Many Christians would have been opposed to such discussion from a fellow Christian. But Angela understood and respected Rachael's background of superstition. Angela herself had wrestled with the thought that if the presence of God's Holy Spirit—a force never seen but often felt—was a reality, then why was there not the opposite force present in the world? She believed there was but also knew that the power of Jesus Christ far surpassed all others. After struggling with this for a long time, she had finally left it all in God's hands. She did not fear the evils spirits as Rachael and others did, but then she had not been tormented by them in childhood—as they had been.

Angela's heart was overjoyed when Rachael bashfully opened her tattered Bible and began to read from Psalms. "Let all those who take refuge in God be glad, let them always sing for joy. Spread your protection over them so that those who love your name may rejoice in You."

Angela and Rachael got up from their chairs and knelt on the damp leaves in the shade of a great tree and prayed. Neither knew that Joel had entered the menacing forest on his return trip. All they recognized was the desire to pray for him. Rachael's prayer was unpretentious and filled with her intense love for Joel and her profound trust in God. Angela also prayed earnestly for Joel. She had found herself drawn so quickly to this quiet, godly young man with the intensity of youth and the wisdom of the elders. Her heart went out to Rachael, who was experiencing love for the first and only time in her life.

The early missionaries had made some mistakes through their zeal to share Jesus Christ with these people living in darkness. But among the magnificent things they had done was to elevate young girls like Rachael from the status of slaves and objects of unbridled lust to equality and the full beauty of womanhood.

Tears flowed down both their cheeks as they spilled out their hearts to God for Joel's strength and protection. As they stood with their hands clasped tightly, they suddenly saw Ben standing near them. His head was bowed in reverence to their prayers.

"Dr. Ben, we did not notice you! We did not know you had arrived. Forgive us please!"

"No, Angela, it is I that should ask forgiveness. I should have let you know I was here, but I did not want to disturb your prayers." Even though it was not been long since they had been apart, they embraced as long missing friends. Anxiety and fear entangles time into meaningless periods where moments can seem like ages and ages seem like a moment.

"Have you received news from Joel?" Ben asked.

"No nothing!" Fear pierced Rachael's voice. "I think he should have reached the Ngangu by now. Oh, we are so frightened for him!"

"He has to be in great danger, we know," Angela interjected. "The route is difficult and extremely treacherous, but he knows the dangers of the route. We are not so worried about that. Mostly we are terribly frightened by the possibility of him running into some renegade soldiers. Also, we do not trust the Ngangu!"

"He will return safely. Through your prayers, God will protect him!" Ben spoke with a certainty that comforted Rachael and Angela. "Now, I came to tell you that I am returning to Kikungu."

"Please don't go! You must not!" Angela and Rachael blurted out almost simultaneously.

"Why must you go to the Station? You will be in such great danger! The patients will be safe for a few days!"

"My dear friends, you know I must. But not only because of my patients, but because I must be there when Colonel Ching arrives."

"But why? He will either kill you or throw you in prison. Why must you meet him?"

"I don't believe he will kill me or imprison me. First of all, he would be afraid to because of the presence of what we hope he believes are foreign dignitaries. Secondly, I think he must fear me a little because of the way I escaped from him. Do you remember how terrified I told you he was when Joel rescued me? I think he must still believe in the spirits that attacked him and his men that night. Thirdly, he must have sick and injured men who need attention. I will offer that medical aid. Some of his men know me and trust me. I sincerely believe these things will keep me safe, at least long enough to carry out our plan."

Angela and Rachael were not as certain of Dr. Ben's safety as he, but they also knew that there was no way to change his mind. They both embraced him tightly before he departed, trusting he would reach Kikungu before the darkness had become too ruthless. Rachael spent the remainder of the afternoon and evening helping the village woman gather wood, pound manioc, and start the evening fires. Despite the heat of the day, when the sun disappeared behind the curtain of darkness, the night air would bring a disquieting chill.

Angela and Rachael had consumed their meal and were sitting by the open flames of the fire outside their hut. They had shared many experiences and feelings, and the time had passed swiftly. The village was quiet except for a few voices coming from nearby huts. Suddenly, fear crept into Angela; she sensed, rather than saw anything. All of a sudden, the silence was pierced by a deep, throaty sound. It was unmistakably the snarl of a leopard. Then there was another, and then another. From all directions of the village, murky images began to form in the darkness. Rachael muffled a terrified cry and drew back toward the wall of the hut. As the ghostly silhouettes became clearer, the women saw what appeared to be the glowing, sinister eyes of large cats. But yet, they walked on legs—the leopard men had arrived!

The encounter with the village and with the white woman was very accidental. As per the directions given them by *le Diable Noire's* courier, they had gathered from their villages to convene in a sinister rite that few had ever seen and only the rare had experienced. Three days and nights had been spent calling upon the powers of darkness and the roving spirits of leopards. Powerful drinks and hallucinogenic drugs accompanied evil incantations and furious dances. By the end of the third day, this small group of ferocious man-animals slept the sleep of the totally drained. The following evening, they left the secreted camp fully clad in their carefully prepared and menacing attire. The six men would sleep by day and travel by night to execute their task—to terrify Colonel Ching's soldiers into submission. The unexpected meeting with this small village was to them an exhilarating digression. However, the presence of the white woman was a problem and could be dangerous to them. To deal with this threat, they determined that no one be left alive to tell what happened.

Now, as the hideous beasts approached the two women, Angela stood brashly, her jaw firmly set and her eyes burning with defiance. Rachael arose on trembling legs to stand beside her friend. Angela took her hand and squeezed it tightly, trying to impart courage that she herself did not feel. Within seconds, two of the repulsive creatures towered over them. Nearby, others blew their earthenware reproducing the deep growl of the leopard. Never had Angela been so devastated by fear—or the certainty of death. Simultaneously, the two fiends raised their brutally clawed hands in order to sweep down, shredding flesh from the faces and bodies of these frail women. Angela and Rachael stood unyielding before the attackers, awaiting their destruction and death. They could hear the screams from others of the village as the same fate moved toward them. Suddenly, horrifying snarls erupted from the dark of the forest edge and rapidly moving shapes were seen. Yellow eyes come forward from all directions.

A mature male leopard can weigh as much as 73 kilograms (160 lbs) and measure 2.7 meters (9 feet), but the huge cats that attacked that night seemed to be much larger. Angela knew the power and ferocity of leopards but inexplicably felt no fear. The devastation was over in minutes and the two women and village people stared in horror as ten or more male leopards milled around, snapping at one another as they tore the flesh from the bodies of the leopard imposters. In very little time, they had dragged the mutilated remains of the leopard men to the forest and into caches far above the ground.

"How? Why? How is this possible?" Rachael murmured more to herself than to Angela. Then she stopped. She suddenly knew and smiled. "It was Joel. Joel must have reached the great Ngangu. It must of have been he that called forth the real leopards. Why else would they have attacked just the leopard men?"

"Do you think this means Joel is safe? He must be; why else would the medicine man have helped him," Angela said, hopefully answering her own question.

How unexpectedly and rapidly can stark fear turn to hope and hope to praise! The two young women hugged and whispered prayers of thanks to God. Both also knew that exaltation can quickly turn to anguish and anguish to desperation. However, the wonderful thing felt by both was the security they had in God.

Well into the night they worked to find the remains of the grotesque men so that they could give them a proper burial. These two women, along with the entire village, were thankful beyond measure for the destruction of the creatures. There were some, however, who did not understand why the mondele and her friend wanted to bury the creatures. "Leave them to the jackals and vultures!" Nevertheless, the few that helped them understood. They could not celebrate their deaths, no matter how evil they were. They were still human beings who were now lost for eternity. They might have become part of God's family if they could have only heard His Word.

It was near dawn when their grisly work was finished. They had only briefly slept when awakened by an unfamiliar sound; a grating noise that seemed to stop and start. Only after it came closer did it sound more like a motor. Breathlessly, they recognized it as that of a motorcycle. They both rushed to the doorway in time to see it and its rider burst from the forest edge. Joel's gestures could be seen even from the distance. There may be no more powerful emotion than that experienced when suffering changes to joy and when loss finds reunion. After the tears of happiness dried, Joel shared his experiences with the celebrated Ngangu Ankisi. They, in turn, told him of the leopard men and the attack by the large cats. Yes, he was sure that it was the medicine man that had sent the large cats to save them. He also shared with them the reasons why the Ngangu felt he had to do so. The three slept very little of what remained of the night. The following morning, as daylight dissolved the cool mist from around them, they shared excitedly as they drank viscous coffee and nibbled on parched, tasteless bread.

"We observe the hawk only when he is bearing away a prey," Varstan shared an African proverb he had learned months ago. "I'm sure this Colonel Ching is a clever fellow. We might think he is several days' march away, but we cannot be sure he has not sent scouts far ahead of him. It seems to me we should watch our backs and flanks at all times."

"I appreciate your thoughts," Zack said, "and it is possible that he has moved some of his army closer than we realize. Moreover, I agree, he might have scouts out. If he does, we must detect them first and *neutralize* them. Hopefully, we can capture them before they would have time to report back to the Colonel." Zack found he emphasized the word *capture* not *neutralize*. Was he getting soft?

"I will rotate some of my men around the perimeters. They will know exactly what to do." Varstan spoke with assurance.

"Tomorrow," Zack said, "I will leave to pull the village people together— those willing and able to help us. I know that many of the men have already collected some of the necessary items such as ram's horns, pottery, and drums— —enough to make ol' Gideon proud." Zack had a slight, roguish smile. "Also, these men have managed to find some weapon—primitive as they are." Zack grinned to himself as he thought what his marine buddies would say if they saw him leading a rag-tag unit armed with spears, machetes, ancient single shot rifles, and carrying pieces of broken vases, drums, and goat horns. Nevertheless, they would be ready for the attack!

◇◇◇◇◇◇◇◇◇

Much of Colonel Ching's intensity had lessened. He had not anticipated the rapid change in his men. It seemed that overnight they had become soldiers. They were now a skilled fighting force! He sat in the shade of a large banyan tree dressed in full military uniform. He calmly observed the troops carry out various maneuvers; bayonet thrusts, target practice, and hand-to-hand combat. His chief lieutenant, Mumga, had asked for three more days for intense training exercises, and he then felt the men would be ready. When a man from a town west of them arrived with the news that the leopard men had been killed, Ching felt little regret or disappointment. Nor did he question the reported cause of their death by wild animals. He did not need them now. What he did not know was that Ben had sent the village *runner* to deliver the news to the Colonel's men. Very little would disturb Colonel Ching, for he was feeling too self-assured, almost manic in his certainty that he would soon be advancing to the very steps of power in Leopoldville. He was now far too powerful—no one could stop him!

Pascal and Varstan halted their troops long before sunset. They did not want to venture further than about a two-day drive from the Mission Station. The less time they spent with the colonel, the better chance they had of pulling off their scam. In addition, by being stationary they could better protect their perimeter. The reconnaissance they had deployed would be returning within the next few hours, giving them information about location and composition of the rebel force. As they waited, the two men rehearsed their plans with David Mbote, Maludi, Pastor Ndela, and the others. It was essential that Ching's soldiers detect none of Varstan's men. The presence of several white men would raise too much suspicion and would bring disaster. Neither Zack nor Varstan thought the colonel would use scouting parties once they rendezvoused and began the voyage back to the Mission. They anticipated that he and his group would feel there was no danger. In the meantime, Varstan's men would be required to live in the forest, stationed in key areas around them. They were tough, hardened soldiers who found this responsibility to be of little hardship.

CHAPTER 35

At the approximate time Pascal and Varstan were planning their confrontation with the insurgent army, Angela and Rachael had just finished the burial of the remains of the leopard men. The two women had spent as much time as possible with the village leaders, and now they were preparing to make the one-day walk to Kikungu. Only two of the community leaders knew anything of their strategy. They were prepared for a few of the leaders from the Station to come soon to obtain a portion of the food and water stored there. Joel would be going ahead of them on the motorcycle, leaving Angela and Rachael to make the shorter but much more grueling trip on foot. Following a well traveled path cross-country the distance was only twenty kilometers (twelve miles), but much of it was over rough slopes and required a great deal of difficult rock climbing and forging rapid flowing streams. In order to take the motorcycle, Joel would travel a much wider and more level route but would surely arrive before them.

The two women were exhausted, suffering bruises and painful muscles when they finally entered Kikungu from the west. They were greeted with great joy and tremendous relief. Ben had been anticipating their arrival, so it took little time for the dog-tired women to shed filthy clothing, shower, and sit down to a hot meal.

"They are only two or three hours away!" The bearded man standing in front of Pascal and Varstan smelled of sweaty clothes and tobacco breath. His eyes were saturated with fatigue, but his voice was resolute.

"Thanks, Jerry. Now get yourself a shower and some hot food before you have to go back to the forest. Good job!" Varstan spoke with genuineness.

Within thirty minutes, the band of men was loaded and maneuvering down the wide path to their encounter with a shadowy fate. They left no sign that anyone had encamped there. Their first encounter with the rebel army came in the presence of five young, uniformed, and able-bodied soldiers. They appeared nothing like those who had been described by Ben, Maludi, and others. These men were capably dressed, organized, and they appeared well disciplined. The soldiers rapidly surrounded the Land Rover with menacing movements. They were definitely dangerous!

"We take you to Colonel Ching," one soldier barked in accented English. "But first we must check you for weapons!" They did not seem to be taken back at all by the *official* emblem on the vehicle, or by the white men and the important appearing Africans. After satisfying themselves there was no threat; they ordered them to start driving to the east—but slowly enough for the rebels to walk at the same pace. There were about twenty soldiers in front and behind the Land Rover. Occasionally some would jog beside the truck windows, banishing their Chinese made automatic rifles.

As the moment of their rendezvous with *le Diable Noire* became precariously closer, both Pascal and Varstan began experiencing increasing anxiety and doubt. Varstan did not concern himself with these feelings; after all the things he heard about this Black Devil, he knew the thoughts were normal. He had experienced them before—in other encounters. On the other hand, Pascal was undergoing the same tormenting fear and unnerving anxiety that he had been experiencing the last several days. He knew the anguish crushing him was disproportionate to the situation . . . or was it? Within an hour of driving, the road deteriorated into a corridor filled with cavernous potholes and bone-jarring rocks and tree roots. The soldiers no longer had to jog to keep up with the struggling Land Rover. As the route descended, enormous vine-covered trees surrounded them. Colorful birds shrieked their annoyance at the intrusion and diverse monkeys scurried from branches to creeping vines.

The bravest of men can be beaten down by painful memories. Pascal's fears from the forest rushed on him with devastating force several minutes before they saw the large man standing before them. He was regally dressed in full military uniform. Ching's vicious eyes smoldered as his scarred face contorted into a sadistic smile.

An even more violent weight crushed at Pascal's chest as they exited their vehicle. Fleeting memory after memory flashed through his mind. He knew this man, this devil! This monster! This servant of Satan! How could he ever forget this cruel face and haunting eyes? Yes, he knew this man! The memories continued to flood his mind—of his own charred flesh, the terror of coiled serpents and scorpions in his bed, and the torture by evil spirits. He now stood before the scourge of the middle Congo! The legend whose presence could strike dread into the hearts of the bravest—the Ndoki who could *eat* human beings. This was Colonel Ching, who was the center of continuing myths and widespread brutality. Suddenly, Pascal knew why he had been experiencing the baffling fear! Now he knew why the onslaught of horrid childhood memories! The grotesque shape before them was the oldest son of his own father. This was Antonio Ansaka, his long believed dead and virtually forgotten brother! Pascal knew that his emotions were incredibly powerful, and he prayed silently that Antonio would not detect his reactions. He knew his brother was extremely astute. But the colonel seemed not to be all interested in Pascal. He had turned his interest toward Varstan.

"Bon jour monsieur. Je suis enchante vous rencontrer." Colonel Ching's voice was disarmingly pleasant, even if the cruelty in his eyes was not. "You are American, I believe. But you speak French?"

"Je parle bien le francais, monsieur Colonel."

"C'est bien. It is good because my English is a little weak. We will speak in French and you will tell me who you are and why you are here in my country!" The military commander and self-appointed liberator spoke with great authority.

"My name is Varstan. I am with an organization from America called *Physicians for Freedom and World Care.* We are sanctioned by the United Nations to bring medical care to underdeveloped countries, particularly those in the midst of war or revolution. We have no political affiliations or agenda." Varstan turned to Pascal standing at his side. "This is Dr. Mutamaya. He is volunteer American surgeon with our organization."

Pascal held his breath as Ching shook his hand. The colonel's eyes revealed no hint of recognition. Pascal willed his handshake to be steady and dry. The colonel started to turn away and then suddenly looked back into Pascal's face.

His stare was terrifying. Pascal felt certain that he was able to extract his every thought. But this brief confrontation of psyches ended and the colonel turned back to Varstan.

Pascal relaxed imperceptibly. Had he recognized him? Were memories being restored? He did not think so, yet he knew this man facing him possessed instincts far above the ordinary. A man of lesser determination and inward strength than Pascal could not have mandated his feelings to be so indistinguishable. As Antonio shifted his attention to Varstan, Pascal felt certain that he had not recognized him. However, Varstan sensed the distress in Pascal and intentionally took over the conversation. Soon he and the colonel were chatting like old friends and allies. Ching was pleased that this *important* organization was interested in his *Freedom Movement.* The three rebel officers who stood with them said nothing but somberly listened to every word. Their faces often displayed caution and possibly some suspicion. However, they had been trained to never interrupt or question their commander.

"We are going to the American-run hospital near here. The name of the village and Mission Station is Kikungu, I believe." Varstan's voice was very relaxed. "Do you know this place, Colonel?"

Antonio smiled disarmingly. "Si. Je la connais—I know it. We tried to help these people a few months ago, but they did not allow us to. They attacked us and we had to fight them to protect ourselves." Ching avoided saying anything about the ravaging of homes, the murder, the rapes, and the plundering of the hospital. Nor did he mention the capture of Dr. Ben. "But now we have returned because we have some sick and injured men who need medicine and care."

"We also want to visit the hospital and staff there. Possibly, there is something we can do to help them." Varstan sounded genuine. "We have many medical items at Leopoldville for distribution and we want to help your country. Also, maybe we can be of assistance to an army like yours that is fighting for freedom"

Colonel Ching did incredibly well in masking his immense pleasure. Already he was mentally calculating the wealth and supremacy he could gain with such medical supplies

"Is there a surgeon at Kikungu?" Varstan asked.

"I believe there was, but I do not think he is there now. However, there are many competent nurses. I am certain they will want your assistance." Ching seemed so encouraging.

CHAPTER 36

Almost at the exact same time Pascal and Varstan were in conversation with Colonel Ching, Zack was advancing down a narrow, well-worn trail. He was sweating profusely with his exertion. Nevertheless, his muscles were responding well and his judgment was strongly primed by the magnitude of his assignment. Their scheme had to work! Too many lives depended upon it! Yet, as focused as he was, he could not keep his mind completely away from Angela. Where was she? Was she safe? Maybe she was sick or hurt! It had been so many years since he had genuinely cared about anyone but himself and his dedication to medicine. Where was life taking him? What was he becoming? These were questions that would have to be answered. And they would be—but at another time!

The route had become rugged and he was climbing over rocks, twisted tree roots, and thick undergrowth. Without warning, he encountered the inexplicable *being*. It was again like the encounters in the small call room at County Hospital. In the past, they had created apprehension and a menacing feeling. Strangely, this *presence* seemed to be the same manifestation but was more comforting and reassuring than ever before. Memories of Desiree suddenly flooded his mind. Now there was no guilt or enormous anger directed at himself or toward his murdered wife. Also, he felt no hate of her killer! He only felt a tremendous love for his precious little girl. He longed to hold her. Yet, at the same time, he was inundated with a great peacefulness! He suddenly *knew* she was where she was completely happy!

Out of the blue, an overpowering thought invaded his consciousness! Had this *presence*—in the gloomy call room and on the creaking stairs—been God trying to reach him? Could it be? Swiftly and without explanation,

Zack knew that truth! How else could one explain it? God had been pursuing *him* all this time!

Zack realized that he had to keep going. Too much depended upon keeping on schedule. But as he again moved rapidly along the trail, he readily permitted his mind to conjure up vivid memories of Desiree; her sparkling blue eyes and joyful smile. Her image became more and more vivid. She was waving at him. Her long blonde hair curled around her face—she was running toward him. Although he heard no sound, she seemed to be speaking. "Thank you, Daddy. Thank you, Daddy. I love you, Daddy!" She was holding out her tiny hands and seemed almost close enough to take her into his arms. Then she turned, and suddenly there were many children around her. They were all African children—running, skipping and singing together. Suddenly, they were gone. Zack broke off his trot and rested on a fallen tree. By all rights, he should be feeling very sad, but strangely he was not. Somehow he now knew that, with God, separation from his beloved daughter was not really separation at all. She would always be with him and soon, within days or years, she *would be* in his arms again!

Zack was abruptly shaken from his beautiful reflections by a sound behind him—the faint snapping of a twig. Instinctively he dove, his 38-caliber revolver removed from its holster before he hit the ground. He quickly rolled to his left side and glanced in the direction of the sound. He saw nothing. Cautiously he raised his head to peer above the elephant grass. About twenty yards away stood a large male Okapi staring insolently at him. He knew this to be the largest and most magnificent of all the antelope. It was a rare and solitary animal. Very slowly, he stood up. The huge animal watched him closely; its ears and nose searching the air. Then, with astonishing quickness, it turned and disappeared into the tall brush. The chances of ever seeing this splendid antelope were extremely small. Zack wondered if, for some reason, God had allowed him to share a few moments with his precious daughter *and* to be near one of His most splendid creations. In his mind he could not identify any connection, but still sensed it was from the Creator.

He would have very much liked to have spent time reflecting on this but knew that he had no more time to spare. He had to get back to the assignment! Yet, as he moved rapidly down the trail, he found himself silently whispering a brief prayer, "Thank you, God."

Many believe that future events spin through time and space in random fashion and then burst out into circumstance beyond anyone's control. But the Bible teaches the extreme opposite. From Genesis to Revelation, it declares that God is in total control. What may appear chaotic is a perception that is restricted by the human mind. God sometimes allows *apparent* confusion and chaos to emerge, but they are never out of His control. What may seem catastrophic to man never catches God unaware. Faith reveals this truth. The incidents about to occur in an obscure, inconsequential region of the Belgium Congo were no less in the Creator's charge.

◇◇◇◇◇◇◇◇◇

Unknown to the group of white people at the Mission, Joel's journey had been delayed by motorcycle difficulties, causing the three of them a lot of worry.

At this same moment in point in time, Zack was a full day's journey away from his destination. He had been actively gathering his *army* from the various villages.

Almost at the same point in time, Ching and his staff were feeling comfortable with their new *collaborators* as they traveled toward the hospital. Most of the colonel's soldiers marched behind and were completely unaware of being silently flanked by Varstan's mercenaries. As they trekked closer and closer to the Mission Station, Pascal and Varstan were glad they did not have to converse much with Ching. The fierce throbbing of the Land Rover's diesel engine blending with the loud music from its radio—the colonel demanded it—made conversation impossible. Pascal was particularly grateful for the lack of exchange because he was not sure how long he could keep his identity from Antonio. This *silence* gave him freedom to fervently pray that the awful loathing for his crazed brother would not overcome his ability to hide his identity. How easily experiences from the past can overpower what we are *now* and change what we are *to become*. Pascal knew that he was a child of God. Never would he permit repressed anger and hate to destroy that. Nevertheless, he intuitively recognized that he and the eldest son of his father must soon endure a dreadful conflict from which there might be no survivor.

CHAPTER 37

Ben exited the hospital as the Land Rover pulled up in front. He downed the few steps to greet them just as Colonel Ching was getting out. When their eyes met, Ben had the advantage of foreknowledge that Ching did not. When the colonel saw Ben, his scarred face distorted into instant rage and suspicion. His dark eyes narrowed angrily and for just a split second Ben thought he saw panic in his expression. He quickly decided to give the man very little time to react. He stepped forward and offered his hand. He willed his actions to convey no hostility—Ben had to disarm his mortal enemy! Thankfully, the colonel's manic mood was not easily daunted. He knew he was far too powerful for this simple missionary doctor to be of any threat to him!

"Bienvenu, monsieur Colonel. J'espère que vous et vos soldates sont bien. Je ne vous vu depuis plusieurs semaines. (Welcome. I hope you and your soldiers are well. It has been a few weeks since I last saw you). Some village people told us you were coming, and we have prepared a house for you and for a few of your officers. Some of your men may sleep in the surgery wing of the hospital. There are some comfortable beds available. But most of your soldiers will have to bed-down in the church over there." He pointed toward the metal roofed building.

Despite feeling relatively secure, Ching gave the orders to Lieutenant Mumga. His commands were in a language that Ben did not understand—probably Swahili. It was a few minutes later that Ben saw the officer lead a small band on what was clearly a reconnaissance operation. The colonel was far too experienced to take chances. When Ching returned to where Ben was visiting with Pascal and Varstan, his behavior seemed more challenging.

"Why do you greet me like this, monsieur Doctor?" He looked intently at Ben, and they both knew his meaning.

"I would like to hate you, Colonel, but I cannot." Ben spoke the truth. Without God's help, he *would* hate this fiend. Yet, he would still have to try to bring his bloodbath to an end! Ben continued. "You and your men are welcome here. We will try to make your time with us comfortable. We can feed you, but our water supply is very limited. Some enemies have damaged the springs in the valley, and the women must carry water from long distances. For now, you and your soldiers may drink from the cistern by the hospital. But when that is gone, the water must be carried in."

He was certain this experienced military leader would quickly investigate his story. He hoped and prayed they had gotten everything in order. Colonel Ching would overlook very little.

Pascal's mind raced as he listened to Ben and his brother talk. Though many years had passed, Pascal understood well the Kituba words that Antonio intermingled with his excellent French. Ben's remarks about hating struck him almost like a physical blow. The hate, fear, and loathing he believed he had conquered were pervading every fiber of his mind. Long obscured feelings had been resurrected so abruptly and effortlessly. Pascal realized how easily hate can be inadequately repressed and possibly never extinguished. Every thread of Pascal's body was taut, wanting to spring in a ferocious assault. Yet, his eyes revealed nothing, and his face remained benevolent.

◇◇◇◇◇◇◇◇

Darkness was encroaching as Ching and three of his most trusted aids were finishing their meal. He had relaxed after Mumga returned to report there was no obvious danger surrounding them. He also confirmed the destruction of the springs. The colonel was proud of himself for his vigilance and leadership.

Angela and Rachael had made their presence briefly known, but they stayed in their own house. They wanted to avoid the lecherous stares of the soldiers and to avoid their repulsive leader.

It was near 10:00 p.m. and the night held a strange murkiness. Ching and the three officers sat in the living room. Earlier that evening, one of the soldiers had made the one-mile trip to the market and returned with several bottles of whiskey. Two kerosene lanterns threw flickering shadows on the walls. Sounds of revelry from the soldiers in the church building drifted in through the open windows. The small group of men was well into a second bottle of scotch when there was brisk knock on the door. The sergeant arose and staggered to the door. Moments later he brought a stranger into the room.

"Monsieur Colonel, vous avez un visiteur. Il pourrait visite avec vous pendant quelque minutes." (You have a visitor. He wants to talk to you for a minute).

The stranger held his lantern up near enough to his face so that Ching could see him clearly. The colonel arose to greet the guest, and as he did, the blood drained from his face. Devastating fear assaulted him, and he began to tremble violently! One word squeezed itself from his constricted throat, "Vous!"

Joel stood immobile and stared aggressively into the *le Diable's* terrified eyes. He made no sound.

"You are dead!" Ching's voice was a rasping whimper.

"I am what you say I am." Joel's voice was low and menacing. Then he set his lamp on the table and abruptly turned—and was gone.

"Stop him! Bring him back!" Ching was screaming. The three soldiers moved as quickly as their intoxicated bodies would permit, but when they burst into the heavy darkness, their caller had vanished. The next twenty minutes were spent searching the vicinity, but they discovered nothing. When the men returned, they found their leader sitting with his face in his hands. He was mumbling over and over again the same phrases, "I killed him. I killed him. I shot him in the heart!"

Ching suddenly stood. His face was contorted from fright. He began screaming meaningless gibberish at his cohorts! They knew from awful experience that it was best they leave. This would not be a night spent in comfort.

The maniacal leader was alone in the dark house. He paced from room to room like a caged animal. Violent and disorganized thoughts ravished his tortured mind. Was he going mad? Were the spirits of the dead molesting him? No! It could not be! *He* controlled the spirits! But he could not stop the fright that was breeding within him. Antonio spent a sleepless, terror-filled night struggling with thoughts of insanity and the terrifying presence of the dead. How quickly mania can turn to overwhelming despair. The colonel met the next day with eyes bloodshot from lack of sleep and a body racked by the horror of apparitions only he saw. He appeared a mere shadow of the person he had been the day before. Fatigue, panic, and uncertainty wracked his brain. But it was a tribute to his inner strength that he dressed in full uniform and stood ramrod-straight as he ordered his officers to bring the mondeles to him!

◇◇◇◇◇◇◇◇◇

The white men and women were meeting with Pastor Ndela in his barren office that occupied the small front corner of the church. They were unsuccessfully trying to shut out the snores of soldiers coming from the large hall. Dawn was breaking, but the undersized, windowless bureau was still too dark for reading their Bibles. They had gathered for discussion and prayer. Suddenly they heard shouting and commotion coming from the area of their homes. Ben went to the door just in time to see several soldiers heading toward them. They were fully armed and appeared menacing. Angela and Rachael joined Ben at the doorway. Pastor Ndela and two Congolese church elders stood determinedly behind them.

"Kwisa! Kwisa na beno! Come with us. The colonel wants you, now!" Two of the soldiers aimed their weapons at them.

"Pourquoi? Why? What does he need us for?" Ben asked calmly.

The largest and more vicious appearing of the soldiers grabbed Ben by the shirt and yanked him forward. The others raised their rifles and aimed them threateningly.

"Kwenda! Kwenda yanda! They pushed the group of men and two women in the direction of Dr. Ben's house where they knew the Colonel waited.

As they entered the house, Ben noticed his cook, Tshikiluka, trembling in the corner of the kitchen. "Would you please prepare us some coffee and bread?" he said kindly to the frightened man. "Enough for all of us," he added.

Colonel Ching stood in the middle of the living room with his back to them. It was several seconds before he turned to face the group. His features were forbidding, but the tone in his voice once again disowned the fury in his eyes. He glared directly at Ben.

"Your young friend visited us last night. You know whom I mean. Where is he!" Ching's tone of voice carried a near irrepressible rage.

"I am sorry, Colonel. I don't know who you are talking about." In fact, he did not. Joel had not had the time to share his plan with Ben. "If you will relax for a few moments, my cook is preparing coffee and bread for us. Then we can discuss your problem."

Antonio was taken back by Ben's calmness in front of his grim assault. For a few moments, he was immobilized by the goodwill, and Ben made use of this brief advantage. "Please, may we sit down and Tshikiluka will bring us le pain et café."

Ching sat, struggling to restrain his rage. No words were spoken until after the cook served them. Just as they began to sip the coffee, Pascal and Varstan knocked and entered the room. They looked vigorous and rested. "May we join you?"

No one in the room could even sense the complexity of the emotions that were developing within Antonio. But for now he was able to adequately conceal them. As the others in the room calmly drank coffee and ate bread, his violent insanity struggled inwardly with his immense, but perverse intellect. How could he pursue his need to obtain his night visitor's identity and location without disclosing unnecessary information to these United Nations *Officials?* He must not lose what they had to offer. He turned to Ben.

"Monsieur, docteur, last night at about 2300 hours a young man came to my house—this house. My men and I offered him our great hospitality, but he stood near the doorway and waved a pistol at us. He shouted angrily and said he would kill us all. Then something must have frightened him because he suddenly ran and hid somewhere. We searched but could not find him. This morning I sent for you to ask if you know where he is." Colonel Ching sounded incredibly honest.

"Will you please try to describe him? Maybe we can help you," Ben asked politely.

Angela sat on the couch next to Rachael listening carefully to the conversation. They too had been brought here by Ching's orders. They were trying to provide each other comfort. They knew! Joel had shared his idea with them the night before.

Ching had remained sitting, giving the appearance of being totally undisturbed. Now he abruptly stood. He appeared on the brink of flying into a frenzy. His scarred face was again made more revolting by his anger. Everyone in the room was now personally experiencing how the energy around this crazed man could strike fear into even the bravest. Even Pascal and Varstan were briefly unnerved. But the two of them independently recognized that this was good! There would be no underestimating him! Yet, they were also seeing firsthand the instability in him, and this could definitely be used to their advantage.

As quickly as it had erupted, Ching's mood changed. He was again in total control. "It is not important. He was probably some crazy man who is harmless. My men will capture him if he shows up again."

CHAPTER 38

During the following three days, Ben tried to establish some semblance of a normal routine to the Mission Station. He and Angela made rounds on the medicine and tuberculosis wards and treated some of the more complicated cases in the dispensary. They purposely spoke loudly about their cases of tuberculosis and leprosy. This had the curbing effect on the colonel's men they hoped for. Fear kept the soldiers from venturing too near the patients, and they left Angela and Ben alone while they were on the wards.

Dr. Ben performed a few minor surgeries and taught a couple of his courses to the nursing students. Establishing a more usual routine helped the colonel and his men relax. Even the more suspicious officers seemed to have lightened up. However, none of them knew what was taking place in Ching's life. He spent the nights alone in the house. Several of the inhabitants of the Station, who passed by at night, reported an eerie glow and uncanny noises coming from within. By day the colonel appeared natural and spent a great amount of time with Pascal and Varstan. In his distorted mind, he began to believe he was convincing them of his vision to lead the Congo in becoming a powerful nation. Now he felt that these important representatives would help him.

In the late evenings, when everyone felt *le Diable Noire* was firmly fixed in the house, Rachael would steal down to the tiny village of Kikolo where Joel was hiding—taking him food and water. He was staying in a hut that was isolated several meters from the others. The little house had been deserted for many moons because of the strange deaths that had occurred there. The village inhabitants felt many evil spirits infested it. Joel and Rachael were in little danger of being discovered, and they spent this precious time sharing their love for one another.

By the fifth day of their arrival, the soldiers were becoming edgy and ill tempered. This was partly due to inactivity but mostly as a result of their lack of water. The hospital's cistern had been emptied by the middle of the third day of their invasion. On the sixth day, they came to realize they had not seen their leader for more than seventy-two hours. But this bizarre behavior by him was not unusual and aroused no suspicions in the officers. At the week's end, Lieutenant Muyembe took the Land Rover and eight enlisted men and left for Lukema, a village about twenty kilometers (twelve miles) to the south. They were led to believe they could get water there. When that evening arrived and they had not returned, no one became suspicious because they all knew the roads were difficult and breakdowns were frequent. However, the next morning when they saw the empty Land Rover parked at the edge of the Mission Station, a tremendous fear descended on Ching's army.

It had been an easy exercise for Varstan's *dogs of war* to destroy the nine soldiers that had crowded into the Land Rover. The brief fight was silent and deadly. The bodies of the soldiers were buried and then they drove the vehicle as close to the Station as safety permitted. Afterward, under the cover of darkness, they had pushed the Land Rover onto the road near the hospital. They anticipated the kind of reaction it would produce. There had made no attempt to clean its interior of the gruesome sight of blood and death.

Le Diable Noire sat on the floor of Dr. Ben's bureau. He was in some type of bizarre trance that was intensified by the foul incense that burned near him. He was dressed in his filthy and unkempt military uniform. He had not removed it for more than three days. It took several moments of pounding by the officers to shake him from his spell. The person who answered the door shocked the soldiers. How can one's appearance be changed so drastically over such a short time? The man that stood before them was a mere apparition of the leader they knew. He was unshaven and the flesh of his face drooped, forcing the ugly scar to twist his mouth into a hideous sneer. His shoulders were bent and his legs seemed flaccid. His breath was fetid and reeked of liquor. In spite of this, his eyes glowed with power and authority. These eyes held the men in fear and submission.

"You are disturbing me! I did not send for you! What do you want?"

A very frightened sergeant by the name of Bopenda fought back his terror and stepped forward. In a trembling voice, he briefly related what had happened. The blood drained from Ching's face as he was told of finding the empty Land Rover and the disappearance of nine of his soldiers. The men before him could not begin to comprehend just how unbalanced their leader was becoming. They had no way of knowing that during the night, the face of the *dead man* had appeared to him again.

Sometime after midnight, a tapping at Ching's window had awakened him from a fitful sleep. When he looked, there was Joel's face silhouetted in the window by the iridescent light of a lantern. The great Colonel Ching had been diminished to a cowering, childlike creature. The remainder of the night, he was tortured by horrid images of dead ancestors and the wandering souls of those he had murdered. A lesser man would have been totally mad by morning and definitely incapable of answering the door as he had.

"Get some of your best men and follow the trail back from where it came!" Color had returned to his face and his voice sounded remarkably authoritative. "I want to know what happened to those men! I also want to meet with the two men from the United Nations. Bring them here in about one hour!"

Pascal and Varstan sat across from one another drinking their third cup of strong coffee. Varstan had never seen Pascal as preoccupied or strained as he was right now.

"Do you want to spit it out, Pascal? I think I've gotten to know you well enough to think that there is something beyond just our present situation that is troubling you. Do you want to tell me what it is?"

Pascal looked up and his dark brown eyes examined Varstan's face. He must have seen the sanctuary he was looking for because he felt open to respond.

"There is something you must know, and you are the only one besides me who will know it for now. Even this *Diable*, with all his supernatural powers, does not yet know. It pains me to tell you this." He studied Varstan, watching him for his reaction. "Colonel Ching is my brother!"

No matter how hard Pascal studied Varstan's rugged features, he could not ascertain his reaction; there was nothing more than a slight tightening of his jaw. His only response was to say, "We've got some problems, haven't we? Tell me about it—at least, what you are comfortable sharing."

During the next several minutes, Pascal sketched some of his past. He shared a few of the details of his childhood filled with fear and hate for his older brother, Antonio. He told of the torture, the intrusion on his sleep, the nightmares, and the pain. He disclosed to Varstan the belief of some that Antonio would become a great Ngangu Ankisi—as their father had been. He spoke of Antonio's disappearance and assumed death. Without explanation, Pascal felt free to reveal to Varstan how he had begun to forgive his brother after accepting Jesus Christ as Savior. He finished by revealing why the recent, inexplicable nervousness he had been experiencing now made sense—and the fear had ceased. He did not disclose to Varstan his conviction that there would have to be a final encounter with Antonio Ansaka—the Ndoki.

"I pray that I have not revealed anything in my actions to jeopardize our operation." Pascal was clearly concerned.

"I saw nothing in your actions that would have given you away," Varstan said. "Looking back, I think you have done fantastically concealing you feelings!"

The sun made its appearance well above the mango trees lining the sandy road that dissected the Mission Station. The colonel's men did not even knock on the door where Pascal and Varstan sat talking. They just coarsely barged into the house. The soldiers aimed their rifles menacingly. The oldest of the three officers barked orders, "You come with us, now!" For no apparent reason, except for their inherent cruelty, the soldiers cursed and shoved the two men toward where Ching waited. Both Pascal and Varstan calmly endured the verbal and physical abuse. When they got to the house, Ching did not appear. However, they heard his voice from within—forceful and ominous.

"Take them to the storehouse up by the hospital and lock them in. Guard them well, and send some men to get the doctor and the two women and lock them up also." Unwisely, he did not include any of the indigent staff or pastors. He did not fear them, for he was certain they were too terrorized by him to be of danger. The soldiers waited a few minutes, hoping the colonel would appear, but now only eerie sounds came from within. These men had heard the *voices* before and they were terrified. If they had known the Devil's plans, they would have been even more frightened. Ching was planning to spend the next hours with his foul and malevolent *friends*.

On the way to the storehouse the soldiers were too scared to pay much attention to Pascal and Varstan; they only wanted them locked up and out of sight.

CHAPTER 39

Fierce thirst can have an overwhelming and devastating effect. In the tropics, the direct rays from the sun rapidly dehydrate the human body. One's dry tongue adheres to the roof of the mouth. Parched lips fissure and muscles become flaccid. The mind drives out most all thought except the desire for water. Many of these marauding soldiers had reached this point. They were becoming increasingly more irritable and agitated. A few of the officers spoke of going for water but the memory of the bloodstained Land Rover held them back. By mid-afternoon, the scorching sun was causing erratic and belligerent behavior. They had not seen their chief for several days. Captain Muyembe attempted to strengthen and encourage the men, but he lacked any real enthusiasm. By evening, many of the soldiers were wandering aimlessly around the Mission Station and grounds of the hospital. Some were drinking whiskey but others longed for the local beer—the market place had none. In their dehydrated body, the alcohol was having especially vile side-effects. It was only their terrible fear of reprisal from the colonel that kept them from going on a rampage of stealing, burning, and raping. They were particularly attracted to the white woman and the nursing students.

A tolerant darkness settled on the area, but turmoil intensified among the army. With drunkenness came less fear of the colonel. They had attacked and ravaged many villages, but never without his orders. The antagonize effect of alcohol on parched minds was creating an atmosphere of madness ready to explode.

Without warning, a loud commotion erupted from the surrounding darkness. The sounds seemed to be coming from all directions. A few of the confused men ran for their weapons, but others just stood, paralyzed by fear. The noises they heard from the distant shadows sounded like a large army marching toward them. Then followed the sound of trumpets and guns being fired.

Within minutes, total mayhem reigned! As the loud noises came closer, several of these young, drunken, and superstitious men began fleeing. On the east of the station, Vartstan's warriors encountered and *neutralized* many of the escaping soldiers. However, many they did not kill—they told them to leave and return to their villages. In that way they could live!

Zack led his *troops* from the northern direction. The strategy of Gideon was even more effective than anticipated. The dread of having to kill that had taken hold of Zack was honored by the desertion of the soldiers. A few of Ching's men tried to resist and were shot or hacked to death with machetes. The humble, untrained villagers fought heatedly and bravely. Zack could not have been more proud of them if they had been a unit of highly-trained marines. Ching's army, officers and recruits, believed a strong, well-armed militia was attacking them. Zack was grateful that it was over quickly and that he had not been forced to kill anyone.

Suddenly and seemingly from nowhere, Joel appeared at his side. He had a large ram's horn to his hand. As he placed it to his mouth, his amplified voice pierced the night.

"Leave! Go back to your homes and your families! Your war is over! Your chief is finished. He can no longer lead you! Kwenda! Go!"

Fear, thirst, superstition, and the haze of drunkenness all combined to further drive the young soldiers into complete confusion. Within days or weeks, many would be back in their own regions and villages. Some would drift to large cities, like Leopoldville or Kikwit. The more hardened of the fighting men would join the government forces or wander to Angola in the south or across the Congo River to Central African Republic. Colonel Ching's dream of great conquest was dissipating like the mist as it is driven from the massive Congo River by the morning sun

In the storage building, Pascal, Varstan, Angela, and Rachael could hear the pandemonium around them, and through cracks in the wall they saw their guards running away. It took little effort to break the lock and leave the storeroom. There were no guards. Cautiously, they walked back toward the homes but saw no one and heard only a few gunshots and some yelling in the distance.

The powerful Antonio Ansaka had spent most of the day communicating with the spirits. Supernatural strength had begun to return. His satanic trance was deep, and for a long time he was unaware of the uproar outside. For much of the evening he had been in communication with his departed father and other hideous spirits he called from the dead. It was a loud pounding at the door that finally shook him from his foul spell. He had been seated for hours clothed only in a loincloth. Grudgingly, he arose and covered himself with a robe. He moved silently to the door. When he opened it, he quickly drew back as he stared into the face of the *United Nations* physician. He did not see the others behind Pascal. It was if an unseen force grasped him, holding him in icy fingers. As their eyes met, inexplicable desperation shook Antonio. By knocking on the door, Pascal had created the destabilizing effect on Antonio for which they had hoped.

"Guards! Guards!" he screamed.

"They cannot help you." Pascal's eyes never left his bother's face.

Gradually Ching became conscious of the bedlam in the region around them. In the partial moonlight he could see the silhouette of people of running. Shots were being fired, and muffled screams drifted to him from the shadows. Pascal raised his lantern and stepped toward his brother. He did not miss the fear in the man's face.

"Your army is crushed. Most of your soldiers are on the run. Many of them are dead!" Ching just stared, his fear creating immobility.

"Please, go back inside. We must talk." He turned to the others. Only Varstan grasped the full meaning of this moment. Angela took Rachael's hand and stepped back ever so slightly. Never had she seen such dangerous resolve in a person as she now did in Pascal.

"Let's go; we have much to do." Varstan was obviously used to having his orders obeyed. However, Angela hesitated for a moment, spellbound by the interchange between the two men—she wanted to understand more. It was with reluctance that she turned away to follow Varstan and Rachael.

The two men stood a few feet apart. Pascal held the lantern so that light revealed both their faces. "You do not recognize me do you?"

No, should I?" Antonio's voice had regained some self-assurance.

Pascal Mutamaya held the flickering light closer to his face. "You should remember the youngest son of your father! Remember the boy you tortured and humiliated so many times?"

Slowly, memories materialized in Antonio's mind and then recognition slammed against him like a fist.

"Yes, I remember. I remember you now! Nge kele Pascal!" Astonishment made him briefly revert to his mother tongue. "Oui! I know you. You are my dear brother!"

Antonio raised his arms to embrace his brother. Pascal held the lantern in his left hand. Then—with the strength driven by the years of loathing—he swung. His fist struck the side of Antonio's jaw with a sickening sound. The scourge of the Congo collapsed into a pathetic heap on the cement floor. Pascal dragged the unconscious body to the bedroom and with ease placed him on the bed. He found rope and quickly secured the unconscious man. Swiftly, he searched the house for weapons and found only the Colonel's revolver. He made a hasty search of his brother's fétiches and charms but found nothing of danger. Pascal shivered ever so slightly as he touched these appalling objects. Even after so many years of absence from the heart of dark Africa, he had not entirely vanquish his inherent fear of this arsenal of satanic worship.

It was Angela who found Ben. She had no doubt where he would be. After leaving Pascal, she walked directly to the hospital. The mission grounds were quiet. No sounds of fighting could be heard. Thankfully the moon was bright and she could see the outline of the poorly dressed villagers and a few white men, whom she assumed were Varstan's men. She ached to see Zack, to hold him, to know he was safe.

Angela found Ben where she had anticipated. He was on the medical ward, moving from one bedside to another. He was trying to comfort the sick, assuring them there was no danger. She ran into his arms and hugged him tightly. She actually thought she felt a tear fall into her hair, but she did not look at Ben's eyes; she did not want to embarrass him. Instead she gazed over the ward filled with patients as she spoke. "I think we are out of harm's way now. It seems most of Colonel Ching's army has fled."

"Where is the Colonel?" Ben's voice was anxious.

Angela quickly related the confrontation between Pascal and Ching. "Pascal seemed very determined and quite in control of the situation when I left."

Ben turned and spoke loudly so that the ward full of patients could hear. "Do not be afraid, you are safe now. Soon, the nurses I and will return to care for you." Then he faced Angela and said, "Come, let's find the others." Ben took Angela's diminutive hand as they strode down the tree-lined path toward their houses.

CHAPTER 40

Neither the Americans nor Varstan's men had slept for at least three days. Angela and Rachael took the chill from the room with burning logs in the fireplace. They had managed to have some water brought and made coffee and baked bread. Conditions were relatively calm except for a few isolated incidents between the mercenaries and escaping soldiers. By late morning, all the fighting had died away. One of Varstan's men had been killed—a young man from Rhodesia. He had been found with a bullet wound in his back. Another man had a nasty gunshot wound in his thigh. As nearly as they could determine, at least three of the *village* army had been fatally wounded, and several others were seriously injured by gunshots, knives, and machetes. Much of the damage had occurred as the result of accidental encounters with the fleeing soldiers. Later that morning it would be determined that several of Ching's soldiers had been *neutralized* by gunshots. But spears, beheadings, and strangulation had also killed many.

With dawn had come a cool mist and an overcast sky. Soon wind and rain assaulted the Mission Station and with it came a thick fog that obscured the buildings—a phenomenon that was rare in the dry season. Just before dawn, while the two women were trying to grab a few minutes sleep, an alarming knock had awakened them. Cautiously, Angela peered through the window. There at the doorway stood an exhausted and bedraggled man—Zack. All the terror and fatigue of the last few hours melted with their embrace. Love can so incredibly erase revulsion and neutralize fear. They held each other in a silent intimacy until dawn broke. Neither needed to speak—they just enjoyed their embrace and incredibly grateful hearts.

Later that morning, the small house belonging to Angela and Rachael was crowded with Zack, Pascal, and Ben. Also, with these men were the pastors and village elders. Varstan and four of his men also stood quietly in the background.

Some of the others had gone to the house where the colonel lay captive. Zack and Varstan had stationed a couple of soldiers to guard him well.

Angela and Rachael provided a large amount of coffee and bread to the hungry, exhausted, and chilled men. They ate with relish. Several pastors and other locals talked about how unusual rain and fog were during this time of year. As the falling rain struck the corrugated metal roofs, it flowed to the eves and surged to the corners of the house to fill the large barrels. The water that had been so laboriously stored in the village would no longer be needed. They could not help but think how things might have been different if the rains had come sooner to Colonel Ching's soldiers. Would their plans have been ruined? Was it just coincidence that the rain did not come earlier? Would they ever know the answer?

Varstan and his rugged team used most of the day to give a proper burial to fallen colleagues and to bury those of the Ching's men. Ben, Zack, and Angela spent much of the day treating Varstan's wounded and the few injured soldiers of Colonel Ching's army who had not escaped. These medical people once again blended their skills to assist the wounded. Zack and Angela took every extra split second to briefly touch one another as if the piercing fear they had been experiencing could be swept away by the touch of a cheek or brief brush of a hand.

A dreary afternoon sky cast gloom over the Station when Varstan came back to the women's house where he found Zack, Dr. Ben, Pascal, and three Congolese pastors sitting in a circle. Several open Bibles lay on the table in front of them.

"Pardon Messieurs and Mesdemoiselles. I have come to ask if I can take the colonel now. He will be going to Leopoldville, although not exactly in the manner in which he had planned."

Zack, Pascal, and Ben stood up almost at the same time. "Why must you go so soon? Please, stay with us for a while. You need rest," Zack spoke with great feeling.

"Yes, please do. Besides, a couple of your men still need some medical care," Ben added.

Varstan stood calmly. Everything about him conveyed resolve. "Our work here is finished. Now we must take the murderer back to the Capitol, collect our payment, and then decide where life is going to lead us." He turned to face

Ben. "Can my wounded stay here until they are well enough to travel? I will pay you for their care."

"You can leave your men. We will care for them gladly. But pay us? No, you will not; not after all you have done for us!"

Varstan saw that there would be nothing accomplished by pursuing the matter of compensation, so he simply said, "Thank you."

Similarly, the group all realized they would not break Varstan's determination to leave and agreed to let him send three of his men to get the Colonel.

"Before you leave with him, would you please bring him here so that we can talk briefly?" Of all the people present, only Varstan knew the full complexity of Pascal's request. "Sure, I will bring him myself."

Varstan and two of his companions found Ching securely tied to the small bed. However, if they had expected to find a frightened, beaten-down man, they were greatly surprised. Antonio seemed to be every bit the great Ngangu Ankisi, even in captivity. His swollen jaw was set firmly and his sinister, dark eyes emanated hate. Varstan and his colleagues experienced an uneasiness as the untied him.

"Permettez-moi a m' habiller, si vous plait."

"Go ahead and get dressed, but be careful of any moves you make!" Varstan's voice was ominous. The colonel quickly dressed himself in full military uniform.

"Si vous plait, je voudrais apporter mon fétiche." He held a harmless appearing statuette in his hands. It was a wood carving with the body of a man and the distorted face of some creature. It looked completely innocuous.

"Sure, bring your doll," said the mercenary standing next to him.

As they left the house with prisoner between them, the rain suddenly stopped, but the fog thickened. They could see only the shadowy image of the houses and church building. As they walked, Ching's hand moved imperceptibly on the carved figurine. Within a split second, he had removed a threadlike, razor sharp stiletto from it hiding place in the base of carving. He slipped it up the sleeve of his uniform.

As they escorted him onto the veranda, Pascal came out the door. Behind him stood Ben, Zack, and Angela. Pascal gazed calmly at Antonio's hate-filled face. "Your army has been destroyed. There are no more men for you control with your madness."

"Where are they? Where have they gone?" Seething insanity was ready to burst out.

"Back to their families, to their homes, or to the cities. They will never follow you again."

Ben and Varstan stood behind Pascal as he spoke, carefully watching the colonel. They saw rage and hate surge within him, distorting his face into even worse repulsiveness. Without warning, and too quickly for the mercenaries to stop him, he lunged at Pascal, the slim dagger in his hand aimed at Pascal's throat. Pascal reflexes allowed him to deflect the blade, and with astonishing swiftness, he twisted Antonio around and clamped a powerful arm around his neck. The others saw Ching switch the thin stiletto to his other hand, but before they could move, he drove the slim blade into Pascal's lateral chest. Pascal's eyes darkened for a split second, and then he applied pressure to Antonio's neck with a twisting motion. They all heard the nauseating snap of bones as the cervical spine shattered. After several moments, Pascal released his grasp and the lifeless body collapsed to the floor. The dead eyes still held hate, but there was something else—disbelief!

"Oh, thank God!" Angela left Zack's side and rushed to Pascal as le Diable Noire fell to the ground. There was a sad expression on Pascal's face and tears formed in his eyes. It was a great effort for him to speak. "I am sorry . . . I am so sorry." They leaned closer to hear him more clearly. "It had to be done!" He drew himself erect for a moment, gazing briefly at each of them with sorrow in his eyes. "C'est fini!" He exclaimed in a firm voice. "It is over!" His eyes showed a wonderful peace—then nothing. They moved to his side as his knees began to buckle. It required all of Angela's strength to hold him during the few seconds it took Zack and Ben to reach her side. Together, they eased him to the floor of the porch. It was only then they saw the handle of the thin dagger protruding from his chest. Its threadlike blade had passed through a small edge of his lung and its tip entered a few centimeters into the muscle of the heart; not far, but just enough to cause a severe and fatal irregularity of heartbeat. Pascal was dead before they had gently laid him down.

CHAPTER 41

A full week had passed since Pascal's death and the departure of Varstan's group. They had taken with them photos of Ching's dead body and sufficient identification to collect their reward. The impenetrable fog had lingered far longer than any of the indigenous people could recall. The dampness and cold mist only added to the anguish that gripped the village of Kikungu. The day following his death, they had laid Pascal's body on a newly constructed bamboo platform—in typical African fashion. The usual grass roof needed for protection from the sun was not used because of the overcast days. He lay there for a full day and night as mourners came and went to view the body and comfort his loved ones. He had no family in the immediate region, but his courage and leadership had gained many friends and admirers. At noon of the second day, they placed the body into a rough-hewn wooden coffin. Dr. Ben, Zack, Angela, and many others stood at the gravesite with memories inundating them with excruciating pain.

Ben spoke a few words at the gravesite—his voice breaking several times. "We are saying farewell to the boy I knew; to the human being he was; to the healer and surgeon he became; and to the man of God we all loved."

◇◇◇◇◇◇◇◇◇

Even though a month had passed since Pascal's death, the grief and melancholy that gripped the small community had actually grown deeper. It was early nighttime as Zack and Angela walked hand in hand down the long grass landing strip where the natives continued to fight back the elephant grass and brush. This airstrip was the only means of obtaining future medical supplies and providing for the arrival of missionaries and visitors—it had to remain open for contact with the outside world. They were lost in thought as they strolled. Finally, Zack broke the silence.

"Angela, have you wondered what Pascal meant when he said 'I am so sorry'?"

Angela's voice was husky with grief. "I felt that he meant he was feeling very guilty for killing the colonel, despite that fact that it had to be done. That madman couldn't be allowed to go on gathering more men under his depraved control. Yet, he was a human being. I believed that to the very last, Pascal respected the value of human live. He hated everything his brother stood for. However, that isn't the reason he had to kill him. In this country, there are no laws, no judges, and no prisons to hold a *maniac like he*. He would have never stopped his rampage of murder and devastation until arriving at the very seat of power. Who knows what would have happened after that." Angela paused and stopped walking. She gazed directly into Zack's face. "I'm sorry; I have been spouting my thoughts without letting you speak."

Zack gently press her soft hand in his. "No reason to apologize. I guess I had come to the same conclusions, but I appreciate hearing you express it." He was silent for several moments. "I still do not know how we Christians ever justify killing? Man, I have been grappling hard with that lately."

Angela's heart skipped as she heard him say *we* Christians. She had no way of knowing of the many nights Zack had laid awake in the flickering light from his lantern, reading Dr. Ben's well-worn Bible. He had made many quiet decisions and had come to the clear conviction that the multiple *manifesta-tions*—the *presences*—that he had experienced, beginning back at the county hospital, were from God. All this time, when he thought that he was looking for God, it was actually God searching for him.

Without warning, lightning flashed. The two young people had been so engrossed in their sharing, they had failed to notice the dark clouds building up over them. Within seconds they found themselves drenched with rain. The dry season would end early. Trees would leaf-out, flowers would bloom, and the grasses would mature. The earth would be nurtured. New life would begin!

They ran the entire distance back to the houses. Despite the fierce rain that drenched them, they held each other close, not wanting to surrender another moment of their time.

That night, as Angela slept, she dreamed of angels rejoicing in heaven because of Zack's acknowledgement of Christ as Savior. A hundred yards away, Zack lay awake, staring at the rotting beams above him. In his thoughts he saw Pascal so clearly and heard his voice saying, "I am sorry. I am sorry."

It was after midnight before Zack fell asleep. Dreams came quickly, and he saw his beloved Desiree. She was waving at him, and clearly he heard her say, "I love you, Daddy, and I love Dr. Pascal too."

CHAPTER 42

The rainy season had been on them for a full month. Much of the life at Kikungu had returned to normal. Unrestrained grief can last for only a time, even though the barrenness left by death can be forever. During the weeks, Pastor Ndela had delivered some remarkable sermons on faith. The courageous village people had returned to their lives, free of fear from the rebel army. Dr. Ben had very quickly filled the wards again with medical and surgical cases. He, Zack, and Angela worked superbly as a team with Rachael assisting; they worked long hours to fulfill the medical needs of the enormous region. When not displaying love for his new wife, Joel spent hours assisting in surgery and teaching his people about nutrition, sanitation, and basic agriculture. David Mbote had become valuable as a handyman, repairing many things on the Station. Maludi, the rebel soldier who had gained all their respect had gone to his home village. Nganda, the young man who had aided Zack in attacking the colonel's men, had become a first rate chauffer.

As time permitted, Zack and Angela spent every occasion gaining further insight into one another. Contrary to many relationships, the more time they spent together, the more their love intensified. Three months after Pascal's death, they chose to spend their lives together. Pastor Ndela, together with Dr. Ben, married them in a small church a few kilometers from the Kikungu. They chose this place of worship, with its mud walls and thatched roof, because for them it surpassed the most exquisite cathedral. The congregation was royalty in ragged clothes—barefoot, poor, and sickly. The *royalty* smiled graciously and shared their great happiness for the couple. God had placed on Zack and Angela's hearts a love for these people that went beyond understanding. After completing their vows, they turned from the makeshift pulpit to face the congregation and acknowledge their warm smiles.

As they walked down the aisle of the primordial church, Zack looked over the congregation—the man there with the deformed leg; the emaciated woman holding the malnourished child; the older mama with the face disfigured by leprosy; the pot-bellied child with spindly legs. Throughout this village, if one has a few cows, he is rich; if three of their five born children were still living by puberty, they are greatly blessed. *God has given Angela and me such a wonderful gift,* he thought, *the opportunity to serve Him through these deprived people and allowed me to spend my life with the most precious woman God ever created.*

As the service came to an end, the sun was setting, creating a brilliant red glow across the horizon. In the distance, drums were heard. Were they announcing a death, a birth, or a dignitary's visit, or were they announcing a union made in heaven?

Zack and Angela found leaving their loved ones much more difficult than they had anticipated. In addition to Ben, Joel, and Rachael, several pastors and mission personnel were present. There were nearly two hundred men and woman from nearby villages. A large, diverse group of inhabitants surrounded their loaded truck. Some people had walked two or three days to be present when the couple departed. Singing and clapping surrounded them and tears flowed from eyes of people they had never seen before. The larger assemblage pressed tightly around the smaller one of Dr. Ben, Joel, Rachael, the pastors, and church elders. Zack and Angela stood in the middle of them with heads bowed in prayer. In the crowd, Zack had seen the faces of David Mbote, Nganda, and others standing back, half hidden in the masses as African culture decreed—strong and brave men and loved friends.

The pain of separation and loss was crushing Zack and Angela's hearts. Would they see them all again soon? The distance between them would not be great—four-hundred miles at the most. But this was darkest Africa where time stood still. Life was precarious and often fleeting, like a light bulb's fragile filament. Small distances were often insurmountable. Wild animals, thieves, or deadly microbes could attack the most experienced of travelers. As the newlyweds drove away from the throng, their hearts were filled with love, but were also heavy with parting. Life's normal experiences can create intense bonds; living through incredible danger unites people in ways that others cannot feel—or even begin to understand.

Zack and Angela spent their first night sleeping in the back seat of the Land Rover. They held each other close against the chill of the night but also from the surge of their love. The following evening they reached the Catholic Mission of Kaninga, where the nuns greeted them with enormous affection and hospitality. Zack and Angela spent the next two days and nights in the mission about one-hundred and twenty miles from Kikungu. Their unchained love and passion for one another was flawless and exquisite; a perfect balance of intense passion, gentleness, and enormous unity. The Catholic sisters treated this young couple with benevolent excess by serving delicious meals and caring for all their needs. The kindness and warmth lavished on the young couple by the Catholic sisters helped them complete the miracle of love found, love expressed, and love fulfilled.

The ensuing days of travel were arduous and slow. While driving, neither tried to speak much because, as usual, the loud thumping of the diesel engine and road noise made conversing nearly impossible. A great deal of Angela's energy was used just holding on to keep from being thrown about in their metal prison. Each of them was left to their thoughts. Angela was reflecting on what she and Zack had read from the Bible the night before. They had used a flashlight, draining some of their precious batteries. But it was too important not to read well. For no particular reason they had chosen 1 Samuel and learned how God had used King Saul so mightily in ancient Judah. But then they read how he had returned to his former sinful life. Angela was familiar with this. Many times she had seen the embers of the new Christian life flame brightly, and then die away to faint incandescence—then to cold ashes. Just as in Saul's life, it is often seen in the life of new Christians—the result of the ancient battle between the old life and the new. *But if there is defeat*, Angela thought, *it is not from God.* God gave King Saul, as he does to all His people, the means to battle the sinful nature. But just like King Saul, many choose to ignore God's outstretched hand.

With her left hand, Angela grasped the bar in front of her and held tightly to the armrest with her right. It was still taking a great amount of strength to prevent being thrown about. There was almost no road here, just a path between stumps and rocks. But despite the roughness, her thoughts remained peaceful.

She looked at the profile of the man beside her and for the thousandth time thought how handsome he was. She felt with all her heart that he would never flame out. She had never seen anyone come to God with the conviction that he displayed. Zack was used to making life and death decisions, and he had now made the supreme decision of all. There might be some stumbling blocks along the path, but there would be no turning back in him.

The young duo drove for another three days, pausing only to take brief repose and fill the trucks tanks from their barrel of diesel fuel. They lost track of the number of times they had dug the Land Rover out of the sand. Several times they wished they had brought some of the workers from the Mission to assist them. Their food and drinkable water were nearly exhausted when they turned off the road they had followed for so long. The falling sun was deserting the daylight as they climbed out of the Land Rover and stood together in the path. Zack put his arm around Angela's waist as they gazed intently at the two stakes and the hideous skulls attached to them. Once again they read the uncompromising words.

Beware; you are entering a place of roving spirits of the dead, and the remains of the tortured.

Zack kissed her forehead. "Are you certain this is where you want to stop?"

"Yes, darling." Angela's voice was bursting with excitement. "We are home."

They both knew with complete certainty that this forbidding land of lepers would be their home, their labor, and their destiny.

The sun was hiding behind the forest as they stood sharing a union that few would ever know. Through the limitless silence they could hear the rushing of a river about one-hundred yards in the distance. A damp mist began to rise from the vegetation bordering the rushing water. It condensed rapidly making the trees shadowy silhouettes. Suddenly, Zack and Angela saw an image appear in the thick fog. It chilled their blood and immobilized them. As they stared, the figure moved like that of a man. It was their imagination, they knew—just a manifestation created by trees through the mist. Then the shadowy silhouette moved toward them and seemed to be speaking. Inexplicably, they heard no sound—yet, both sensed a voice. Simultaneously, the young lovers felt warmth, peace, and an incredible joy. There were no spoken words, nor would they ever be able to confirm that it was the form of Pascal. Yet, they would *forever remember* and *ceaselessly share* the message that radiated from the mist on that murky African eve.

My dear friends always remember what God teaches. God says, "Be holy as I am holy." Always remember the true purpose of life—the final purpose of man is not to be happy, rich, or even healthy—it is to seek holiness. The figure paused as if reflecting and then continued. *So many people want to do great things on their own. That is a fine calling but also one that God must weaken in those that follow Him. First and foremost, God wants us to be in a right relationship with Him. Right now you are preparing to be holy—but it cannot be a holiness you have created. True holiness can only be the expression of what God has given you—please, never let go of that!*

The apparition turned, and as it did, the outline of a petite girl could be seen. She was reaching up to take its hand. As she did, she turned, and her beautiful smile shimmered through the fog. *I love you, Daddy. I love you, Angela.*

Unexpectedly, a breeze arose in front of them. From the village it brought with it smoke of the evening fires—and the odor of decaying flesh. The gentle wind drifted by, dissipating the mist. Nothing but the forest stood before them as they embraced, experiencing completely their love for one another and the full grace of God.

TATE PUBLISHING & *Enterprises*

Tate Publishing is committed to excellence in the publishing industry. Our staff of highly trained professionals, including editors, graphic designers, and marketing personnel, work together to produce the very finest books available. The company reflects the philosophy established by the founders, based on Psalms 68:11,

"THE LORD GAVE THE WORD AND GREAT WAS THE COMPANY OF THOSE WHO PUBLISHED IT."

If you would like further information, please call
1.888.361.9473
or visit our website
www.tatepublishing.com

TATE PUBLISHING & *Enterprises*, LLC
127 E. Trade Center Terrace
Mustang, Oklahoma 73064 USA